INSIDE

THE WIRE

A Delta Force Unleashed Thriller

Also by J. Robert Kennedy

James Acton Thrillers

The Protocol	Blood Relics	The Cylon Curse
Brass Monkey	Sins of the Titanic	The Viking Deception
Broken Dove	Saint Peter's Soldiers	Keepers of the Lost Ark
The Templar's Relic	The Thirteenth Legion	The Tomb of Genghis Khan
Flags of Sin	Raging Sun	The Manila Deception
The Arab Fall	Wages of Sin	The Fourth Bible
The Circle of Eight	Wrath of the Gods	Embassy of the Empire
The Venice Code	The Templar's Revenge	Armageddon
Pompeii's Ghosts	The Nazi's Engineer	No Good Deed
Amazon Burning	Atlantis Lost	The Last Soviet
The Riddle		Lake of Bones

Special Agent Dylan Kane Thrillers

Rogue Operator	Black Widow	State Sanctioned
Containment Failure	The Agenda	Extraordinary Rendition
Cold Warriors	Retribution	Red Eagle
Death to America		The Messenger

Templar Detective Thrillers

The Templar Detective	The Sergeant's Secret	The Black Scourge
The Parisian Adulteress	The Unholy Exorcist	The Lost Children
	The Code Breaker	

Kriminalinspektor Wolfgang Vogel Mysteries

The Colonel's Wife	Sins of the Child

Delta Force Unleashed Thrillers

Payback	Kill Chain	The Cuban Incident
Infidels	Forgotten	Rampage
The Lazarus Moment		Inside the Wire

Detective Shakespeare Mysteries

Depraved Difference	Tick Tock	The Redeemer

Zander Varga, Vampire Detective

The Turned

INSIDE
THE WIRE

A Delta Force Unleashed Thriller

J. ROBERT KENNEDY

ISBN: 9781990418273

First Edition

For the girls still missing.

INSIDE
THE WIRE

A Delta Force Unleashed Thriller

"People sleep peaceably in their beds at night only because rough men stand ready to do violence on their behalf."

George Orwell

"Allah said: 'The rulers of the infidels, their leaders, must be killed. They must be killed because they doubt your religion.' If you kill the leaders, they will subside. Among those who doubt your religion, you must find the highest leaders and cut their throats because they don't keep their word. Find the leaders and kill them because they doubt your religion. Allah said: 'That's how they will stop doubting your religion.'"

Muhammad Yusuf, Founder of Boko Haram

PREFACE

Jamā'at Ahl as-Sunnah lid-Da'wah wa'l-Jihād is one of the most brutal terrorist groups in the world. Translated, their name is Group of the People of Sunnah for Preaching and Jihad. It is a name known to few outside the intelligence community. Instead, the world knows them by a far simpler name.

Boko Haram.

The name is a combination of Hausa and Arabic. Many will recognize the Arabic 'Haram' as meaning 'forbidden,' but Boko is a little more difficult. It literally means 'fake.' Culturally, however, it takes on a different meaning. In the region, for decades, 'ilimin boko' means 'fake education' and referred to Western education. Over the years, it was shortened to simply 'boko' and has now been coopted by these lunatics.

For they are lunatics.

Founded in 2002, they are directly responsible for over 35,000 deaths, and the strife they have caused in the region has resulted in the death of over 300,000 children and the displacement of over 2.3 million people.

In the 2010s, they were declared the world's deadliest terror group according to the Global Terrorism Index.

Their most notorious attack took place over two days, starting April 14, 2014. Boko Haram kidnapped 276 schoolgirls from Chibok, Nigeria, and announced they intended to sell them all into slavery. It would not be the last time they kidnapped large numbers of young girls to be sold into the sex trade, married off to their members, or exchanged for large ransoms.

With as many as 20,000 members, this vicious organization is opposed by multiple nations in the region, with the assistance of the United States, United Kingdom, and France.

Yet as always, politics gets in the way.

And today, it just might cost the lives of hundreds of innocents, including Bravo Team.

North of FOB Ugurun, Nigeria

Two days from now

Sergeant Carl "Niner" Sung grinned as he guided Sergeant Zach "Wings" Hauser in for a landing using two glowsticks in the dim light, the ancient Bell Huey helicopter beating at the air, the sound no doubt carrying for miles. It was the entire point of this secondary LZ he had set up, away from any prying eyes that might be watching the vulnerable Forward Operating Base they were trapped at with hundreds of defenseless civilians.

They needed manpower, supplies, and most importantly, time. Boko Haram was gathering hundreds to throw against their barely two dozen. The arrival of this chopper meant another eleven were entering the fight, and if they could successfully begin ferrying soldiers and supplies in, and the civilians out, it could be a game-changer.

"Get those wounded ready!" he ordered, three of the Nigerians shot earlier the first to be evacuated. No one wanted to risk the civilians, especially the children, until they had proven this lifeline safe.

The chopper landed with a bounce and idled down slightly. There was no time to waste. The doors were thrown open and the rest of Bravo Team along with six Nigerians poured out, lugging three large crates of ammo for the unavoidable fight ahead. The team's second-in-command, Master Sergeant Mike "Red" Belme and Wings had a brief conversation inside the cockpit as the wounded were loaded aboard before Red stepped out.

"Clear the LZ!" ordered Niner, then once he had confirmed everyone was safely out of the way, he indicated Wings was clear to depart. The chopper rose then banked away, quickly lost in the dark, though the hammering of the rotors could still be heard. Niner tossed the glowsticks on the ground then used his boot to cover them with dirt—there was no point giving their enemy a juicy illuminated target.

Wings' voice squawked in his ear as his friend contacted Control. "Control, One-Two. I'd appreciate it if you'd thread this needle, over."

"Copy that, One-Two. Proceed west, bearing two-seven-zero. The Reaper is overhead and we're showing no heat signatures in your direct path, over."

Niner pointed at two troop transports nearby. "Your chariots await, Sergeant."

Red turned to the others. "Everyone load up. I want to be inside the wire ASAP."

A round of "Yes, Sergeant!" responded as Red and Niner peered into the distance, attempting to pick the chopper out in the night sky. With each passing second, Niner rested a little easier, then something flashed and he grabbed Red's arm.

4

"Oh shit!"

His comms squawked. "One-Two, RPG coming in from your six o'clock. Take evasive action immediately. Repeat, RPG coming in from your six o'clock. Take evasive action immediately."

Niner spotted a point of light racing skyward, the rocket propellant carrying the unguided but deadly Rocket Propelled Grenade into the air. Everyone turned to face the action, every breath held as they waited to hear the all-clear.

But it wasn't to be.

"Control, tell my family—"

Niner's stomach churned and his heart pounded at the brilliant flash on the horizon as the RPG's warhead found its mark.

Killing one of his best friends.

And any hope of making it out of their situation alive.

Behind 1st Special Forces Operational Detachment—Delta HQ

Fort Bragg, North Carolina

A.k.a. "The Unit"

Today

"It only hurts when I breathe."

Sergeant Leon "Atlas" James regarded his best friend with concern. "I tried to warn you, but instead you decided to be an idiot."

Niner wiped the tears from his eyes. "You didn't warn me, you merely baited her trap."

Atlas' girlfriend, Vanessa Moore, rushed up with a small carton of milk pilfered from the children's table. She handed it to Niner. "I'm so sorry. I must have overdone it with the hot peppers." Niner took a large swig of the milk, swishing it around his mouth in a desperate attempt to neutralize the ungodly hot chili he had just sampled.

Command Sergeant Major Burt "Big Dog" Dawson shook his head. "You know, one of these days somebody's going to get hurt."

"Somebody did get hurt," protested Niner. "And tomorrow it's going to be worse."

"How's that?"

"Because my colon's going to get to taste that again on the way out."

Several better halves groaned in disgust, including Niner's girlfriend, Angela Henwood. "Carl, be polite!"

He gave her a look. "I thought I was. You don't want to know what I was going to say."

"I probably don't." Angela took another spoonful of her chili, labeled prominently as 'mild.' Vanessa, an aspiring chef, was experimenting on Bravo Team, an elite group of warriors, members of 1st Special Forces Operational Detachment—Delta, commonly known to the public as the Delta Force. The families were gathered behind the Unit on a beautiful Saturday, everyone here except for Sergeant Will "Spock" Lightman, who had recently lost his wife. He had bowed out. It was just too soon to have fun, and his daughter wasn't ready. Apparently, she was taking things extremely hard, which was understandable at her age. Dawson didn't press him, and was pleased when Vanessa said she would drop off a care package so Spock wouldn't miss out.

And while Spock's loss was in the back of everyone's mind, today was a day to relax, enjoy each other's company, and forget their troubles. When Vanessa had asked if she could test out some chili recipes, everyone was eager to accept. The woman was a phenomenal cook, and the last chili Dawson had eaten was from a can. In fact, he could not remember the last time he had had homemade chili.

He took a bite of cornbread, one of his absolute favorite foods in the world. He moaned. His fiancée, Maggie Harris, smiled at him. "I didn't realize you liked cornbread."

"Love it, but I rarely see it anywhere."

"I'll get the recipe from Vanessa."

He tapped what remained of his piece. "If you learn how to make this, I'll figure out some way to love you even more."

Red, Dawson's second-in-command and best friend, groaned. "Would you two love birds knock it off. You're making us old married men look bad."

Dawson leaned forward in his lawn chair so he could catch Red's wife Shirley's eye. "Learn to make this, and you might just get that romance back in your life."

Shirley patted Red's hand. "Oh, he still knows how to romance me."

Red gave Dawson a toothy grin. "Thank you, dear."

"Besides, he doesn't like cornbread."

Dawson eyed his friend. "Since when do you not like cornbread?"

Red shrugged. "Never have, never will."

"Really?"

"Have you ever seen me eat cornbread?"

"Can't say that I have. Huh. I'm not sure we can be friends anymore."

Red shrugged and extended a hand. "Well, it's been a good run."

Dawson shook it. "It had its ups and downs. In fact, now that I think about it, we've got nothing in common but the job. How we've been friends for so many years, I have no idea."

"That's what happens when you're forced to work together. You overlook all the things that annoy you."

Maggie rolled her eyes. "Will you two stop it? You two have so much in common, both on and off the job, that I swear if Shirley and I weren't in the picture, you'd be dating."

Red tilted his head forward, looking up at Dawson. "He could do worse."

Dawson reached out and clasped Red's hand. "But I could never do better."

They both roared with laughter, Shirley and Maggie joining in, Maggie's laugh cut short with a gasp. Dawson spun toward her, immediately concerned. "Are you all right?"

She rubbed her jaw. "I guess I'm not fully recovered."

Dawson ran his hand through her hair with a sympathetic smile. She had been brutally beaten not even two months ago. She was recovering, her physical reminders mostly gone, but it was the emotional scars that had him concerned. She was tormented by nightmares and would flinch at the slightest, unexpected sound. What had happened to her should never have happened, but at least she was alive.

Unlike Spock's wife, Joanne, who had lost her life that day.

"Can I get you anything?"

She shook her head. "No, I'll be fine. Just take it easy on the jokes. Apparently laughing too hard still hurts."

He chuckled. "Well then, we'll leave the jokes to Niner. Those usually fall flat with the ladies."

Niner's head spun toward them. "I heard my name. You better have been saying nice things about me."

Red grunted. "Why start now?"

Niner and Atlas continued to shovel chili into their mouths. Sergeant Eugene "Jagger" Thomas pointed at one of the large pots. "This is my favorite. It's got that perfect blend of meatiness and heat. Satisfying, but not too overpowering."

Vanessa smiled at him. "Thanks, Jagger, that's helpful."

Jagger jutted his large lips toward the two competing friends. "I don't know how you're going to get any useful feedback out of those two. They're going to lose their taste buds if they keep scarfing down that hot batch."

Sergeant Trip "Mickey" McDonald frowned. "If you two don't slow down, when we get on that tin can of a Herc tomorrow, it's going to be a recreation of Blazing Saddles."

Niner giggled, as did Atlas, and even Dawson had to join in. One of the all-time classic scenes in the history of movies was the farting around the campfire chili scene. "I can hold it in," said Niner, noticeably slowing his spoon, apparently not so confident.

"You better," said Dawson. "Save it for when you two zip your sleeping bags together tomorrow night."

Vanessa's eyes shot wide. "You two zip your sleeping bags together?"

Wings snickered. "We established that fact in India when they refused to deny it."

Atlas held up a massive hand, a lone finger held up in defense. "That's BS, and you know it. We just didn't get a chance to deny it, what with the Chinese missiles that were inbound."

Angela leaned in and gave Niner a kiss on the cheek. "I think it's sweet."

Niner grinned. "So do I." He turned to Atlas. "Don't you?"

Atlas growled. "Don't you get started."

Niner patted him on the knee. "He loves me."

Vanessa threw her head back, groaning. "Sometimes I wonder if Niner is actually his soul mate and not me."

"Certain questions are better left unasked," said Shirley.

"Well, you're right about that," agreed Dawson. "You two better be on your best behavior. I don't think the Nigerians are going to understand your brand of humor. If you two start Dutch ovening each other in your tent and giggle like schoolgirls, you're going to seriously affect the reputation of the—"

Shirley interrupted. "Dutch ovening?"

"I'll show you tonight," said Red before he turned and grinned at Dawson.

Maggie's eyes narrowed. "What *is* Dutch ovening?"

Dawson turned to her with an equally toothy smile. "I'll show you tonight."

Vanessa groaned. "When I was introduced to Niner, I should have known you were *all* terrible."

Flexible wrists all slapped against chests. "Who? Us?" echoed the team.

"Yes, all of you. You're terrible." Vanessa stared at Shirley and Maggie. "A Dutch oven is when you throw the covers over your heads in bed and fart so that your partner gets to suffer."

Shirley groaned. "Oh, God, he's done that before, the pig. I just didn't know it had a name."

Red frowned at Vanessa. "Gee, thanks for ruining my fun tonight."

Vanessa eyeballed him. "If that's your idea of fun in bed when you've got a gorgeous wife like that, I feel sorry for Shirley."

Shirley frowned at her husband. "Yeah, maybe I should get that cornbread recipe from you."

Red turned toward her. "But I don't like cornbread."

Shirley eyed him. "I never said I was making it for *you.*"

Everyone roared with laughter as Red's cheeks matched his nickname.

"You got burned, buddy, you got burned!" cried Niner.

Red finally joined in. "Okay, I deserved that. No more Dutch ovens." He jutted his chin toward Niner and Atlas. "But you two sweethearts better put corks in them, because if you start stinking up that Herc tomorrow, I'm lowering the ramp and kicking you two out on harnesses."

Niner batted a hand at him. "I'm sure there's some regulation somewhere that says you can't do that."

Atlas agreed and tapped his chili. "A much wiser course of action would be to arm yourself, otherwise this Howitzer is going to blow you out the back of the plane."

Red stared at Atlas for a moment then cursed. "Okay, give me another damn bowl. This means war."

Shirley's head sank and her hands covered her face. "I married into a family of man-childs." She turned her head to look up at her husband as Vanessa delivered a bowl of chili. "You're sleeping in the guest room tonight."

Red took the bowl then hesitated. "You'd deny me the night before I deploy?"

She sat up. "No, you're right. You don't deserve that." She looked at Vanessa. "Give me a bowl of whatever recipe has the most beans. If I have to sleep with Farty McFartFace here, I'm going to Dutch oven the shit out of him."

Over the Atlantic Ocean

Dawson groaned as Atlas leaned over and cocked a cheek, ripping something that had to have a clause in the Geneva Convention against its use. At least he had aimed it at Niner, but gas respected no boundaries, and just as easily could come back on friend or foe. Fortunately, all twelve of them were loaded to bear, and many a story had been told of refined women performing Dutch ovens all night, giggling as much as Niner would.

Niner leaned away, covering his mouth and nose with a hand. "Oh my God, I think I can taste that one."

Red turned to Dawson as he grimaced. "Sergeant Major, I highly recommend that when this mission is over, you ask the colonel to ban any methane-inducing cuisine the night before."

Dawson finally let one go that he had been holding for hours. He sighed in relief. "Sorry about that. I'll be meeting with the colonel the moment we get back stateside." He stabbed a finger at Atlas. "I blame you for this."

Niner squeaked one out and giggled. "I make no apologies. I blame him too."

"How is it my fault?" protested Atlas.

Spock cocked an eyebrow. "You're the one who started dating a woman who believes in human experimentation."

"Hey, I didn't see anybody complaining. You're only uncomfortable because you're all trying to hold it in." Atlas leaned forward, extending a hand then clenching it. "Embrace the fart side. You know you want to." His ridiculously deep voice was made even deeper by his Darth Vader impression that would have made James Earl Jones sound like a soprano by comparison.

Niner agreed wholeheartedly. "Fart away, gentlemen. It's both liberating and fun. The sooner you do, the sooner your suffering is over."

"Oh, to hell with it," said Mickey, a long high-pitched ripper following his surrender. Someone else farted, then another, and within minutes they were all wishing they had gas masks with them. But the intestinal cramping had been relieved. Red groaned in ecstasy as he launched an air biscuit that Dawson swore rattled the airframe.

Atlas' eyes shot wide as he rated the effort with two thumbs up. "Holy shit, Sergeant, you've been holding out on us."

Red's shoulders slumped as every muscle relaxed with the exquisite release. "You have no idea." His head lolled to the side and he stared at Dawson. "My recommendation stands, however."

Dawson waved his hand in front of his nose. "Oh my God, it definitely does." He directed his attention at Atlas. "And you tell your girlfriend to stop experimenting on us."

Atlas grunted. "Yeah, right, like I can tell her what to do."

Niner eyed him. "What, are you scared?"

"I didn't say that."

"You *are* scared. Have you looked at yourself in a mirror lately? How the hell does anything scare you?"

"I am *not* scared, but have you looked at her in a mirror lately?"

"I don't know. Have you found my hidden camera yet?"

"Huh?"

"Forget about it. No, I haven't looked at her in the mirror lately. What's that got to do with it?"

Atlas gave a toothy grin. "If you had seen her in a mirror, there's no way you'd ever say no to that woman."

Mickey nodded in agreement. "He's got you there. Vanessa is one fine-looking woman and one hell of a cook. Don't you dare tell her to stop experimenting on us. Though I do agree with Red, lay off the gas-inducing ones the day before a mission, especially one that has us flying in a tin can with no windows to open."

Atlas held up his hands in mock surrender. "Fine, fine, but when you're eating MREs for the next week, you're going to be missing my woman's chili."

Wings executed a one-cheek squeak. "Just adding my vote. More experimentation, better timing."

"Seconded," said Sergeant Gerry "Jimmy Olsen" Hudson, his trousers coughing.

Dawson rolled his eyes but didn't dare sigh because that would require inhaling. "Okay, enough of this." He checked his watch. "We're landing in an hour at Kano. Let's review the mission. We're splitting into two teams. I'll be leading Team One, Red, Team Two. We each have a list of Forward Operating Bases that the Nigerians have asked us to consult on from a security perspective. Uncle Sam has graciously volunteered our asses—"

"I think he knew we were going to be loaded to bear so planned ahead," rumbled Atlas.

Dawson gave him a look. "Our *asses*, loaded or not, were volunteered because Boko Haram is so active. The Pentagon is concerned that with the collapse of ISIS, Boko Haram might attempt more kidnappings to raise funds for their operations. We all know what these animals are capable of and how many schoolgirls they've kidnapped, how many people they've murdered, all in the name of their twisted version of Islam. Our job is to make sure these new bases have a shot at allowing those stationed there to defend themselves. We'll review, make recommendations, then move on to the next base."

"Are we expecting another UN Peacekeeping operation?" asked Niner.

It was well known in the military world why peacekeeping operations were often undertaken by Third World countries. They would show up ill-equipped, often with nothing at all, and it would be up to a NATO ally to provide them with everything they needed to survive and prevent the inevitable slaughter if the warring parties they were there to keep apart ever discovered that those manning the ramparts had no weapons or ammo.

Dawson shrugged. "No idea. However, if past experience dictates, I'd say we're going to show up at some of these new installations and find canvas fencing. The Pentagon wants us to assess the situation, make recommendations on how to improve things, and supplies will be sent in if the Nigerians agree."

"Why wouldn't they agree?"

"They seem touchy about letting anyone operate on their soil, though I think they'll happily take anything materiel that we offer them."

"Are we expecting any problems?" asked Atlas.

"Always expect problems, but the Nigerians insist they can handle anything Boko Haram might attempt to throw at us."

Spock cocked an eyebrow. "If they can handle anything, then why do they need us there?"

Dawson smiled slightly. "Exactly. So, heads on a swivel, gentlemen. There could be an AK-47 around any corner."

Jimmy grunted. "And let me guess, ROEs are that we can't fire unless fired upon?"

"Welcome to the modern US Army."

Niner grinned. "Where we give the best hugs."

NAF Kano

Kano, Nigeria

Dawson stepped off the C-130 Hercules' ramp and onto the tarmac at Nigerian Air Base Kano. He had been here before and was certain he would be here again. He smiled at the sight of Sergeant Major Yemi Buhari, a man he had dealt with before. Competent, capable, and friendly. He was standing beside a colonel, who judging from his expression, wasn't too pleased to be here. He could understand the man's feelings. No one liked having to admit they needed someone else's help.

Nigeria was a poor but proud country, with the largest population in Africa, approaching two-thirds that of the United States, wedged into an area less than a tenth its size. They were dealing with a significant Islamic fundamentalist problem, and after over twenty years of war, nobody had more experience in that area than the United States. His country was only too happy to help, especially when China and Russia were attempting to exert influence in Africa, the Russians through discounted weapons sales, the Chinese through their Belt and Road Initiative, which merely saddled Third World nations with massive debt.

"Sergeant Major White, so good to see you again," said Buhari, addressing Dawson by his codename. "This is Colonel Oguntade. He's in charge of the FOB expansion program."

Dawson and the others snapped to attention, saluting the senior officer. He returned the salute. "Sergeant Major, on behalf of the Nigerian government, I welcome you to our country and thank you for your assistance."

"It is our honor, sir."

Oguntade indicated Buhari. "The sergeant major will be your liaison. Should you require anything, speak to him."

"Yes, sir."

Oguntade turned on his heel and left them without saying another word. He climbed into a nearby jeep that sped away, leaving the NCOs to themselves. Buhari shrugged. "You'll have to forgive the colonel. He feels things like this are beneath him."

"Well, a senior officer receiving a bunch of sergeants probably isn't something he's accustomed to."

Buhari grunted. "No. If you were a Nigerian, he wouldn't have said a word to you unless he wanted you to polish his shoes."

Dawson held out a hand toward Red. "My second-in-command. Master Sergeant Grey."

Buhari shook Red's hand. "Good to meet you, Sergeant."

"Likewise."

"Are you and your men ready to go?"

"We're always ready," replied Dawson with a slight smile.

Buhari chuckled. "I have no doubt. Change of plans, however. We had some extremely heavy rainfall yesterday that's made some of the roads to your first base impassable. We'll be taking you in by chopper instead."

"Always preferable than half a day on a bumpy road."

"I thought you might like that." Buhari turned to Red. "Unfortunately for you, your roads are perfectly fine."

Red rolled his eyes. "Gee. Don't I feel lucky?"

Buhari laughed. "At least you're only looking at a couple of hours in the back of a troop transport." He turned and whistled. "Sergeant!" A man standing nearby with several other soldiers jogged over. Buhari indicated Red. "This is Master Sergeant Grey. He is in command of the team you'll be partnered with. Sergeant Grey, this is Sergeant Akintan. Anything you need, you ask him, and he'll do his best."

Red shook the man's hand. "Got a helicopter hanging around that's not being used?"

Akintan jerked his head at the lone chopper in sight. "You're lucky we were able to get approval to use this one. I think the colonel would have been happy with you walking to your destination."

Buhari gave Akintan a look, the same look Dawson would have given any of his men if they criticized a senior officer in public. Akintan's jaw clenched and he pointed at a nearby truck. "When you're ready, Sergeant, I'll be over there."

Red nodded. "Thank you, Sergeant. We'll be with you shortly."

Akintan jogged back to the truck, orders snapped to others in the vicinity. Buhari lowered his voice slightly. "I must apologize."

Dawson dismissed the apology with a flick of his wrist. "No need. NCOs complaining about their officers among other NCOs is common the world over."

"Yes, but not to another country's NCOs."

"Consider it forgotten."

Atlas tossed a duffel bag on the large pile the team had been unloading, and Buhari frowned. "I didn't realize you'd have so much equipment." He glanced over his shoulder at the chopper. "There's no way we're fitting you and all that on there."

"How long a round trip?"

"Two hours."

"Do you have permission for two trips?"

"No." Buhari grinned. "But I've always found it's better to apologize after the fact than to ask permission before."

Dawson chuckled. "I think I've heard that somewhere, and I tend to agree." He turned to his team. "Break it down, gentlemen. Essentials only. The rest will be two hours behind us."

His team went to work, setting aside anything they would not need in the next several hours, and when they were done, three duffel bags remained to be loaded on the chopper, containing mostly items they would require for self-defense should things go south.

Red approached, his team already loaded in the back of the transport with their equipment. "We're heading out now. See you in a week."

"See you in a week," replied Dawson, exchanging a fist bump.

Buhari jerked a thumb over his shoulder at the chopper as it powered up. "I suggest we leave now before the colonel figures out that this pile of equipment is going out on a second unauthorized flight."

Dawson eyed the hoard. "We're going to need guards on this. There's some highly classified stuff in there like changes of underwear and new MRE recipes."

Buhari smiled, reading between the lines. He turned and whistled, rhyming off four names. The men in question rushed over and Buhari pointed at the equipment. "Nobody gets near this stuff. This is United States Government property. When the chopper returns, load it, then return to your posts. Understood?"

A chorus of, "Yes, Sergeant Major!" was the reply.

"Men I can trust," explained Buhari as they strode toward the helicopter.

"I have no doubt. I meant no disrespect."

Buhari slapped him on the back. "And you gave none. Nigeria is a poor country, and unfortunately, sometimes things such as a pile of American equipment can prove an irresistible temptation to someone whose family is desperate."

Dawson stood by the side of the old Bell Huey and watched as his team boarded. He gave a wave to Red and Team Two as their truck rumbled past accompanied by two jeeps, front and back. Buhari climbed aboard the chopper and Dawson followed, the last boot off the ground. He took a seat as they lifted off, then stared down at the base below and prayed for an uneventful mission.

But when Boko Haram was involved, anything was possible.

Boko Haram Staging Area

Outside Maiduguri, Nigeria

"The infidel is weak, for he does not have Allah in his heart. Only through Allah can we have the strength necessary to be victorious. The infidel, he rejects Allah, he rejects His words as they are written in the Koran, and it is because of the constant state of sin they live in that they will be defeated. It is only a matter of time, and it's why we win victory after victory."

Ibrahim Muhammad ran his hands down the backs of two spoils from previous victories, two girls, favorites in his harem. His group, founded by the great Muhammad Yusuf, was famous—some might say notorious—for kidnapping schoolgirls by the hundreds. And with the death of Yusuf, he had continued the tradition. Choosing schoolgirls was an intentional decision. It not only shocked the world, which brought Boko Haram respect among its peers, it saved the girls from the satanic teachings they were subjected to by a government intent on adopting Western ways.

24

And it also had advantages in other ways.

Many of the girls, once taught the Koran and what was expected of them as good Muslim women, embraced the teachings. Some married their captors and bore their children. Those who truly resisted were punished in other ways. Some became rewards for his men that served him well, and the rest were sold as sex slaves or returned when ransom was paid. Everyone gained in the end. His own collection numbered a dozen, ranging in ages from ten to twenty, some willing participants after they had been broken, like the two girls with him now, others still intensely resistant, which he found deliciously exciting.

The men that surrounded him were fiercely loyal, and all had been rewarded with the pleasures of the flesh. The Koran gave the victor the right to take the women of their enemies as slaves, and they had plenty. But all these girls cost money—food, water, clothing. It had their coffers running low. Not to mention the provisions required by his men, along with weapons and ammo. With the collapse of ISIS and Al Qaeda, the generous donors in Western countries that secretly supported Islam and its jihad against the ways of their adopted countries were mostly Arab, and had yet to fully embrace donating to organizations comprised of black Muslims.

One didn't have to be white to be racist.

The lack of funds meant they had to take action, and they had to take action now. He smiled at those sitting around him. "If we are to be heard, we need to act. And in order to act, we need money. It's time for another scoop."

Smiles spread across the room at the prospect.

"This afternoon, we'll hit Ugurun before the school lets out. It's small, but has a new camp set up by the infidel government that they hope will scare us off. We'll show them how we have no fear of them and how we are unstoppable with the power of Allah in our hearts. And over the coming week, we will hit a village each day, taking their girls, and then on Friday, we will pray and thank Allah for his generosity. And as word of our victories spread around the world, the donations will flood in. We will teach the girls the way of Allah, then decide what to do with them, as we always have." He rose and the others joined him. "Now, prepare yourselves for battle, for this afternoon we may die in Allah's name and win our entry into Jannah, where only the true warriors of Islam are welcome." He thrust his fist in the air. "Allahu Akbar!"

Fists rose around him, his men repeating the chant, growing in volume each time. "Allahu Akbar! Allahu Akbar!"

And he smiled as the two girls he had broken over a year ago thrust their own fists in the air, screaming the words that filled any good Muslim's heart with religious fervor. "Allahu Akbar! Allahu Akbar!" He squeezed them tight against him, eager to return to his bed, the two of them his reward for his service to Allah.

And it was true.

God is greatest.

FOB Ugurun, Nigeria

Dawson stepped off the chopper first, continuing his assessment of the new Nigerian Forward Operating Base that had begun from the air. Their briefing had indicated the bases were ready and that the Nigerians wanted advice on how to improve upon what they had already built, though what he was looking at could never be considered complete, at least not by American or NATO standards.

An area perhaps the size of two football fields had been carved into the forest then ringed with chain-link fencing topped with barbed wire. Within this cleared area were half a dozen sandbagged positions around the perimeter, and a handful of hastily erected buildings clustered in the center, likely containing barracks, a mess hall, and various other administrative offices. A few troop transports and a couple of jeeps were lined up along the north end of the compound. The opposite end appeared reserved for PT, a group of about twenty soldiers currently being put through their paces by a seasoned sergeant.

And there was an inexplicable massive mound of dirt outside the fence line, blocking any line of sight from the south.

Sergeant Major Buhari stood beside him. "So, what do you think?"

If Dawson hadn't already known the man, he might have minced words, but Buhari preferred things straight, so that's what he would get. "Answer me one thing. Is this considered ready for our review?"

Buhari chuckled. "I'm afraid so."

"Run me through the thinking."

Buhari pointed toward the PT area. "Boko Haram is known to have fighters in that direction. We put our vehicles as far away from where we expect them to attack, clustered our buildings in the center so they're as far away from the fence line as possible and can act as a fallback position, and we have six permanently manned positions, all with fifty cals."

Dawson jutted his chin toward the group exercising. "They look young."

"They are young. Raw recruits."

Dawson cocked an eyebrow a la Spock. "You have raw recruits on the front line?"

"This isn't exactly the front line, but we put them here, train them, and let them live here for a few weeks knowing that at any moment they could die. It teaches them to be careful, to pay attention to the rules, and to listen to their sergeants and officers."

Dawson grunted. "I suppose that's one way of doing it." He jerked a thumb at Atlas helping unload the chopper with the others. "Usually, we just send in a scary son of a bitch like him, and nobody dares not pay attention."

28

Buhari laughed. "I can see how that might work, but in America, you don't have environments like this where you could send your recruits. If you did, maybe you'd adopt our methods."

"You haven't seen our inner cities."

Buhari regarded him. "What do you mean?"

Dawson waved a hand. "Never mind."

Atlas walked up to them, pointing at the pile of gear as the chopper lifted off, carrying a lieutenant that appeared under the weather. "Everything accounted for, Sergeant Major."

"Copy that." Dawson turned to Buhari. "Where can we set up camp?"

"Your pick, Sergeant Major. Anywhere you want." An AK-47 rattled in the distance and Bravo Team spun toward the sound, readying their weapons. Buhari laughed. "If you react every time you hear a gun go off here, you'll get nothing done."

"That sounded like it was only a few miles away," said Atlas.

"Probably taking some pot shots at the helicopter. Nothing to be concerned about."

Spock cocked an eyebrow. "Unless you're on the chopper."

"It's why we rarely use choppers in this area, and the only reason we did today was because the road is out."

Dawson pursed his lips. "When do you expect that to reopen?"

"They're working on it. Probably a couple of days."

"How often do they shoot up the camp?" asked Niner.

"Every couple of days. Usually it's just a drunk."

Dawson reassessed the area with this new piece of information. He pointed at the buildings. "You've got corrugated metal on all of these."

"Yes. What we've found over the years is that most of the shots taken at us are from a distance. These provide enough protection against a stray shot that comes at us from the maximum range. Pretty much useless if we were to come under direct attack, but our men rest a little easier at night knowing the occasional stray will likely be stopped. If you want, I can put some of our men in tents and your team can bunk inside."

Dawson shook his head at the proposition. "I'll never take another man's rack." His chin jutted toward the vehicles. "Are the keys in those trucks?"

Buhari smirked. "Why, are you planning on leaving?"

Dawson smiled. "The thought had occurred to me, but no, we'll reposition them to provide cover for our tents." He pointed at the far too close tree line. "Do you have chainsaws?"

"No, but we have axes and strong men."

Dawson indicated the soldiers now doing jumping jacks. "I suggest then that you end the dance routine and put them to real work. Get that tree line back. Minimum another hundred feet in all directions."

Buhari's eyebrows shot up. "That far?"

Dawson chuckled. "That's only the beginning."

Boko Haram Staging Area

Outside Maiduguri, Nigeria

"Stop your crying!" snapped Ibrahim Muhammad as he dressed. His two favorites lay in the bed, wearing nothing but smiles, but he had forced two of the younger girls that he had yet to break to watch—they needed to learn what to expect and what he liked.

Though he didn't have to listen to their sniveling.

If they didn't smarten up soon, he'd break them the hard way. He turned to the girls on the bed. "Clean yourselves up for when I get back." He gestured at the two students. "And talk to your sisters. Tell them what's in store for them if they don't accept their fate."

He stepped out of the room, if one could call it that. They had taken over an abandoned warehouse and he and a select few had sheets hung to provide a minimal sense of privacy. He had a home in a nearby village that he would visit often, where everyone knew what he did, but didn't dare say or do anything about it. The authorities certainly had no idea he lived there, otherwise they would have raided it long ago. It meant his neighbors could be trusted to not say anything, though he had no doubt it was out of fear, not loyalty. His wife never spoke of it, and their children knew nothing. It was his haven from the constant jihad.

His current quarters were uncomfortable, though had their benefits, namely in the supply of girls. It was a sacrifice he made willingly. He was doing this for his family, for those villagers that feared him. He was fighting back against the constant encroachment of Western civilization and its decadent, ungodly ways. As more were drawn to the cause, they would succeed. Afghanistan was proof. It might have taken decades, but Muslims like him had forced the Russians out, and now had forced America out.

What Westerners, with their idealistic beliefs, could not process was that true Muslims had no desire for democracy. It was fundamentally incompatible with Islam. The West had its separation of church and state, had elected governments, had laws set down over time, had their churches that they worshipped in that didn't govern them. While Islam was the religion of the people, it was also the laws of the people, and the government of the people. Everything was laid out in the Koran, the Hadiths, and the Sunnah. There was no room for votes, no room for dissent. His people would constantly fight back, constantly fight the invader, no matter what they claimed their intentions were, for there was no room for them in the world of Islam.

When his people won this war purely through demographics, and outnumbered the Westerners they would then surround, it would be a glorious blood bath, triggering the final war. He wasn't sure if he would be around for it, for it might take decades more, perhaps even centuries of struggle, but it would happen one day, and if he died in battle serving Allah, he would witness the great day of the Worldwide Caliphate from Jannah, while fed grapes by one of his 72 *houri*.

He strode through the warehouse, clapping his hands together rhythmically, the others rising and grabbing their weapons, joining him as they headed for the large doors at the far end and the collection of motorcycles that would carry them into battle. As more hands joined, the sound echoed off the walls like the war drums of his ancient ancestors. Goosebumps raced across his flesh in anticipation of what they were about to do. He expected success, but always in the back of his mind prepared for failure. Yet he never feared it, for failure meant entry into Jannah as long as he died with honor. But success had similar appeal, for success meant new girls, and after every kidnapping, he always chose the most terrified and took her to his bed, making all the others stand nearby and listen through the sheets at what their future would be should they not cooperate.

He reached down and adjusted himself, already excited over what the evening might bring. He raised his AK-47 over his head as he mounted his motorcycle and started the engine. "Allahu Akbar!" he cried as he roared out of the warehouse, his men behind him, Allah's power flowing through him.

Today would be a good day.

Today would be a *great* day.

Leroux/White Residence, Fairfax Towers

Falls Church, Virginia

"I didn't like it the first time I watched it."

CIA Operations Officer Sherrie White popped an eyebrow at her boyfriend's surprising statement. "You of all people didn't like The Big Bang Theory the first time you watched it?"

CIA Analyst Supervisor Chris Leroux shook his head. "Nope. Everybody kept talking about it so I finally said, okay, fine. And mind you, the show had been on for years, so it was just some random episode, I don't even remember what one. I watched about ten minutes and I turned it off. I remember saying out loud, 'this is one of the most popular shows on television?'"

Leroux's best friend, CIA Operations Officer Dylan Kane, chuckled over the video hookup, joining them from an officially unknown location that Leroux was privy to due to his job—Jordan. "If there was anybody who I thought would be devoted to that show from the moment it was announced, it would be you. It's all computers and Star Wars and Star Trek and comic books."

Leroux gave the laptop a look. "Do you see any comic books here?"

Kane wagged a finger at his friend. "Your bedroom in high school was filthy with them, so don't go pretending you weren't an uber dork when you were younger."

"I'm still an uber dork and proud of it, but I lost my taste for comic books along the way. Just no time. I get my fill now through the movies."

Kane's girlfriend Lee Fang, a former Chinese Special Forces officer now living in exile, took a sip of her coffee. "In China, we used to watch it as part of our training."

Leroux's eyebrows shot up. "Huh?"

"Well, we were trained in the pop cultures of our enemies, so if we had to do something undercover, we could blend better. We'd watch popular TV shows, movies, music. Before I came here, I was up on all the celebrity gossip, latest movies, TV shows, music, I knew it all."

"And now?"

She flicked her wrist. "I couldn't care less about that crap. While I like to sit down and watch a good movie or laugh at a TV show, why would I ever care about who's dating who? I prefer a good book regardless. I like to let my imagination fill in the blanks rather than someone in Hollywood."

Kane leaned closer to the camera. "What books did they have you reading in spy school?"

"None."

Sherrie's eyebrows shot up. "None?"

"It was felt it wasn't necessary."

Leroux's eyes narrowed. "Why wouldn't it be necessary?"

"Because not enough people actually read more than a few books a year, so you had almost no chance of dealing with someone who had read a book you had."

Leroux grunted. "That's appalling, if you think about it. Then again, I don't have much time to read anymore either."

Fang shrugged. "I'm not judging."

Sherrie leaned back. "It does kind of make sense though, doesn't it? We're introduced to reading usually by our parents when we're young, and then by the time we reach high school, we're being forced to read books that are unbelievably boring to a teenager, and then we have to write a report on it, sometimes do a presentation in front of a class, so the school system basically turns what should be a fun activity into a task that you hate."

Kane agreed as he tossed a finger toward Leroux, who had tutored him in high school. "You're preaching to the choir here. Just ask him. I hated reading the assigned books. They should have just let us pick a book to read and then write a report on it. Leave the classics for when you get older."

Leroux finished his Diet Dr. Pepper, putting the empty can on the coffee table. "I liked the classics."

Kane tilted his head, giving him a look. "Yes, but we've already established you're an uber dork."

"True, but I still didn't like The Big Bang Theory when I first watched it."

"But now you love it," said Sherrie. "What changed?"

He shrugged. "I don't know. A couple of years later, people were still talking about it, and when I said I didn't like it, they said I must have just got a bad episode, so I tried it again and it just clicked the second time. Now I can't get enough of it. I'll watch all twelve seasons straight through, and by the time I finish the finale, I'm ready to start episode one again. It just goes to show, I guess, how first impressions aren't always correct."

Fang giggled. "You're right there." She jerked a thumb at Kane. "The first time I met him, I thought he was a stupid, arrogant American."

Kane flashed her a toothy smile. "But drop-dead gorgeous, right?"

She laughed aloud. "Not at all! I did *not* like white men back then."

Kane slapped a hand against his heart. "I think I just died a little inside."

She reached over and patted the laptop. "Don't worry, dear. It wasn't you that I didn't think was attractive, it was all white men."

He glanced at the others. "Umm, thank you?"

She snickered. "You don't understand. In China, we're taught that anybody different from us is inferior and wants to destroy what we have out of jealousy. Pop culture has been easing that somewhat, mostly through Hollywood, which is why the government is so eager to partner with Hollywood studios so that they can portray China in a positive light so it's not always the Americans saving the day."

"Now how do you feel about us unattractive, illiterate Americans?" asked Sherrie.

Fang giggled. "After I lived here for a while, I realized everything I had been taught was a lie. Then a certain American man made me fall in love with him by being the kindest person I had ever met."

Kane glanced over both shoulders. "You're talking about me?"

"Of course." She sighed. "It just shows how the prejudices of those who surround us affect us so deeply. If only people could see the other side without the bias, they would realize we're all the same all around the world. At the end of a long week, people just want to get together with friends and family, share a meal, maybe see a movie or go dancing, and laugh. Everywhere you go, people just want to laugh and forget their troubles. In China, we're taught you are the enemy and we learn to hate, and it's just so sad that so much time and energy is wasted on ridiculous things like this."

"Well, it's not that much better here in America," said Kane. "In China, you're taught the outsider is the enemy. Now in America, we're taught the guy who voted for the other party is the enemy."

"It wasn't always like that?"

"No, it's a recent development. A few decades ago, you cast your vote and then you threw your support behind whoever won. You'd criticize him domestically for policies you disagreed with, but on the foreign stage, you backed your president. Now, everyone spends their time tearing down whoever's elected at all levels. The guy gets a bad haircut, he's derided on social media and the late-night talk shows. An old man stumbles on a set of stairs, and it's replayed over and over as a commentary as to how he's unfit to be president. It's both sides tearing each other down and tearing this country apart."

Leroux grunted. "I even see it at the office. Politics never enters the operations center, but afterward in the coffee room, at the water cooler, in the parking garage, you hear the conversations and sometimes the arguments. I even have team members at each other's throats sometimes."

Sherrie's eyebrows shot up. "Seriously? Your team?"

He nodded. "Oh, yeah. There are a few of them on both sides of the spectrum that you just can't talk to anymore. I've told them to do the BBC challenge, as I call it, but they refuse to. I'm guessing because they're afraid I might be proven right."

Kane regarded him. "The BBC challenge?"

"One of the major problems is that most of our news sources have become polarized. They only tell one side of a story and quite often they make up the other side. And both sides are guilty of it. This isn't a Fox issue or a CNN issue. This is *all* of them. And what most Americans don't realize is that where they get most of their news, which is social media, have algorithms that show them only what the artificial intelligence thinks they want to see, and people want to see articles that support their opinions.

"So, I tell them to do the BBC challenge. Get BBC World News added to your cable package and only watch it for a month. See what's actually going on in the world, and see what the world thinks about America, and get relatively unbiased reporting about what's actually happening. And after a month, turn back to your favorite news channel, whether that's CNN or Fox or whatever, and see if you even recognize the country that the world sees, and ask yourself what the news is supposed to be?

"What were you taught as a child when Tom Brokaw, Sam Donaldson, and Peter Jennings read you your nightly news? Were the reports dripping with opinion and sarcasm, or were you just getting the straight facts? Back then, the news was the news, because it was thirty minutes long. As soon as you watch a newscast where the anchor reads you the news then gives you their opinion on it, you know you're watching a bad news station. Turn it off, switch the channel, whatever, because you're not getting the news. We need to smarten up and stop hating each other, otherwise we could be in for a world of hurt."

Everyone sat in silence for a moment before Kane finally broke it. "You really know how to kill a mood, dude."

Leroux flushed as he rose and headed for the kitchen, getting another Diet Dr. Pepper. "Sorry," he said as he returned.

"All I can say is that being someone who travels around the world a lot, I've noticed over the past decade that people's perception of our country has changed for the worse, and not just among our enemies, but our friends as well. That's not to say it's sunshine and lollipops everywhere. Europe certainly has its problems with extremists on both sides, but we seem to have taken it to a whole new level."

"You're right," said Fang. "You need to start getting along again. You need a good dictatorship. What's going on here wouldn't be tolerated back in China."

Sherrie's eyebrows rose. "My God, Fang, don't let anyone outside this room hear you say that!"

Fang chuckled. "I was merely pointing out the absurdity of it all. You live in a country free enough to hate each other to the point where you want to kill each other and still get to choose your leaders. Isn't that what freedom is all about? I thought freedom of speech was something you held dear?"

"It is," replied Kane. "But too many people don't understand what freedom of speech actually means. Freedom of speech means you have the right to say whatever you want without interference from the government, however, nowhere in the Constitution does it say you have freedom from consequences. If you libel or slander someone, there are consequences. If you call upon people to hurt or kill an individual or a group, there are consequences. The problem today is with the Internet, which is where most of our discourse, civil or otherwise, takes place. It's anonymous. So, for over a decade, people have been able to post whatever they want without consequence. If you took that anonymity away and you suddenly knew it was your neighbor calling on your wife to be raped and murdered because of how she voted in the last election, then what would you do? You'd go over there and lay a beating on him that he'd never forget, then call the police and have him arrested for what he posted. But today, you don't know that it's your neighbor posting that. The day we finally do solve this problem and take away anonymity, it's going to be like the Purge, when people who don't understand the change continue to post and then face the consequences. I tell you, the day that happens, there's going to be a lot of canceled asses all over the place."

Leroux took a swig of his soda. "It's really too bad. The Internet was supposed to be this wonderful tool that would allow the sharing of information and be the great equalizer, letting anyone in the world have access to all the knowledge of mankind. Instead, like typical stupid humans, we turned it into a way to hate each other. Unfortunately, it's almost impossible to put the genie back in the bottle. We have the technology to remove the anonymity side of things, but until people start to make a conscious choice and demand consequences, nothing's going to change, and it's a change you can't have governments impose. It has to be something that comes from the individuals using the platforms, and the platforms themselves, otherwise, it'll never work." His phone vibrated on the table and he picked it up. "It's the office." He swiped his thumb. "This is Leroux."

"Hey, Chris, it's Braxton. Just thought you should know, a flag came up on one of your files. I sent the details to your secure messenger, but I thought I'd give you a call since it's your day off. I'm in OC3 if you want to come in and monitor."

"Okay, I'll check it out and let you know. Thanks."

"No problem."

Leroux ended the call and brought up his secure messenger on his CIA-issued phone. And frowned.

"What is it?" asked Kane.

"Bravo Team is in Nigeria on an advisory mission, reviewing the security of some new Forward Operating Bases the Nigerians have set up to combat Boko Haram."

"Sounds routine. What's the problem?"

"Apparently, a large group has mobilized and is heading toward their position."

Kane leaned closer to the camera, concern for his former brothers-in-arms written on his face. "ETA?"

"The CIA is watching the staging area and they just left it. Twenty, maybe thirty minutes, by the looks of it."

"Does Bravo Team know?" asked Sherrie, her own concern evident as she had worked with the team several times in the past, including just a few weeks ago in an off-the-books operation.

"I don't know, but I think I'm going to head in, just in case I can be of any help. My team's worked with them more than any other."

"I think you should."

"Is it a CIA op or Pentagon?" asked Kane.

Leroux rose. "Pentagon. Braxton's team wasn't even monitoring the mission. They were monitoring Boko Haram activity along with a dozen other groups. The system just flagged activity, then an alert was triggered that I had set up concerning Bravo Team and high-risk activity in areas they were deployed."

"Expecting trouble?" asked Fang.

"I always expect trouble, but I watch out for my friends. You'll have to excuse me." He headed for the bedroom to change, a pit forming in his stomach as the details of the alert replayed in his head. Bravo Team was outnumbered three-to-one, but if they were abandoned by the apparently inexperienced Nigerian troops, those numbers changed to ten-to-one. And with the ROEs they were operating under, they could not proactively protect themselves. He sighed as he pulled off his T-shirt.

"Bureaucrats."

FOB Ugurun, Nigeria

Dawson walked the perimeter with Buhari. All around them trees were being felled, and with each one, the encampment became slightly safer. He came to a halt at the gate, merely an opening in the fencing flanked by two sand-bagged positions—it wasn't holding back anyone. In fact, there was nothing here to hold back much of anything. He indicated a village just down the road. "What can you tell me about them?"

Buhari shrugged. "Ugurun? Nothing much. Mostly rice farmers. A few hundred people, peaceful. Nothing to worry about."

"No Boko Haram sympathizers?"

"Not likely. There isn't a family in this region that hasn't had someone they know kidnapped or killed by Boko Haram. It's villages like this that we're here to protect. They're too small to fight off the terrorists. We're hoping these bases will serve as a deterrent, but unfortunately we can't be everywhere at once."

A bell rang in the distance and moments later the sound of excited children carried down the road. Dawson frowned. "Is that a school?"

"Yes, they're calling them back from lunch. Every day when those children are gathered at the school, I don't rest easy until that final bell lets them out. Boko Haram loves to grab the children from schools. They're all in one place with very few adults."

Dawson sighed. "It's not right that your people have to live like this."

"No, it's not, and I'm not sure what we're supposed to do about it. We don't have the manpower to protect every town and village, every school. Even if we could put a platoon at every site where children gathered, it wouldn't be enough. Boko Haram only has to hit one place at a time, but we have to defend them all. They'll come into a village like this with a hundred armed men, and while a dozen highly trained men like us might be able to hold them off, the average Nigerian soldier simply isn't trained well enough. They're taught to take care of themselves from a hygiene and health standpoint, how to properly put on their uniform and how to fire their weapon. For too many of them, the first time they come under fire is the last time. It's sad, really. If we had a professional armed forces like America does, we might be able to protect our children."

Dawson felt for the man. Children shouldn't have to live in fear that they might be kidnapped then raped or sold into slavery. Mothers and fathers shouldn't be forced to choose between sending their children to get an education, or keeping them home where there was safety in lack of numbers. Unfortunately, this was the reality in too much of the world, and while America and its allies could project their power anywhere, they could not do it everywhere—exactly as Buhari had said of his own troops. Those who would do harm only had to target one location with everything they had, while those putting their lives on the line had to be spread thin to offer a small sense of protection everywhere, that was, unfortunately, no protection at all. "Well, your government reaching out to us was a step in the right direction. These bases are a good idea, and the more you can set up, the more quickly you can react to an attack. I assume you have scouts?"

Buhari nodded. "We have half a dozen out at any given time, spread throughout the area. If they detect any movement, they radio it in, and that hopefully gives us enough time to get our men in position to repel an attack." He waved a hand at the soldiers pushing back the perimeter. "But you've seen what I have to work with. I can muster a couple of dozen men, almost none of them with combat experience. In a real fight, even if we succeeded, a heavy price would be paid."

"Then I suggest you train them beyond the manual."

"What do you mean?"

"I mean, stop rotating them through here and doing just the basics. Your NCOs have these men doing jumping jacks. This is Nigeria, not Brooklyn. Your young men are already fit. Teach these men hand-to-hand combat, teach them how to use and take care of their weapons, what it's like to be in a fire fight. Let them hear the sound of an AK-47 going off ten feet away from them so that when they hear it for the first time in battle, it's not as terrifying. Ask your superior officers to extend the training course, and if they won't, double the hours you're doing during the day. Send these men off with a fighting chance. They'll hate you for it by the time they leave, but after they survive their first battle, they'll be writing you love letters."

Buhari chuckled. "Now that would be something. You're right, though. Quality over quantity I think is how you say it."

"Sergeant Major!"

They both spun toward the guard at the gate, the concern in his voice suggesting urgency. "What is it?" asked Buhari.

The man pointed down the road. "It's Garba, sir!"

Dawson spotted a man in civilian attire running toward them, soaked in sweat, gasping for breath as his arms dangled limply at his sides. "Who is that?"

"Corporal Garba. He's one of my scouts."

Buhari jogged toward the man, increasing his pace as Garba slowed, an arm outstretched. He finally collapsed and Buhari reached out, grabbing him before he hit the ground. Dawson turned and whistled. "We need some water and a stretcher!"

"Yes, Sergeant Major!" responded one of the Nigerians. Orders were shouted and Dawson joined Buhari, still holding Garba in his arms.

"What is it? What's happened?" asked Buhari.

Garba continued to gasp for breath, though was slowly catching it. "I'm sorry, Sergeant Major. There's something wrong with my radio. The battery, I think." He sucked in several lungsful of air. "Boko Haram, they're on their way, at least sixty men, maybe more."

Buhari exchanged a concerned glance with Dawson. "Where are they headed?"

"For the village."

Buhari cursed and twisted his head toward the base. "Raise the alarm!" he shouted, and moments later a siren wailed, speakers on top of a large pole spreading the broadcast far and wide, warning not only those at the camp, but the village as well. "How far behind you?"

Garba shook his head. "Not far. I ran all the way. Less than ten minutes."

A stretcher arrived and Garba was loaded on it. "Take him to the infirmary. Food and water until he's ready to fight."

"Yes, Sergeant Major."

Two men carried Garba off as he worked hard at draining a canteen. Buhari strode quickly back toward the wire, Dawson at his side, Bravo Team already sprinting toward the fence line and climbing over the chain-link, defeating the entire perimeter security in a matter of seconds as they abandoned helping the Nigerians push back the forest and instead prepared for battle.

Dawson waited for Buhari to finish giving orders to his men. "What's your standing orders for a situation like this?"

"If we were a functional unit, we'd head into the village and repel any attack, but we're hardly functional."

"We can't just leave those people there defenseless. Between your men and my team, we've got over thirty people. We could put up one hell of a fight."

Buhari hesitated then gave a curt nod. "I'm with you, Sergeant Major, unfortunately, my commander is in Lagos and his second-in-command was just flown out on your chopper with malaria."

"So that leaves you in charge?"

"Until a replacement can be sent."

"Didn't you say something about asking for forgiveness after—"

48

"Yes, yes." Buhari pointed at Dawson's comms. "I think the bigger problem is at the other end of your earpiece."

En route to Ugurun, Nigeria

The wind swept through Ibrahim's hair as he and scores of his men raced toward the small village of Ugurun and the bounty it promised. They could hit a bigger town and grab more girls at once, but that would be risky. Today, he wanted an easy score, twenty or thirty children, bringing them back to their base and divvying them up into whatever would be the most profitable, and perhaps pleasurable, manner. They needed money desperately, and a small operation like today would raise them enough funds to keep them going for a few weeks. They didn't need many of these operations to keep them going.

But it was more than just the money and the sex. It was about reminding people what was right and wrong, and putting girls in school and teaching them how to read and write and do math was against the Koran, was against the will of Allah. Girls should only be taught what their faith expected of them, what their communities, their families, and their future husband expected. Their heads shouldn't be filled with Western nonsense. And the same could be said for the boys. Their teachings should be restricted as well. Yes, they needed to know how to read and write in order to study the Koran properly, but other than that, everything they needed to know could be found in the teachings of the Prophet Muhammad, peace and blessings be upon him.

This was their way of fighting back throughout the region where they operated. Families kept their daughters home, unwilling to risk putting them in a setting where they could be scooped with others. Yes, occasionally, one of his men would grab a lone child against orders. She would be interrogated and returned if it were found she didn't attend school. They weren't heartless, after all. The entire point of Boko Haram was to have parents stop educating their children by keeping them home. If the children were getting kidnapped at home regardless, parents might begin thinking there was safety in numbers, where at least there were soldiers assigned to protect the schools.

The village they were heading for had a new encampment nearby designed to deter him and his men. He had already had it scouted. Every few days, he'd have one of his men take a few shots at the camp to sow fear among those who would oppose him. From what he had been told, there were only a couple of dozen men stationed there, most young and poorly trained. His men were hardened warriors who didn't run from a fight, who didn't cower in fear at weapons fire.

His men were willing to die for the cause because they knew the rewards in the afterlife an honorable death provided. He had roughly sixty men with him. They would easily overwhelm any opposition, though if he had to hazard a guess, he suspected most of those they would face would run away, for those without Allah in their hearts were cowards by nature.

He closed his eyes for a moment, enjoying the wind on his face. He inhaled deeply, breathing in the countryside, then opened his eyes and exhaled, his heart pounding with excitement as they neared the village. He might live, he might die, but either way, the day would end in ecstasy.

They sped past farms on either side of the road and he smiled at a woman working in the fields with her daughter. It was a school day, so the message had been received by this family. The woman grabbed the girl, perhaps twelve, and rushed toward the farmhouse set far back from the road. He was out of sight long before they reached the door.

The whine of the motorcycles ahead of him changed pitch and he finally paid attention to where he was. The village was just ahead, and while he had supreme confidence in the capability of his men and that victory would be theirs, it was never wise to enter a village blindly. He came to a halt at the crossroads where the lead riders had stopped, and pointed at two of his men. "Go check it out."

They both gunned their engines, racing ahead, the pitch easing as they entered the village. He cocked an ear, listening intently for any signs of trouble. He could barely hear them now, and he raised his hand to signal the advance when suddenly the engines revved hard. Shots rang out and he cursed.

Perhaps this would not be easy after all.

FOB Ugurun, Nigeria

Dawson stood inside the gate, pissed. The Pentagon didn't want American troops engaged in combat on Nigerian soil, and he and his team had been ordered to stay on the base and let the Nigerians deal with their own domestic problem. They were there as security advisors only. It would not be the first time he had been given orders like this, and it would not be the first time it had enraged him. This wasn't a situation where there were varying degrees of bad guys. If they were in Yemen or Saudi Arabia, and the other side were attacking, things might be different. Both sides were bad, just varying degrees of it. But here, it was clear cut— local troops defending schoolchildren from terrorists who would kidnap them and sell them into sexual slavery.

"Bureaucrats," he muttered.

Niner eyed him. "You hearing voices, BD?"

Dawson grunted. "If our job isn't to defend schoolchildren, then I don't know what is."

"Yeah, this is bullshit," rumbled Atlas as they watched a tactical column of Nigerians led by Buhari hurry down the road toward the village. "Are there any circumstances where we're allowed to engage?"

"Only if we're fired upon, and then it's only to repel. We're not allowed to pursue."

"Complete and utter bullshit."

"Is that direct from the colonel?" asked Spock.

Dawson nodded. "Yeah, but he's working on getting our ROEs changed now that we know an attack might be imminent and children could be involved."

At least one motorcycle whined loudly in the distance, the chorus of high-pitched wails they had heard earlier having settled down. "Something's happening," said Niner as they all turned in the direction of the sound. Weapons were readied and Dawson resisted the urge to join in on what he feared could become a blood bath.

Shouts followed by the easing of the engines indicated those approaching were now slowing. More shouts then several shots, and the engines whined once more. In the distance, they could see the Nigerians sprinting toward the village as more gunfire erupted. Then a sound that sent a shiver down Dawson's spine screamed out in the distance—scores of motorcycle engines revving.

Whatever was going to happen had just started.

And they were stuck on the sidelines because of politics.

Operations Center 3, CIA Headquarters
Langley, Virginia

Leroux entered the state-of-the-art operation center, having rushed all the way here, calls going out to his team to report in as soon as possible. Analyst Supervisor Braxton Phelps waved at him from his station at the center of the room.

"Just in time." Phelps jerked his chin toward the massive displays that arced across the front of the operations center.

Leroux stared at the screens as he joined Phelps at the center of the room. "What am I looking at?"

"On the left is the Forward Operating Base. The cluster of identified targets at the front gate are the six members of Bravo Team. Just to the south, we've got about twenty Nigerian regulars that are now heading into the village. They just challenged two guys on motorcycles sporting AKs. They fired at them, but they got away. However"—Phelps indicated the second image and Leroux frowned at the sight of dozens of motorcycles, most carrying two men, all armed with rifles, racing north—"we've got a horde of Boko Haram heading their way from just outside of town."

"ETA?"

"I'd be surprised if it's sixty seconds."

Leroux cursed. "So, do these Nigerians stand a chance?"

"Unlikely. Our reports are that they're barely trained. Most are raw recruits."

"And let me guess, Delta's ROEs are that they're not allowed to engage unless engaged?"

"Exactly. The Pentagon said to leave it to the Nigerians. Apparently, the Nigerians don't want American soldiers involved in combat on their soil."

Leroux rolled his eyes. "Bureaucratic horseshit. We're talking about children here! They're innocent in all of this." An idea occurred to him. It was a long shot, but it was the only one they had. He turned to one of Phelps' team members. "Get me the Chief."

"Yes, sir."

Phelps handed Leroux a headset and he jacked in.

"Director Morrison is on Line One, sir."

Leroux pressed the button. "Hi, Chief, it's Leroux."

"Isn't this your day off?"

"A little birdie told me Bravo Team was involved in something in Nigeria that looked like it was about to get out of hand."

Leif Morrison, National Clandestine Service Chief for the CIA, chuckled. "I don't know why we bother with compartmentalization here.

My phone is indicating you're in the building so it must be important. What is it you want?"

"It looks like at least fifty or sixty Boko Haram are about to engage twenty Nigerians with little experience. Bravo Team is within literal spitting distance and wants in on the action, but their ROEs are preventing them."

"Yes, I'm aware of what's going on. The Nigerians don't want our people engaged in combat on their soil. They're concerned about blowback from the local population in that area."

"Well, I had a thought on that."

"Go ahead."

"Get the op reclassified as a CIA operation, then all these problems go away." Leroux could almost hear Morrison smile.

"I'll get back to you. Get your team in place."

Leroux smiled. "Yes, sir."

Approaching Ugurun, Nigeria

Sergeant Major Buhari cursed as the sound of dozens of motorcycles raced toward them. The schoolhouse was just ahead, containing two rooms with separate doors, the back for boys, the front for girls, where students from several villages in the area attended class. There was already crying from inside the thin walls, the children likely no strangers to gunfire, though probably had never heard it so close. The two terrorists on their motorcycles had no doubt been sent in to scout the school. Unfortunately, they had escaped and were now informing their friends just how many they were facing.

He pointed at the school and addressed his men. "Our mission is to defend these children. You know what will happen to them if they're taken." He deployed his men in groups of four, each with an experienced man, someone who had seen combat in the past that might steady their nerves and keep them an effective fighting force. Yet as the whine of the engines grew louder, the fear in his men's eyes also grew.

He pulled open the door of the schoolhouse, praying their American friends would be allowed into the battle, for he feared it might be the only way they could save these poor children, children now staring at him, tears staining their cheeks as they all huddled under their desks, holding each other, no doubt having heard the stories of what would become of them, some too young to understand, some old enough to fully comprehend the nightmare in store.

And as he made eye contact with one of those teenage girls, he vowed then and there that he would die before he let harm come to any of them.

Operations Center 2, CIA Headquarters
Langley, Virginia

Leroux entered Operations Center 2, the first of his team to arrive, the automatic muster transmitted by the system to the rest not long ago. Though his team wasn't there, the operations center was manned, as it always was, in case of emergency, and he had worked with every one of them at some point in his career. "Good afternoon, everybody."

A variety of acknowledgments were returned as he headed to the center of the room and joined Avril Casey, Control until the moment he had stepped through the door. "Hey, Chris, couldn't stay away?"

He chuckled. "Hey, Avril, I'm a glutton for punishment."

"What's up?"

He turned to face the room. "Okay, people, we're prepping for a priority takeover of an existing Pentagon mission that could be about to go south. Bring up mission Sierra-Golf-Victor-4744."

Casey tapped at her keyboard, the displays at the front of the room refreshing with the satellite feeds and status reports he had just seen across the corridor.

"Everybody start orienting yourselves. You're looking at northern Nigeria. On the left are the Nigerian forces. On the right is Boko Haram. We've got a schoolhouse full of children that we believe they're going to be targeting. The base, at the top left, has six Delta operators on an advisory mission under Pentagon command with ROEs that don't allow them to engage unless attacked. We have approximately twenty inexperienced Nigerian troops who will attempt to protect the school from at least sixty armed hostiles. I've asked the Chief to have the mission reclassified as a CIA op so we can change the ROEs, and if he's successful, we could be taking over the op at any moment."

Casey looked up at him from her station. "And if you succeed in becoming Control Actual?"

"I'll give the Delta commander on the scene discretion to act as he sees fit."

She checked her display. "That's Command Sergeant Major Dawson. You know he's going to act."

Leroux agreed. "If he does, we need to be prepared to provide him the best intel we can, so his team cannot only survive, outnumbered as they are, but also save those girls."

The door opened and his second-in-command, Sonya Tong, entered. She flashed him a smile and he returned it as Casey turned to her team. "As your replacements arrive, head over to OC One and prep for standby."

61

The analyst manning Tong's usual spot grabbed his personal items then quickly brought Tong up to speed. Tong sat in the vacated seat and logged into the system before facing Leroux and giving a thumbs-up. "I'm in. Good thing I have no social life."

Leroux laughed. "I think that's why most of us were recruited. Start analyzing the footage. I want to be able to tell Bravo Team exactly what they're up against. Pull resources as you need them and as they arrive."

"I'm on it."

"Do you still need me?" asked Casey.

Leroux shook his head. "No, now that Sonya is here, I can handle things. Why don't you head over to OC One and I'll send your team over as mine arrive."

Casey smiled at him. "Good luck." She headed out the door as Randy Child, their tech wunderkind, arrived. He appeared disheveled and Leroux was certain he was wearing the same clothes from two days ago.

Child yawned heavily. "This better be good, boss. I had to abandon my team after two days of nonstop battle."

Tong's eyes narrowed. "You were in battle? What, paintball?"

"Call of Duty." He glanced at the displays. "If that's what I think it is, my combat experience should come in handy." Snickers erupted from around the room. "Hey, it's very realistic!"

"I have no doubt," said Leroux, jerking a thumb over his shoulder at Child's station. "Get up to speed and prepped. We could be in the thick of it any moment now."

Child became serious. "You got it, boss."

Tong raised a hand. "I've got the Chief for you, Line Two."

Leroux jacked his headset in and pressed the button. "This is Leroux."

"Washington approves your plan. The Bravo Team mission has been retasked to the CIA for a covert counter-terrorism operation. We now have control. Are you ready?"

Leroux nodded as one of the senior analysts, Marc Therrien, entered the room. "We're ready, Chief. Just give me the word."

"The word is given. The Pentagon has just released the encryption codes and frequencies. You should have access to Bravo Team's comms now. Just give the Pentagon time to inform them of the handover."

"Copy that, Chief."

"Now get on it and save those girls."

Leroux's chest tightened at the reminder of what this was all about, and the responsibility he had just taken on. "Yes, sir. You can count on us and Bravo Team to get it done."

"That's what I told the president. Now go prove me right."

FOB Ugurun, Nigeria

Dawson paced in front of the gate as dozens of motorcycles raced toward the village and the small school at the center of it. According to his update, an estimated sixty armed hostiles were en route, and unless Buhari's men could find good cover to repel the attack, and keep their nerve, they would lose this battle.

Niner sprinted up to him, skidding to a halt. "Confirmed. We've got a good view of the school and the road coming into the village from the one-two corner. It's within range. Good thing this is happening after the chopper came back. I got my SWS in the gear and so does Atlas."

"Good. Get set up just in case our orders change. I want you to be ready to open fire with the first shot."

"You got it."

Niner raced toward the pile of gear that had arrived about an hour ago, Atlas already pulling out the Sniper Weapon Systems. "We're on!" he yelled, and Atlas gave a thumbs-up.

Dawson's comms squawked in his ear. "Zero-One, Control Actual. Come in, over."

Spock cocked an eyebrow. "The big man himself?"

Dawson shrugged as he responded to Colonel Thomas Clancy, his commanding officer. "Control Actual, this is Zero-One. Go ahead, over."

"Zero-One, your unit has been reclassified. This is no longer a Pentagon operation, it's a CIA operation. Stand by for your new Control Actual and ROEs. Good hunting, Zero-One. Control Actual, out."

Dawson smiled and he held up a finger, not wanting to miss a moment of what was about to happen as the motorcycles entered the village at the far end of the road.

"Bravo Zero-One, this is Control Actual. Do you copy?"

"This is Zero-One. I copy, over." He recognized Leroux's voice, a man he had worked with on many occasions, and someone he considered one of the best in the business, if not the best.

"Zero-One, as the previous Control Actual informed you, you are now under CIA command and your ROEs have changed. You are now permitted to engage if fired upon or if there is an immediate threat of being fired upon. You are also permitted to enter into joint operations with the Nigerian forces on and off the Forward Operating Base at your discretion. Do you copy?"

Fist bumps were exchanged all around. "Copy that, Control. New ROEs acknowledged."

Leroux's voice became slightly less formal. "What are your intentions, Zero-One?"

"We're going to save those girls."

"Confirmed, Zero-One. Expect significant resistance and potential retaliation. Does your assessment of the current situation require additional forces?"

Dawson unslung his M4 and headed through the gate with Spock, Jagger, and Mickey. "Control, we're outnumbered three to one, and the enemy has additional resources in the area. I'm requesting that Zero-Two's team be brought in to assist."

"Copy that, Zero-One. We'll make every effort to get them there as soon as possible, however, we'll have to rely on local transport, so don't expect them any time soon."

"Understood," replied Dawson as he sprinted down the road with the others. "We're about to engage. Zero-One, out." He glanced over his shoulder at the one-two corner of the compound, spotting Niner and Atlas setting up. "One-One and Zero-Six, this is Zero-One. Open fire as soon as you have targets, over."

Atlas and Niner acknowledged the change of orders, the relief in their voices evident to everyone. Gunfire erupted from around the school as the first motorcycles gunned into the village, the lead two riders dropping. Those behind them with comrades riding bitch returned fire and Dawson cursed as two of Buhari's men, standing in the open, firing their weapons on full-auto, dropped.

The thunderclaps of Niner and Atlas' sniper rifles ripped apart the air behind them, and two more riders dropped. Dawson spotted Buhari standing in the doorway of the school, his sight trained on the hostiles, disciplined bursts erupting from his weapon. At the sound of the sniper rifles, his head spun and he spotted Dawson and the others. A smile spread and he shouted something to his men who cheered, pouring more gunfire on the enemy.

"Zero-One, Control. Be advised you have hostiles leaving the road. They're about to flank the school to the west and east."

"Copy that, Control." He glanced at the others. "Spock, you're with me. Mickey and Jagger, cover the rear of the school."

"Yes, Sergeant Major," echoed his men as Mickey and Jagger split off. Dawson raised his M4 and began firing single shots at the enemy. As they reached the school grounds, he didn't bother joining Buhari at the door—it was too exposed. Half of Buhari's men were in a ditch that ran along the front of the school that provided far better cover. Shots continued to sound from Atlas and Niner, each one true, leaving a tangle of motorcycles with dead or wounded riders now providing a fairly effective roadblock.

Shots rang out from behind them and Jagger's voice came in over the comms. "Zero-One, Zero-Eight. We've got at least a dozen back here. We could use some local help, over."

"Copy that, Zero-Eight. Stand by." Dawson twisted around and waved at Buhari. "Sergeant Major! Send six men to reinforce the rear!" Buhari gave a thumbs-up, snapping out the order, half a dozen of his men redeploying. "Zero-Eight, Zero-One. Reinforcements are coming in from the number two side."

"Copy that, Zero-One," replied Jagger, his and Mickey's M4s engaging a large number of AK-47s and 74s, suddenly joined by the Nigerians, evening out the odds. Even if their aim was less than accurate, it provided suppression fire that would give his men the opportunity to deliver disciplined rounds and quickly thin the herd.

"Zero-One, Control. The rear of the hostile column has stopped, over."

Dawson peered down the road to see the approaching motorcycles slowing, some of them turning around. Shouts from the riders behind those at the lead had heads spinning then wheels. Dawson rose and switched to full-auto, pouring as much lead as he could on the riders as they retreated, knowing that every one he eliminated now would be one less he would face later. Spock and the Nigerians joined in, another half-dozen wiped out before Dawson raised a fist in the air.

"Ceasefire!"

And the guns fell silent.

The Nigerians stood in stunned silence then smiles broke out and cheers erupted at the unexpected victory. But there was no time to celebrate.

Dawson activated his comms. "This is Zero-One. Everybody report in."

The entire team reported in order, confirming they were alive and uninjured, and he rested slightly easier.

A shriek from inside the school had everyone spinning. Buhari and Dawson sprinted inside to find a teacher kneeling over the body of a little girl, a stray round having penetrated her chest, the large pool of blood she lay in indicating she was long past helping.

Buhari kneeled beside the teacher. "Is anyone else hurt?"

But she said nothing, the woman's entire body trembling from fear and shock. Dawson checked for a pulse, confirming the girl, no more than eight, was dead. He rose and smiled reassuringly at the children. "You're safe now. Is anybody else hurt?"

A hand rose from behind the huddled mass in the corner and his chest tightened at the sight of blood running down the extended arm. He stepped forward and the children parted, revealing a girl, perhaps twelve, shaking in place, struggling to maintain her balance as blood oozed from her shoulder. He activated his comms as he rushed forward to catch her before she collapsed.

"One-One, Zero-One. Get to the schoolhouse now. Bring a medkit."

"Roger that," replied Niner, their most experienced medic.

Dawson pressed his hand against the wound as he gently caressed her cheek. She stared up at him, terror filling her eyes at what must be a horrifying sight, for he was in full combat gear, a white man with a gun whom she had never seen before, a stranger for all she knew was responsible for what had happened. A motorcycle engine revved in the distance and her eyes widened further, meeting his.

"Please don't let them take me," she whispered.

Niner burst into the room and took over. Dawson stepped back as more engines revved, Boko Haram sending a message that this day wasn't over.

Outside Ugurun, Nigeria

Ibrahim twisted the throttle repeatedly, as did the others who survived the failed assault. As soon as he had heard the loud claps of multiple sniper rifles, he had eased up. Something was wrong. Other types of weapons he wasn't accustomed to hearing had joined in the fight, and when it was apparent they were losing, he had ordered the retreat. He waited for the last survivors to join them then led everyone away from the village to a safe distance.

He turned off his bike as did the others, the silence only broken by the gasps of the exhausted, shocked, and wounded. "What happened?" he asked the group in general.

"They had help," said one of his men, Maduka, gripping a bloodied shoulder.

"Who?"

"Americans."

The ember of hate he always carried in his stomach flared at the mention of Islam's greatest enemy. "Are you sure it was Americans?"

Maduka shrugged then winced at the motion. "I saw white guys in expensive gear."

"We need to know if we're fighting Americans. If we are, the donations we raise will be greatly increased if we can kill them."

Maduka's eyes bulged. "You mean we're going to try again?"

"We lost the battle, but this is a war." Ibrahim waved an arm at half a dozen of his men. "Take radios and set up positions around the village and that base. I want to know what we're facing. Are they Americans? If not, who are they? How many of them are there? What kind of weapons do they have? How many government soldiers? Gather as much intel as you can, then report in." He turned to the rest. "Those of you who aren't wounded, I want you to visit every town and village in the area and gather our supporters. Our brothers will be avenged, and the great Satan and the corrupt who would seek their aid shall pay the ultimate price. Nobody defies Boko Haram!"

Operations Center 2, CIA Headquarters
Langley, Virginia

Leroux stared at the satellite images and breathed a sigh of relief as the bulk of the remaining Boko Haram force turned tail, but frowned when half a dozen remained behind.

"What do you think they're doing?" asked Child as they left their motorcycles on the side of the road then split up.

"Probably some sort of recon mission," replied Tong. "They just got their asses kicked and they want to know who did it." She pointed at the screen, noticing the same thing Leroux just had. Riders were splitting off at the various crossroads leading back to their warehouse. "That looks ominous."

A pit formed in Leroux's stomach. "They're gathering supporters."

Child cursed as he spun in his chair. "So then this isn't over."

Leroux shook his head. "Not by a long shot." He jacked into his terminal. "Zero-One, Control Actual. Do you copy, over?"

"Control, Zero-One. I copy, over."

72

"Eyes in the sky show six hostiles remained behind and are on foot in your area. We assume they plan on gathering intel. Remainder of the hostiles have left the area, however, it appears they're splitting up. Our thinking is that they're gathering followers for a counterattack. Recommend you prepare to evac the area."

Dawson's reply was immediate and expected. "Negative, Control. We'll remain until the Nigerians can reinforce this area and guarantee the safety of these children. We have wounded here. See if you can get the Nigerians to send in the chopper to evac them."

"Copy that, Zero-One. We'll try to arrange it, however, your local contacts will probably have more success than we will."

"Understood, Control. Zero-One, out."

Leroux pulled off his headset and tossed it onto his station. He turned to Tong. "See if you can arrange a helicopter evac for the wounded. And find out what other assets we have in the area that we might be able to use."

"A nice drone strike on their warehouse when they're all in there partying might be a nice idea," suggested Child as he dropped his foot, killing his spin.

Leroux shook his head. "We don't know who's inside. That could be where they're keeping girls that they've kidnapped. On this mission, collateral damage is unacceptable."

Ugurun, Nigeria

"How many men did you lose?" asked Dawson as the area filled with villagers rushing toward the school to check on their children. Buhari's men weren't letting the children out of the school until they could be matched with parents—the last thing they needed were several dozen unattended children running around the area.

"Four." Buhari sighed. "Four young men, boys, who never should have been here."

Dawson tapped his earpiece. "The voice in my ear tells me we have six hostiles reconnoitering the area, and it appears that the survivors have split up and may be attempting to gather others for a counterattack."

Buhari cursed. "We barely won this one. The only reason we did was because we surprised them. Now that they know you're here, they'll be coming in numbers, using a much wiser strategy than riding in on noisy motorcycles down the only road."

"Agreed. What would you recommend?"

Buhari smirked at him. "You're the advisor. What would *you* advise?"

74

Dawson chuckled. "I'd advise you radio headquarters and get them to fly in reinforcements so that we can immediately bolster our defenses, then get a column of a couple hundred troops heading this way, because they could be hitting this place by nightfall in force."

Buhari grunted. "As I told you before, the roads are out. There's no way we can get reinforcements in by ground."

"Then get them all in by air."

"I had a hard enough time convincing the colonel to free up a single chopper for you."

Dawson bristled. "Then tell the colonel the choppers aren't to taxi American advisors, it's to save children."

"I'll do my best, but I'm not confident."

"Then tell your colonel to do *his* best, because America will be watching."

FOB Hadejia, Nigeria

Red stood near the center of the Forward Operating Base his team had been sent to evaluate, though that job had been set aside the moment he had received word of the change in command. This was a CIA operation now, counterterrorism, and Dawson's team had just engaged in battle with Boko Haram, fending off the terrorists' attempt to kidnap schoolgirls. He turned to Sergeant Akintan. "How long would it take us to get to Ugurun?"

"Eight hours by truck in ideal conditions. Less than an hour by helicopter, but we don't have any available."

"Can you get some?"

"I'll ask my lieutenant."

Red pointed at one of the dozen troop transports now spread around the compound rather than clustered together as a single target. "Are these fully fueled?"

"Always."

"How many of your men are ready to go?"

"Go where?"

"Ugurun."

Akintan shook his head. "We're not authorized—"

Red interrupted him. "That's not what I'm asking. I'm asking, *if* you received the orders, how many men are ready to go, right now?"

"I could put one hundred men on those trucks, armed and equipped, within fifteen minutes."

Red smiled slightly. "That's what I like to hear."

"But it doesn't matter, the roads are out."

"This is the Army, Sergeant. Just like the Marines, we improvise, we adapt, we overcome. Talk to your lieutenant. We need to be prepared to go and provide relief. From the reports I've received, FOB Ugurun is a joke, barely twenty men, most raw recruits with only a chain-link fence to protect them. Boko Haram just got their asses kicked today, but they could be back in greater numbers, and your countrymen and mine will be slaughtered if we don't act now."

The sergeant bristled at the mention of Boko Haram. "They attacked one of our bases?"

"No, they attacked a school just down the road. The soldiers at the base engaged along with the other American team, and they repelled the attack. Four of your men were killed and at least one child."

Akintan cursed. "You are right, Sergeant, Boko Haram never likes to lose. I'll go talk to my lieutenant and see what can be done." He headed for the command hut and Red turned to the rest of his team.

"We could be about to get into the thick of it."

"Good," said Jimmy. "I'd rather be killing terrorists any day than inspecting fence lines."

"Me too," agreed Wings. He pointed at a chopper sitting off to the side of the landing pad. "I talked to one of the Nigerians about that earlier. He said they have the parts to fix it, but they're waiting for the mechanic. I bet you I can get that thing working."

"Do it."

Wings sprinted toward the chopper, shouting to one of the Nigerians. "Yo, bring those parts! We're going to get this baby running!" The man grinned before disappearing inside a storage building.

"Pack your gear, prepare for a change in venue. If we're going by helicopter, we won't be able to take as much with us. Focus on weapons and ammo, and don't forget the night vision. BD's initial report indicated they barely had any separation between the fence line and the tree line. I want to be able to pick these mothers out if they decide to attack at night." He smacked his hands together. "Get to it. I'm going to contact Control."

The others headed to the barracks reserved for them, the accommodations here apparently far better than those on offer for Dawson's team. He activated his comms. "Control, Zero-Two. Come in, over."

"This is Control. Go ahead, over."

He recognized Leroux's voice. "Can I get a status update on Team One, over?"

"Affirmative, Zero-Two. Zero-One reports that his team is secure and is providing first aid to the wounded, over."

"Have they returned to the FOB?"

"Negative, they're still at the school."

"Hostiles?"

"It appears they left six scouts behind, and what remains of their force has fallen back to their original staging area, about twenty minutes away, but a lot of them broke off. We believe they're gathering reinforcements for a more significant attack."

"Copy that. Request permission to redeploy to Team One's location."

"Permission granted if you can arrange transport. At the moment, the Nigerians won't provide clearance for anything of ours to fly over their airspace. Do you have transportation available to you?"

"We're working on it. We'll hopefully know shortly."

"Copy that, Zero-Two. Keep us posted."

"Roger that, Control. Zero-Two, out." Red strode over to the helicopter as the replacement parts arrived, Wings already buried in the engine. "Report."

Wings poked his head out. "I'm not done yet." Red gave him a look and Wings grinned. "If my friend here has all the parts we need, I can get her running, but it's probably going to take me a couple of hours. My guess is you'll be in trucks heading there long before I've got this thing in the air. What do you want us to do?"

"Keep going. If we get permission to leave in the trucks, we will. You stay here and get this bird in the air. Even if we have a two-hour head start on you, if the roads are truly out, we might not be able to get there until tomorrow. Five men stuck on a road with one working on a possible solution is better than six stuck with no solution."

"You're a wise man, Sergeant."

"That's why they pay me the big bucks." Red headed for his rack to prep his gear when Sergeant Akintan burst from the command hut, hailing him.

"Any luck?" asked Red.

Akintan twisted his hand back and forth. "Sort of. Two choppers have been dispatched from Kano. They should be arriving in Ugurun soon with about thirty additional troops plus equipment."

"What about choppers for us?"

Akintan shook his head. "None available." He lowered his voice. "I got the impression that Command wants to solve this problem themselves. They don't want to be seen as needing Americans to protect their own children."

Red frowned. He could understand the sentiment, but this was no time to let pride get in the way when children were at stake. "Well, there's no point in arguing. What about the transports?"

Akintan smiled. "Approved."

Red slapped him on the shoulder. "That's great news. Get your men ready, I want to be on the road in fifteen minutes. Bring weapons, ammo, and anything that might help us clear roads like shovels, axes, chainsaws, anything you can think of."

"Consider it done." Akintan split away, barking orders as Red headed for the barracks and activated his comms. "Control, this is Zero-Two. Let Zero-One know that we're on our way. ETA unknown, over."

"Copy that, Zero-Two. I know they'll be happy to hear that."

"Copy that, Control. Zero-Two, out."

Red checked his watch and cursed as he entered the barracks, praying that Wings could get the chopper working far sooner than he expected, otherwise, they might arrive long after the battle had been lost, and instead of helping friends, they might be relegated to identifying them.

Ugurun, Nigeria

Dawson and Spock stood at respectful attention as the bodies of the dead Nigerians were carried past and back toward the base. Out of the corner of his eye he spotted Niner emerging from the church, his hands covered in blood. Dawson waited for the procession to pass before facing him. Niner shook his head and Dawson's heart broke. He closed his eyes, picturing the young girl's last plea.

"Please don't let them take me."

He squeezed his eyes hard, stemming the tears that threatened to flow. These were innocent children. This shouldn't be their life. And while there was little he could do about it in the grander scheme of things, there was something he could do about it today. He walked briskly over to Buhari. "We have to protect these people."

Buhari regarded him. "I agree, Sergeant Major, and I'm open to suggestions."

"Get them all on the base."

Buhari's eyes bulged slightly. "You yourself said it's not ready."

82

"It's not, but we'll make it ready. All we need to do is hold out until reinforcements arrive." He pointed at the schoolhouse. "I'm willing to die to protect those kids, are you?"

Buhari squared his shoulders. "Sergeant Major, I swore the moment this started that I wasn't leaving here alive, unless it was with those children."

Dawson smiled, extending a hand. "I knew you were my kind of man."

Buhari returned the handshake. "Let's hope God is on our side today." He headed for a nearby cluster of village elders and concerned parents.

Niner joined him and Spock, cleaning his hands. "We need more help if we're going to save these people."

Dawson agreed. "Red and his team are on the way by truck. Eight hours *if* they can get through the roads, which the locals are saying they can't."

Niner shook his head. "Eight hours? This thing could be over by then."

"Wings is working on repairing a helicopter. He thinks it might take two hours. If he's successful, he'll pick them up. But even then, we're talking hours before they get here, and we're only talking six more men against what Langley just told me could be hundreds. They're fearing a repeat of the Koshebe Massacre."

Atlas' eyes narrowed. "What's that?"

"A couple of years ago, in a village about five miles from here, a Boko Haram fighter demanded the locals cook him food, and he apparently wasn't too polite about it. So, rather than put up with his shit, they overpowered him, tied him up, and called in the local authorities. In response, Boko Haram came in force and slit the throats of over one hundred of them to make an example of anyone who would defy them."

Spock cursed. "Well, we just killed about a dozen of them. I'd say that's defiance."

"Exactly. We could be facing hundreds if they hold true to form."

Jagger stared at the mess of motorcycles, the villagers tossing the bodies into the ditch beside the road and lining up the abandoned bikes. "No offense, BD, but while I admire your faith in us, aren't we just delaying the inevitable? If they're going to be sending hundreds against what, twenty-five, then that FOB has no hope in hell of defending against those numbers. It's chain-link. If we had some real walls that we could keep these people behind, we might be able to hold them off, but even if we had fifty or a hundred men behind there, there's nowhere to take cover. These people are going to be slaughtered."

Dawson agreed with Jagger's assessment. "I'm open to suggestions."

"We've got half a dozen transport trucks. I say we load these people on there and get the hell out of Dodge."

Dawson shook his head. "I already talked to Buhari about that. If we head east or south, we're heading deeper into Boko Haram territory, and the roads are out to the north and west. We won't get ten miles, and then it'll be open season on us."

"What if the locals just scatter?" suggested Atlas. "You know, safety in lack of numbers."

"That's what they tried in Koshebe, and they just rounded them up then murdered them. Boko Haram is one of the most vicious terrorist groups currently operating. They've killed over thirty-thousand people. They have absolutely no regard for human life, and I'm willing to bet they're going to kill every man, woman, and child in this village just to make an example of them so the Nigerians will think twice about engaging."

Niner shrugged. "Well, it's not like we have any way of getting out of here ourselves, so if I'm going to die, it might as well be on my feet protecting innocent civilians."

Dawson noticed a round of handshakes in Buhari's cluster then the sergeant major strode quickly over. "They've agreed to take refuge at the base. They're terrified of a repeat of Koshebe."

"How many people are we talking?" asked Dawson.

A group of young men jumped on the still-functioning motorcycles and raced off. Buhari indicated them with a wave of his hand. "Runners are being sent to all the farms in the area to warn them of what's going on. If everyone heeds the warning, we're looking at several hundred."

Dawson cursed. "The bastards won't even need to aim."

"Fish in a barrel," muttered Atlas.

"What would you suggest we do?" asked Buhari. "You didn't see what happened in Koshebe. I was one of the first on the scene, and it was the most brutal thing I've ever witnessed. I'll die before I let that happen again."

Dawson regarded the man, there no doubting his bravery. "We're all willing to die for these people, Sergeant Major, but once we're dead, there's no one left to protect them. I suggest we start thinking in terms of how to survive this."

Buhari sighed. "You're right, of course."

"Let's get back to the base. There's no need for us to stay here now. Everybody knows where to go. We need to start prepping, and it's time for our taskmasters to start earning their keep."

En route to Ugurun, Nigeria

Red swung the axe, the head chipping off another chunk of a large tree that blocked the road. They hadn't even traveled three miles before they had reached the first blockage, the heavy rains having swept away the trees whose root systems weren't deep enough or those that had died. It was an annual occurrence, but it took time to clear.

When they had arrived, local civilians were already at work on it, and were only more than happy to allow fresh soldiers to take over. His team had joined in the efforts. If they were about to enter hopeless combat, he wanted everyone to feel as if they were comrades-in-arms as opposed to arrogant Americans who thought they were superior to their Nigerian counterparts. Everyone was equal when swinging an axe, though what he would give to have Atlas here right now. The man probably would have just picked up the log and tossed it aside. He smiled and Sergeant Donald "Sweets" Peters regarded him.

"If you've got time to smile, I don't think you're swinging that axe hard enough, Sergeant."

Red chuckled. "I was just thinking how it would have been nice to have Atlas here."

Sergeant Danny "Casey" Martin laughed as he grabbed a smaller log and dragged it off the road. "Yeah, you definitely lost out on picking teams."

Sweets eyed him. "What are you trying to say, that we're the B team?"

Casey stared at him blankly. "And you are?"

Sweets grinned. "Not everybody on the team makes the highlight reel, but they all play their part. But yes, I'd trade you any day for Atlas."

Red swung again, the tree finally splitting, and he exchanged a high-five with the Nigerian he had been working the log with in tandem. He stepped back, exhausted, as everyone in the immediate vicinity grabbed the ends of the split roadblock and dragged them out of the way. Akintan snapped orders to his men and everyone headed back to the trucks, the locals lining the side of the road and shouting their thanks as the engines started and they slowly lurched away, leaving the rest of the clean-up to the locals.

Red took a drink from his canteen. "I think I'm going to recommend that chainsaws be added as standard equipment for missions like these."

"Seconded," said Jimmy with a half-hearted raising of the hand.

The truck came to a jerking stop and Sweets groaned. "What now?"

Akintan appeared at the rear of the truck. "We've got another tree."

A round of groans erupted from Americans and Nigerians alike, and Red shook his head as he hopped out of the back of the truck. At this rate, there was no way in hell they would reach Dawson and the others in time to help.

This could take days.

Operations Center 2, CIA Headquarters
Langley, Virginia

Leroux stared at the displays, one set of images disturbing, the other oddly interesting if it weren't for the fact it was appalling evidence of just how desperate the situation was. They were tagging hostiles as quickly as they could identify them, and a large tactical display showed well over 200 targets on the move with more added every minute.

This was quickly turning into a Charlie-Foxtrot. Red's team was rolling with over 100 Nigerian regulars and supplies, but they were stuck clearing roads and had barely made it a few miles from their starting point. Wings was working on repairing a chopper, though it could take a couple of hours and there were no guarantees. And even if he did get it working, it meant a dozen men at a time, less if they brought significant equipment.

The only hope at the moment were the two Nigerian helicopters, now inbound, carrying two dozen men along with critical supplies—a sustained defensive effort would require thousands of rounds of ammunition. He peered at the overhead shot of the Forward Operating Base, scores of civilians streaming through the front gate, clustering around the buildings at the center.

"What are they doing?" asked Child as he zoomed in slightly.

Leroux rose and stepped closer to the displays, his hands clasped behind his back. "Are those logs?"

Tong squinted. "I think so."

Leroux pointed. "They're trying to use the trucks and logs as a makeshift barrier."

"My God. They must be desperate," murmured Tong.

Child pointed. "Those choppers are coming in now."

Leroux glanced over his shoulder at him. "ETA?"

Child adjusted the image, showing the two choppers rapidly approaching the FOB. "Less than ten minutes."

"Good. At a minimum, that'll give them more manpower to build their barricades and hopefully project some of that force outside the wire. If they just hole up inside, no one's making it out of there alive."

Tong threw up her arms in excitement, staring at her screen. "They have one!"

Leroux turned to her. "Who has one of what?"

"AFRICOM Base Camp N'Djamena in Chad has what we're looking for."

A smile spread as Leroux returned to his station. "How soon can they get it there?"

Tong continued to read the message then frowned. "They can't. The Nigerians haven't granted clearance for anything to enter their airspace.

They have the container, they have the heavy-lift chopper, and they say they can have it there in thirty minutes, but they need a pilot and he can't be American military."

Leroux cursed. "Politics. Get me the base commander."

Tong gave a thumbs-up a few moments later. "Colonel Kate Waters is on Line Two."

Leroux plugged in his headset. "Colonel Waters. I assume you're aware of the situation."

"I am, sir. We've got what you need. I have my team hooking it to the Chinook now, but I don't have a crew. The Nigerians have made it quite clear they don't want any American military assets operating on their soil, and I can't violate my orders unless instructed to do so by my chain of command. As I'm sure you know, that request has already gone up and been denied. Nobody wants to rile what could potentially be an important ally in the region."

A thought occurred to Leroux. "Colonel, if we were to supply the crew, would you look the other way if they took that chopper on a joyride with whatever might happen to be attached to it at the time?"

"Sir, I could guarantee you that every set of eyeballs on this base will be checking the polish on their boots."

Leroux smiled. "Happy to hear that, Colonel. I'll get back to you shortly. Langley, out." He disconnected from the call and Tong turned to face him.

"How the hell are we going to get a flight crew there in time that's crazy enough to steal a Chinook with a ten-ton container, and fly it into not-so-friendly territory?"

Leroux smiled slightly, wagging a finger at her and his team. "No, I haven't gone mad. Remember that contractor we used in Afghanistan last year, the one who helped fly Kane and his translator around?"

Tong's eyes narrowed for a moment then her face lit with recognition. "The ex-Aussie Special Air Service guy?"

"Exactly. According to the briefing notes I read at the time, he's worked with Dawson and the others before. After the collapse of Afghanistan, Kane mentioned he had heard he was flying oil company execs around Africa."

Child spun in his chair, staring up at the ceiling. "That guy is just the right amount of nuts for the job. Do you think he'd do it?"

Leroux sat at his station. "I think he would just for fun, but if he knew who he might be saving, he'd probably be mad we took so long to think of him. Sonya, see if you can find him. He could be the key to getting that equipment delivered. If we get that container in position, they might just stand a chance."

FOB Ugurun, Nigeria

Dawson helped direct the flood of new arrivals, the FOB rapidly filling. "Children and nursing mothers to the center of those buildings. Able-bodied men and women, head over to Sergeant Major Buhari, he'll assign you work. We need to prep for whatever Boko Haram is going to do next."

Fear flared in the eyes of the already panicked civilians at the mention of the enemy, but they followed his instructions. Dawson had effectively taken command as there were no Nigerian officers at the base, and Buhari was content to abdicate responsibility to someone else with more experience.

Niner jogged over. "We started siphoning the fuel off from all those trucks. It's going to take a while though. It'd be faster if we could just puncture the tanks and drain them that way."

Dawson shook his head. "No, we might need to refuel them and use them for evac at some point. We need to preserve the fuel in their storage tank. I just don't want one of those trucks erupting into a fireball and taking out a dozen civilians using it as cover."

"Understood. Let's just hope the bastards don't hit the fuel tank."

Dawson glanced over his shoulder at the cinder block enclosure surrounding it. "It should be fine unless they hit us with something really heavy. Let's just make sure nobody's hiding near those walls."

"Roger that."

Atlas dropped a massive log he had single-handedly carried from the tree line. The roar of chainsaws and the thuds of swinging axes filled the air all around them as more locals were put to work pushing back the trees that could be used as cover by the enemy, and shelter for the civilians.

Buhari hailed him, rushing over with one of the villagers. "Sergeant Major, this man says there's a front loader about two miles from here. The government uses it for road clearing in the region, but it ran out of gas. If we could refuel it and get it here, we could use it to push back the tree line far faster."

Visions of The Green Berets with John Wayne flashed and Dawson nodded, pointing at Jagger. "You and Mickey take some jerry cans in one of the trucks and get that loader here. Any resistance, back off and return to base. Don't engage."

"Yes, Sergeant Major." Jagger and Mickey broke off to execute the orders as Spock, carrying one end of a log with a local, stopped and cocked an ear instead of an eyebrow.

"Does anybody else hear that?"

Dawson smiled as he picked out the thunderclap of helicopter rotors beating the air over the chainsaws and axes. Cheers erupted though Dawson tempered his response, for he knew all too well that unless the Nigerians could get at least a dozen roundtrips in to reinforce the area, they didn't stand a chance. The latest reports from Langley indicated at least 200 hostiles assembling, and a couple of dozen extra soldiers were just labor. He pointed to the far end of the base where the men had been exercising when they first arrived. "Clear that area. We've got choppers incoming."

Several of Buhari's men started shouting orders, hustling the civilians out of the way. Dawson peered into the distance, shielding his eyes from the afternoon sun as he searched for the incoming relief.

Spock pointed. "There, two o'clock low."

Dawson adjusted his gaze and spotted the two choppers coming in from the west. Buhari had informed him they contained twelve men each plus weapons, and most importantly, ammo. It would not be enough to hold this base, but it would be a start, and the manpower could prove critical in readying a defensive position for these civilians. The thunder of the choppers grew and more civilians took notice, all now on their feet staring toward what they likely thought were their saviors.

The good news was that they might get out most of the children ahead of the attack, though as word spread throughout the area, more civilians continued to arrive. And if this kept up, scores of flights might be necessary. They needed open roads and heavy transports, as well as a significant force on the ground to not only repel any attack, but to proactively engage.

The lead chopper rapidly approached when the cheering from the villagers abruptly turned into gasps as the smoke trail from an RPG streaked up from the ground. Dawson cursed as it slammed into the tail, erupting into a fireball. The chopper tipped forward then collapsed out of the air. The ground shook as the fuel ignited, the heat from the fire setting off the ammo, thousands of secondary explosions killing any hope of survivors. Gunfire from an AK-47 rattled across the landscape and the second chopper banked hard to the right. Smoke poured from the tail and the rotor sputtered then failed. The pilot struggled to control the descent, and it began to spin as it dropped below the tree line. The sound of the airframe hitting hard reached them as black smoke billowed into the air.

But there was no explosion.

Dawson pointed at Buhari. "Get two of those trucks and a dozen men. There might be survivors." He grabbed his M4 and sprinted with Spock down the road toward the crash site as he activated his comms. "Control, Zero-One. Come in, over."

"This is Control. Go ahead."

"I assume you saw what just happened."

"Affirmative, Zero-One, both choppers down."

"Find me whoever did that."

"Already on it, Zero-One. We'll have that intel shortly."

They continued toward the crash site, the dark gray smoke billowing into the sky continuing to thicken. Engines behind them roared to life, drowning out the wails of despair and disappointment that had replaced the cheering. This was a stark reminder they were in the heart of Boko

Haram territory. This was the entire reason why these bases were being built—to project government power into these regions and force out the vicious minority bringing misery to millions.

A terrific explosion erupted, a fireball clawing at the air, eating through the oxygen that gave it life. Dawson slowed up slightly as they neared, praying that at least some of those on board had managed to escape to safety before their time had run out. The crackling of bullets detonating from the heat had them hitting the ground as strays fired in every direction. Dawson rolled onto his back and held up a hand as a warning to the transports now approaching, the lead driver hammering on his brakes. Dawson scrambled over to a ditch and rolled inside, Spock crashing into him a moment later as the cacophony of thousands of tiny explosions continued.

His comms squawked in his ear. "Zero-One, Control. Come in, over."

"This is Zero-One, go ahead."

"We have your shooter, Zero-One. He's one of the six that were left behind."

Dawson cursed. He had plans to take them out using some of the new arrivals, his intent to send them out to degrade Boko Haram's intelligence capabilities as opposed to eliminating a threat. Nothing had indicated that any of these men had heavy weapons, let alone RPGs. If he had known that, he would have taken them out an hour ago. "Understood, Control. We're going to need to do better. Does anybody else have RPGs or high-caliber weapons?"

"We're double-checking that now, Zero-One. It appears there was a weapons cache that the shooter used. He only had an AK when he arrived."

"Give me his location."

"Two hundred meters north-northeast of your current position. There's a tree line just to your left. If you can make it there, follow it for one hundred meters then he'll be on your right. He seems pretty pleased with himself. He's on his feet cheering."

"Understood, Control. Are there any signs of survivors?"

"Affirmative, Zero-One. We've got at least half a dozen."

Dawson smiled and exchanged a fist bump with Spock. "Copy that, Control. We're going to engage the target. Zero-one, out."

The secondary explosions were dying down and Dawson didn't want that bastard responsible for so many deaths to get away with it. Using the continued distraction as a diversion, he climbed out of the ditch, remaining low, and shuffled toward the tree line, though it didn't provide much cover. This wasn't some forest like back home. These were trees with large trunks and huge canopies with little overlap. But it was something. He reached the first tree and rose, staying behind the massive trunk.

Spock joined him. "What's the plan?"

"Make our way along the tree line, first person who gets a clear shot of the bastard takes it." Dawson pointed in the general direction of where Leroux had indicated their target should be. "Control says he's over there. We'll go one at a time, covering each other."

"Copy that." Spock readied his weapon and peered out from behind the trunk. "I've got you."

Dawson sprinted to the next tree then continued for several more when he didn't come under fire. He came to a halt then took aim, scanning the area. He smiled as he spotted the piece of shit, still celebrating his success and still not paying attention to what was going on around him. Dawson signaled for Spock to advance, keeping his weapon trained on the hostile the entire time. He could take the shot and probably hit him, but if the man had access to a weapons cache, Dawson had no idea what they might be up against if he missed on his first attempt.

Spock sprinted toward him, and as he approached, Dawson gave the all-clear to continue past. His friend came to a halt another thirty feet past his position then took aim. There was no indication their target had spotted them yet, but with the secondary explosions finished, he showed signs of settling down. If they were to take him by surprise, they had to do it now. Using hand signals, Dawson indicated for Spock to cover him then he advanced, his target in his sights at all times as he walked as quickly as a good shot would allow, for he would need to squeeze the trigger on a moment's notice if spotted.

The target ended his celebrations, his back still to them. The man checked left and right and Dawson stopped as the man's foot twisted for the inevitable turn. Dawson froze and aimed at the man's torso, now barely fifty yards out, and steadied his breathing. His finger moved from the guard to the trigger. The man's body twisted, his leg swinging around, and as he faced Dawson squarely, his eyes bulged as he spotted him, the

AK-47 that had brought down the second chopper still slung. Dawson squeezed the trigger twice, both rounds hitting the man squarely in the chest, then rushed forward as the hostile collapsed to his knees, his chin dropping to stare at the wounds. With his last bit of strength, he reached for his weapon and Dawson stopped, firing two more rounds, another in the chest, the final shot in the head. The target collapsed in a heap and Dawson continued forward then made certain the job was done before indicating the all-clear to Spock.

Spock joined him a moment later and covered him as he searched the man, finding little of interest. He checked their immediate surroundings and spotted a hole in the ground nearby.

"That must be the weapons cache that Langley was referring to."

"Watch for booby traps," warned Spock.

Dawson kneeled beside the hole and pulled out his flashlight. "I have no doubt it was booby-trapped, but this guy disabled it to get inside." He pointed at a hook ringlet on one edge of the wooden frame that surrounded the hole, then a grenade on the other, the wire connected to its pin dangling loose. "There it is. We're good." He lay flat on his stomach and poked his head inside, playing the flashlight around what turned out to be a much bigger hole than he was expecting. This wasn't just a weapons cache, this was a spider hole. It was big enough to hold one man comfortably, and there were enough weapons and ammo to equip a platoon, the arsenal including RPGs like the one that had taken down the first chopper. He rose. "If they have a lot of these in the area, there's no way in hell we're getting any choppers in here." He took up a covering position as Spock examined the hole for himself. He whistled.

"Well, there's one thing about rocket launchers."

"What's that?"

"They need a warm body to fire them. Langley told us half a dozen guys are in position around the base, and with almost every soul in this village either already inside the wire or heading there, Langley should be able to spot anyone doing anything out of the ordinary. I say we put together some patrols, clean these guys out, and take the weapons back to the base. Who the hell knows when we're going to get resupplied?"

Dawson shot a wry look at him. "Bucking for my job?"

Spock cocked an eyebrow. "I could never replace you, only succeed you."

Dawson laughed. "If you're Spock, isn't that my line?"

Spock raised a fist and Dawson bumped it. "Good to see you're still on your game when it comes to movie trivia. By the way, that would make you Kim Cattrall."

"I could do worse." Dawson activated his comms. "One-One, Zero-One. What's your status, over?"

Niner responded. "We're secure here, but the civilians are restless."

"Understood. We've got a weapons cache here that could prove useful. Take one of the trucks and half a dozen strong arms. Control will guide you to the location. Watch for booby traps."

"Roger that, Zero-One. We're on our way."

"Copy that. Zero-One, out." Dawson pointed at the spider hole. "Take a second look for tripwires. The last thing we need is Niner getting blown up. I'll never hear the end of it from Maggie."

Spock cocked an eyebrow. "But me getting blown up is okay?"

Dawson shrugged. "Make Maggie laugh more, and she might move you up the list."

"Story of my life. My lack of a sense of humor."

"You'd make a fine Vulcan." Dawson activated his comms. "Control, Zero-One. Come in, over."

"This is Control. Go ahead."

"One-One will be leading a team to recover the weapons cache we discovered here. I need you to guide them in."

"Copy that, Zero-One. We already have him on the line."

"Copy that. Now give me a location on the next closest target. If we manage to get another chopper inbound, I'd like it to at least stand a chance."

Boko Haram Staging Area

Outside Maiduguri, Nigeria

Ibrahim frowned as he stared at the sight before him. He had lost a lot of good men today, and even more had been wounded. Most of those killed were the riders, not the passengers. Those on the back managed to escape the initial onslaught protected by the men in front of them, but as they had made their escape, they had been shot, many in the back, by the cowards that had opposed them. It enraged him that warriors of Allah should suffer wounds like these. They should have died like their brothers, for they would already be enjoying the rewards that awaited them in Jannah. But that was not to be. Today, their wounds would be treated and they would fight for Allah in some future glorious battle.

Word was spreading and other factions were already responding that they were sending men. The opportunity to kill Americans was rare in Nigeria, especially American military, and they would be easy pickings. He had just received word that two helicopters had been brought down by his men, and it was unlikely that the cowardly government would send more.

"Ibrahim, my friend."

Ibrahim turned to see the commander of the Gajiram cell entering the warehouse with several of his men flanking him. Ahmed Lawan had once been a leadership rival when their founder was killed, but he had instead thrown his support behind Ibrahim, guaranteeing the backing he needed to take over. And all that it cost him was the second pick of any girls they kidnapped—first pick, of course, was reserved for himself.

A small price to pay for the power he now wielded.

Ibrahim smiled broadly at the new arrivals. "I see you got our message."

"Indeed, and I've had runners sent throughout the area to find those without radios. The opportunity to kill American soldiers and send a message to any who would defy us, not even your harem would keep me away from that."

Ibrahim roared with laughter. "How many men have you brought?"

"Just twenty. The rest are out gathering more. I suspect we'll be able to add at least a hundred to your numbers by this evening."

"Excellent."

Lawan surveyed the sight of the wounded, his lips pursed. "I see you took heavy losses."

"Yes, they took us by surprise. We had no idea there were Americans stationed at the base. If I had known, we would have done things much differently."

Lawan eyed him. "But you still would have gone in?"

"Absolutely. No godless infidels will ever stop us from acting."

Lawan smiled and slapped Ibrahim on the back. "That's why I backed you for leader. Nothing scares you and nothing will deter you from our goals. So, what is your plan now?"

"I have scouts in the area. We've taken out two choppers bringing in reinforcements, so I suspect no more will be arriving. The government will try to send in reinforcements by ground, but you and I both know the roads are out, so there's no way they'll be there until tomorrow. We'll hit them at night from all sides in full force. Bullets, grenades, RPGs. There's no way they'll survive. Tonight will be a great victory. We will send a message to these Americans so they know never to interfere in our business again. I intend to kill every single man, woman, and child on that base and in that village, and when I'm done with them, remove Ugurun from the map. When this night is through, no one will ever defy us again."

Lawan smiled. "It will be a glorious battle, brother. Allah will be pleased. And tonight, though I have no doubt we will be victorious, many of our brave warriors will be welcomed into Jannah. Perhaps tonight, we too, shall be granted entry."

While the idea of Jannah and the eternal bliss promised was appealing, Ibrahim had no desire to die. He didn't fear it, but life here was good, at least for him. Yet he had to think of the future of his organization. "One of us should remain behind. If we're both killed, there will be too much in-fighting over who should be the next leader."

Lawan's head bobbed slowly. "You're right, of course. And it should be me that stays behind. I cannot deny you the possibility of entry into

Jannah. I will stay behind, and should you fall tonight in your jihad against the infidel, we will honor your name and fight on until the ultimate victory when we will all be reunited." He extended a hand. "You honor us and the Prophet, peace and blessings be upon him, with your bravery and wisdom."

Ibrahim clasped Lawan's hand. He had been painted into a corner by the bastard. Lawan should be the one going into battle, but the man, who was clearly still his rival, had pounced first, and there was no way Ibrahim could refuse. It would suggest cowardice. But this turn of events also gave him a critical piece of information.

Lawan still had leadership ambitions.

If they survived the night, Lawan had to die.

East of FOB Ugurun, Nigeria

Spock pressed against the tree trunk, his weapon ready to provide cover for Dawson as he crawled on his belly toward their target fifty yards ahead. They hadn't spotted him yet, but Langley insisted he was there. Spock breathed in deeply through his nose, steadying his nerves, and caught a hint of something, a memory triggered. His wife was into incense and aromatherapy, their home always smelling of something wonderful. The guys sometimes ribbed him when he would arrive at work, his uniform still smelling of lavender or some other concoction his wife would mix.

A lump formed in his throat with the realization that until this very moment, he hadn't noticed the scents he would come home to were missing. If he thought hard, he was sure he could still smell something, but with each passing day, that would fade.

I miss you. I miss you so much.

He inhaled quickly, forcing the air through his nose, shoving aside the overwhelming grief before it took hold and compromised his ability to do his job. His wife was dead, and had died in terror. Those responsible had been wiped from the face of the Earth, yet that knowledge provided little comfort beyond the fact it meant no one was coming for his daughter or the other witnesses. Things could have been far worse that day. Four families could be mourning instead of one.

But today he had to focus on his job, for hundreds of families were at stake. They had to clean up the kill zone the terrorists had set up so reinforcements could arrive by air, though he had a feeling no more would be coming. The Nigerians wouldn't risk it.

Unfortunately, their best hope at the moment was Red's team reaching them. But the last he had heard, they couldn't expect them until early tomorrow, and he had no doubt the terrorists were aware of that as well. They would attack tonight using the cover of darkness to approach, then use overwhelming firepower to mow down anyone inside the wire.

The villagers didn't stand a chance.

And while he didn't fear death, until recently, Joanne had always been home to take care of their daughter should anything happen to him. But now there was no one, just grandparents. And it broke his heart. Perhaps this was no longer the life for him. Perhaps the Army wasn't a career for a single father. His stomach churned as he adjusted his position slightly, keeping the suspected spider hole in his sights as Dawson was nearly there. The very idea of leaving the Army was inconceivable, leaving Delta even more so. He loved his job, he loved the people he worked with, and he loved that every day he was doing good. Like today, where he had helped save those children from a gruesome fate. And even if all he had done was delay the inevitable, he would die defending little girls like his daughter, as he knew other soldiers like him would lay down their lives for her, because that was why he served.

That was why they all served.

They weren't there just to protect their country, they were there to protect the innocent, and there was nothing more innocent than those amassing inside the wire, no doubt praying that the soldiers whose hands they now placed their lives in could protect them despite the odds.

Two shots rang out from a Glock and Dawson waved the all-clear. Spock sighed with relief and checked his surroundings before emerging from behind the tree. He had some thinking to do about his future, but today he had to focus on the task at hand. Besides, if things went the way he feared, the decision would be made for him. And should this be his final stand, he prayed that one day, someone would tell his daughter how he really died—fighting to save innocents just like her from a horrible fate.

He wiped a tear from his eye and growled at himself as he strode toward Dawson. He forced a smile, once again hiding from his best friends the horror he now lived.

Operations Center 2, CIA Headquarters
Langley, Virginia

Leroux glanced over at a tally of the targets. There were now over 300 hostiles tracked by the computer, and he smiled at the image of Dawson clearing another weapons cache. He turned to Tong. "Radio that location into One-One. They'll want to clear that as well."

She nodded and activated her comms, sending along the report. A zoomed-out satellite image showed a few villagers still making their way to the base, though most who wanted to take refuge were either already there or too scared to venture outside. There were over 200 villagers inside the wire. Walls of felled logs were being constructed, but there weren't enough. There was no way they could protect the civilians.

This would be a bloodbath that he and his team would be forced to watch unfold before their eyes. He had seen death before, of course, had even been responsible for giving the order to kill, but never anything of this magnitude where the killing would last for hours. It was one thing when a large group was wiped out in a massive explosion. There was a single instance of shock, of horror, of grief, but this would be something different. This would be a hopeless, valiant battle against impossible odds that people they had worked with for years would lose, sacrificing themselves in the forlorn hope they might hold out long enough for help to arrive to save some.

This was why he did this job. Heroes like Dawson and his team were out there every day on the front lines, fighting for their country, protecting the innocent, their successes rarely heard of. Those inside this room were dedicated to doing their jobs well by giving Bravo Team and others like them the best intel possible, the best support and guidance possible, and doing everything they could to make sure these men returned home safely to their families, and succeeded in accomplishing whatever the mission might be.

But today, that responsibility weighed heavily on everyone, with the lives of hundreds of men, women, and children on the line, as well as those of people he had placed in this position. The responsibility weighed heavily on his shoulders in particular. It was his idea to reclassify the mission. If he had just left things alone, the Boko Haram raid on the school would have been successful. The girls would have been kidnapped, but the rest of the village would have survived, as would Bravo Team. But even with hindsight, he wouldn't change anything, nor, he was certain, would Bravo Team. Saving those children was the right thing to do, and even if all were to die today, death was far more preferable than the future they would have looked forward to had they been taken.

He glanced back at the screen as his team celebrated another small victory, Jagger and Spock having taken out the last of the Boko Haram moles. He closed his eyes and squeezed the bridge of his nose between his thumb and forefinger. They had to give them a fighting chance. He stared at the map showing Red's progress, and it was minimal, though progress was being made. He sighed and turned to Tong, asking yet again the question he already knew the answer to. "Any word from Ledger yet?"

She frowned, shaking her head. "Nothing."

Leroux muttered a curse and slumped in his chair, praying that whatever was delaying the Aussie's response wouldn't last too much longer. Too many lives depended on this Hail Mary.

Angels 10, Niger

Ben Ledger groaned in ecstasy as he pulled back on the stick, the vibration of the airframe sheer bliss on his aching back and neck. He had been ferrying supplies from the port city of Lagos, Nigeria to various oil fields in the region for three weeks now, the executives at the oil company having decided it was far safer to transport the supplies via air than ground. Too many of the convoys had been hit by gangs intent on replenishing their black-market stock. It was far more expensive, of course, but it kept him in tawny and clean underwear.

After the Charlie-Foxtrot in Afghanistan, his burgeoning little airline of one had been forced to relocate, though not before he managed to evacuate scores of those who would have otherwise been abandoned. What had happened in that country was a disgrace. The capitulation of the Afghan forces within days was one thing, but the breaking of the promises made to those who had worked with the Allies hand-in-hand was another. It was an unforgivable sin, the blood of every single man, woman, and child lost by this betrayal staining the hands of every

114

politician around the world that hadn't cared enough to plan ahead. This wasn't a failure of American leadership, British leadership, or Australian leadership. This was a failure by everyone, politicians of all stripes, politicians who would never pay a price for the blood on their hands. The best those like him could hope for was that the conscience of those responsible would be haunted for the rest of their lives with the knowledge they could have prevented this.

He pushed forward on the stick, leveling out at altitude, smiling at the blue skies ahead. This was where he was most comfortable. He had been Australian Special Air Service before he retired. He had learned how to fly pretty much everything out there that had wings or rotors, and he had fallen in love with the freedom flying provided, especially in countries like Niger, where the rules were fairly lax and the skies relatively uncrowded. Pull some aerial stunts over Canberra and you would lose your license. Do them here, and if anyone noticed, they would ask you to do it again so they could show their buddy.

He was qualified to fly for the airlines, but where was the fun in that? It was a glorified bus driver, where the most excitement you had, unless something was going horribly wrong, was an unruly passenger sneaking a cigarette in the bathroom. Flying in countries like Niger and Afghanistan was far more liberating, far more exciting. Yes, he could die, but that didn't bother him. He had led a good life, done a lot of good, and was comfortable with the legacy he would leave behind. He just prayed that when he did die, it wasn't because he was doing some stupid aerial stunt that went wrong, but instead doing something worthwhile. Saving lives, or bringing in urgent medical supplies under heavy gunfire, something more than what he was doing today, ferrying flash-frozen steak dinners and other luxuries. At least in Afghanistan, every flight he completed he had been doing something useful, especially when he had helped out Dawson and his CIA friend. That had been the most excitement he had had since leaving the military.

His partner in crime, Michael Clarke, entered the cockpit and sat in the copilot's seat. "The cargo is secure. Looks like I did my job flawlessly yet again."

"What, and you expect a bonus for doing your job right, ya arseclown?"

"Bugger off. Isn't that the way things are today?"

"Not among guys our age."

Clarke leaned back and sighed. "Thank God for that. I wouldn't want to be young today. Too much DADS stuff you're expected to follow."

Ledger grunted. "Bloody oath." He tapped his phone, nestled in a holder screwed to the instrument panel. "Can you imagine if everyone had one of these when we were kids? Shit, we'd be in jail."

"Speak for yourself. I was a perfect angel when I was younger."

"Get stuffed! I met your brother. He told me the stories."

"That wanker. I'll be having words with him the next time I see him."

Ledger noticed the phone indicated a message that must have come in while they were loading the cargo. He fished the device from its cradle and brought up the text message.

IRENE! IRENE! IRENE! Urgent you call immediately. SOF friends require emergency assistance.

His chest tightened with the message. 'Irene' was a codeword used among Special Forces Operators the world over to indicate a situation that had gone south badly, just like the Mogadishu mission the name was taken from and immortalized in Black Hawk Down. Things must be extremely urgent if whoever this was felt reaching out to him in this manner was necessary. And the fact they were attempting to reach *him* meant it was local, and it likely meant few if any others were available to assist. "Get me the satphone."

Clarke rose. "Just a sec, I've got it charging."

He disappeared for a few moments and returned, handing the phone over. Ledger dialed the number. It was answered immediately by a woman.

"OC2. Identify yourself."

His heart raced a little at the robotic-sounding voice. "This is Ledger. I received an urgent message to call this number."

"Stand by."

There was a beep and a moment later a man's voice came on the line. "Mr. Ledger, thank you for getting back to us. We have an urgent requirement for a pilot with your background. Are you available?"

Ledger bit his lip. "I'm in the middle of a cargo delivery. It's a short hop. I'd probably be unloaded in about two hours."

"Sir, I'm going to give you classified information. Are you in a secure environment?"

He shrugged. "I'm angels ten. Is that secure enough for you?"

The man chuckled. "I suppose it is. Without naming names, you've previously worked with a group of our people that you saw in Afghanistan recently while helping us out."

Ledger's heart rate picked up a little more. This was the CIA he was talking to, the fact no names had been mentioned now explained.

"Are you aware of whom I'm speaking?"

It had to be Bravo Team. "Yes."

"They're currently in Nigeria, in Boko Haram territory. Hundreds of hostiles are converging on their position and they can't be evac'd as they're protecting hundreds of men, women, and children that we believe Boko Haram intend to massacre."

Ledger squeezed the phone between his shoulder and ear and banked them hard to the right, in the general direction of Nigeria. "I might be able to hold twenty or so people at a time. If there are that many to evacuate, I don't know how I can help."

"We don't need your plane, we need your skills as a pilot. Can you fly a Chinook?"

His eyebrows shot up. "Yes."

"Can you fly it alone?"

"I've got my partner with me. We could manage in a pinch. Why?"

"We need you to go to a base camp in Chad, steal a Chinook and the cargo that's attached to it, then deliver that cargo to the Forward Operating Base in Nigeria, possibly under heavy enemy fire. Are you up for the job?"

Ledger stared blankly out the cockpit window, his jaw slowly sagging as he processed what he had just heard. Clarke stared at him inquisitively, having heard little of relevance from this side of the conversation. "Let me get this straight. You want us to break onto an American military base, steal a heavy-lift helicopter with attached cargo, fly it into Nigeria, and deliver it to a base surrounded by hundreds of heavily armed Boko Haram terrorists?"

"Yes."

Clarke shook his head vehemently and Ledger grinned at him. "Count us in, mate."

FOB Ugurun, Nigeria

Dawson and Spock jogged through the gate, the six Boko Haram left behind to spy on them dead, the weapons caches now resupplying the FOB. In the grand scheme of things, it wasn't a lot, but anything would help, and keeping those weapons out of the hands of the enemy they would soon be engaging could prove even more helpful.

They had been gone almost an hour, and significant progress had been made. The front loader had been successfully retrieved and was knocking down trees, pushing back the cover the enemy could have used against them. The felled trees were being limbed then hauled onto the base, a four-foot-high wall now formed across the south side of the buildings, construction of the west side now underway.

The women were tending to the children and the elderly while preparing to feed the hundreds gathered with the food that those who had planned ahead brought with them, and with that already on the base to feed the soldiers. What was available wouldn't last long, but rationing was of no importance. A hearty meal now could fuel the fight ahead, and should anyone survive until relief arrived, hunger would be the least of their worries.

The younger children were playing, those old enough to understand what was going on assisting by clearing the area that would be their temporary shelter of rocks and sticks and anything else that might prove uncomfortable when lying on the ground.

The men worked hard on the trees, desperate to protect their loved ones. With the exception of the children, the mood was somber. All who understood what was going on were aware of what was coming and that the chances they would see the next sunrise were slim. The spirit of these people was inspiring, and he smiled as a few of the girls they had saved earlier waved at him and Spock, the fear evident in their eyes, their gratefulness on their cheeks. There was no doubt they would rather die with their families than face the horrors Boko Haram intended for them.

It made him all the more determined to hold out for as long as they could.

Buhari flagged him down. "Sergeant Major, congratulations on your successful mission."

Dawson nodded. "Boko Haram won't be receiving any intelligence from those they left behind. That's no guarantee, however, that they don't have sympathizers in the area that are still feeding them info, but our eyes in the sky are keeping a watch for anything suspicious."

"If they have supporters still out there, I'm sure they're few and far between, and even if they aren't, what more could they report than what was already. We're hopelessly outnumbered with virtually no defenses, and despite your efforts, my government has indicated they won't be sending in any more helicopters until they can secure the entire area."

Dawson cursed. "I guess I'm not surprised. But speaking of being hopelessly outnumbered, I have a suggestion. These people have a right to defend themselves. We have a lot of spare weapons now that we've emptied those caches. I recommend you take several of your trainers and any able-bodied man that's willing, and start training them on how to fire those weapons and load-reload. They might not be able to hit anything, but suppression fire can be a powerful force."

Buhari's head slowly bobbed as Dawson explained his idea, and by the time he was finished, his head was bobbing furiously. "Excellent idea, Sergeant Major, though it will mean fewer men building the barricade."

"Then ask some of the women if they're willing. Some of the most capable soldiers my country has are women, and I've found over the years that mothers will fight to the death to protect their children. Let's give them that chance."

Buhari smiled. "I think our odds are improving, Sergeant Major. We may yet survive the day." He jogged off, shouting orders to his men as Spock stepped a little closer.

"While I admire his optimism, I don't think I share it."

Dawson sighed heavily. "Unfortunately, neither do I. All we're doing is delaying the inevitable, but I know I would rather die with a gun in my hand protecting my family than a stick or a stone." He growled with frustration. "These people deserve a chance."

Despite clearing the area of hostiles, the Nigerians were evidently too afraid to risk what few choppers they had and the crews that manned them. It was the cruel calculus too often played out on the battlefield among nations that couldn't afford the modern weaponry they possessed, too often hand-me-downs in a proxy war where the added capabilities were only utilized when the safety of the asset rather than the soldier could be guaranteed. It often meant planes, helicopters, and tanks sat on the sidelines, like today where helicopters could be brought in with reinforcements and used to evacuate civilians. It was a risk, but it should be worth taking. He just prayed Langley came up with something useful that might even the odds a bit.

What that could be, he had no idea.

US AFRICOM Base Camp N'Djamena

Outside N'Djamena, Chad

Ledger and Clarke quickly completed the shutdown checklist, something memorized long ago. Clarke threw open the door and kicked down the steps. Ledger descended into the late afternoon sun, where a colonel stood alone on the tarmac, her hands clasped behind her back, her fatigues crisp, her jaw square. There was no doubt this was a woman not to be trifled with.

He walked over to her. "G'day, Colonel, my name is—"

She cut him off. "Is of no concern to me. As far as I'm concerned, neither of you are here, and your plane was never here." She indicated a Bell CH-47F Chinook heavy-lift helicopter idling nearby. "Can you fly one of those things?"

He eyed it. He had never been in one before, but he had read the manual. "Yes, ma'am."

She glanced at Clarke, whose demeanor never engendered confidence. "With just him?"

"Yes, ma'am, he's a bit of a wombat, but we can manage."

"Have you ever carried ten tons of cargo underneath you?"

Again, he lied. "Yes, ma'am." There was no backing out of this now. The last update indicated the situation was getting worse. There was no way he would let the truth get in the way of helping his comrades-in-arms and the innocent men, women, and children they were willing to die to protect.

He would figure it out along the way if he had to.

She eyeballed him, and for a moment he was afraid she had found him out. "Very well. In exactly five minutes, you're going to hear an assembly announced. Every single eyeball on this base will be looking in the opposite direction. The helo is prepped and ready to go, and the cargo is already securely attached. Do you know what the cargo is?"

"Yes."

"Then you know that's the only hope those people have of holding out until reinforcements arrive." She stepped closer, the taut muscles in her face relaxing, her voice softening as she extended a hand. "Go give those people a fighting chance."

He shook her hand. "We'll give it a fair suck of the sav, ma'am."

She eyed him, puzzled.

"We'll get the cargo delivered."

"Or die trying," added Clarke.

She turned toward Clarke. "I'd prefer to get my chopper back in one piece, mister, so if you're going to be doing any dying, try to do it after you've landed my bird."

Ledger chuckled. "We'll do our best, ma'am."

"Well, good luck then." She turned on her heel and marched back toward a cluster of buildings.

Clarke leaned closer. "Do you think they're going to hold our plane as collateral?"

Ledger grunted. "Something tells me if we lose the chopper, we're dead anyway, so we won't really care what happens to the plane."

"You're probably right. But just one thing."

"What's that?"

"If I survive this and you don't, I'm keeping her."

Ledger laughed. "I knew there was a reason you've been sticking with me, slagger."

The assembly was announced over the speakers, men and women pouring from the buildings and rushing from their posts, all hands, regardless of status, ordered to attend. She stood on a platform facing her entire command as they formed up, but she wasn't watching them. She was watching the far end of the base where two Australians, who had flown in on a beat-up piece of shit that would never be licensed to fly back home, were climbing aboard a $65,000,000 piece of equipment with the intent of stealing it on behalf of the CIA, then flying it illegally into Nigerian airspace in a desperate attempt to deliver the one thing that might just give those people a fighting chance.

Her chest swelled with pride knowing that people like this existed in the world. She had met men and women like this before, she knew their type, she knew what they were capable of, and she knew how they thought. And as the engines powered up and the rotors picked up speed, she knew there was no way in hell she was seeing that helicopter again. There would be paperwork, there would be reprimands, and she might even lose her command, but with hundreds of innocents on the line, her career was the least of her concerns.

Several of those assembled noticed something was going on behind them. "Eyes front!" she commanded, and everyone snapped to attention, directing their eyes forward. Smiles spread as those in the know shared what they believed was happening. She had made sure as many people had heard her orders about prepping the chopper with its cargo in the event the order to stand down was reversed. Everyone knew what was at stake.

The massive helicopter slowly lifted off and gained altitude, the long cable attaching it to the massive container holding the precious cargo slowly uncoiling before becoming taut. The helicopter wobbled slightly and her teeth clenched as she feared she was correct in her assessment that their pilot was full of shit when it came to his level of experience, but then the engines whined louder and the crate lifted from the ground, slowly rising.

Then the son of a bitch turned and flew directly over them all, both the Aussie bastards grinning at her through the tilted forward cockpit. She smiled slightly as she shook her head. The next time she saw them, she was punching them both in the face.

Then buying them a beer.

Ledger exchanged fist bumps with Clarke as he adjusted their course, slowly banking to the west, the heavy cargo below them battling him the entire way, the inertia of the container insisting on continuing to drag them in their previous direction.

"Can you handle it?" asked Clarke, his concern touching.

"Nah, yeah, I'll figure it out."

"Well try not to drop it. Something tells me we can't go back and get another one."

"Ya think?"

"I don't think she looked too pleased with us when you decided to fly right over her head."

Ledger shrugged. "What did she expect? We're thieves."

"She might decide to do a safety inspection on your aircraft."

Ledger slammed his head into the back of the seat and groaned. "That's exactly the type of thing I would do."

"Yeah, it would be an asshole move and you're the biggest asshole I've ever met. The question is, is she an asshole too?"

"God, I hope not, or we're never getting our baby back."

"Maybe we can buy a new one with the reward."

Ledger eyed him. "Reward? Have you got a few roos loose in the top paddock, mate? We're not dealing with the Rebel Alliance here. I'm not Han Solo, and despite the hair on your back, you're not Chewbacca."

Clarke roared with a surprisingly good Wookiee imitation.

"All right, I stand corrected. Chewie, get me the satphone. Let's let Langley know that the Aussie calvary is on its way."

Operations Center 2, CIA Headquarters
Langley, Virginia

"Copy that, Roo Wrangler. Contact us when you're making your approach so we can update you with the situation on the ground. Control, out." Tong turned with a huge smile. "They've got it."

Leroux sighed in relief. "That's the first piece of good news I've heard all day. What's the ETA?"

"Base Camp N'Djamena is just across the border in Chad. It was specifically set up to deal with Boko Haram, so they're already across the Nigerian border. They'll be there in half an hour."

Leroux rose and faced his team. "We have one mission now, and that's to deliver that cargo. Hundreds of lives depend on it. I want everybody monitoring the area. We can't have any more surprises like we did with those other two choppers." He turned to Tong. "Contact the other OCs. See if they can contribute resources for the next forty-five minutes."

She nodded and went to work as he returned to his station, adding his own eyeballs to the mix. They had identified and eliminated the six Boko Haram left behind, but they had no way of knowing how many had already been in the area. Because of how short a hop it was from Chad to Nigeria, the helicopter would be coming in low, and nothing outran a radio. If a Boko Haram member or sympathizer spotted it, scores of hostiles could be sent to take it down. They had to plan for it proactively, not react should it happen.

Tong disconnected her comms. "OCs One and Four can commit resources, Three is too busy on a priority op."

"I'll take whatever I can get. Contact Drone Control. I want to see what we can get in the area in the next thirty minutes."

"I'm on it."

Child cursed behind him and Leroux spun to face him. "What is it?"

"Boko Haram just posted a message on the Dark Web."

Child jutted his chin toward the screen and Leroux faced it, a message appearing.

Calling for all warriors of Allah in the area to join in a glorious battle against infidel American forces.

Leroux sighed, his shoulders sagging. "These people are insane." The end of the message had three rallying points listed in code. "Do we have anything on where those rally points are?"

Child shook his head. "Nothing in the system under those code words, but they should be fairly easy to detect."

Leroux turned. "What makes you say that?"

"Just look for three psycho-conventions held on motorcycles."

Leroux peered at the tactical display, the warehouse still the hub of activity. "I think we can safely assume that one of the three points is that warehouse. Start monitoring for clusters of activity. Let's say a fifty-mile radius. Actually, forget that, we only care about the next thirty minutes for now. Let's have everything focused on a thirty-mile radius. Once we get that cargo inserted and the chopper clear, we can worry about farther out."

Tong moved her mic out of the way. "I've got one Reaper available that can be in the area inside of thirty minutes. Do you want them to deploy?"

Leroux nodded. "Deploy immediately. We'll provide targets when they're identified."

Tong readjusted her mic, tapping a button to reactivate her comms as the orders were delivered. Moments later, a new blip appeared on the tactical map as one of America's most deadly unmanned aerial vehicles launched from a secret CIA facility few Americans were aware even existed. It was moments like these that humbled him, for the power he wielded from this room would terrify most. If he got his way, in the next thirty minutes the drone he had just ordered launched would hopefully kill dozens of people. Some might think that made him blood-thirsty, and he would dismiss their naiveté, for no matter how much those critics might abhor violence, it was a violent world, and killing dozens of fanatics to protect hundreds of innocents was a decision that would always be easy to make.

Yet every time, at the end of a long mission where people had died, many of whom he had given the order to kill, he would press his head against the wall of the shower and pray to God for forgiveness, as the tears rolled with the water. When his life was over, as it inevitably would be someday, and he faced his day of judgment, would his interpretation of "Thou shalt not kill" be accepted and balanced against all the lives he had saved? He hoped so. But even in the end, if he knew he would be condemned for eternity for what he had done, he would do it all again. For he had no doubt that in the grand scheme of things, he had saved far more than he had taken.

And today, the math was easy—hundreds of innocent men, women, and children, versus scum.

The math was *very* easy.

FOB Ugurun, Nigeria

Dawson stopped, pressing on his earpiece. "Repeat that, Control?"

"I repeat, we have an FOB in a can en route to your position. ETA twenty minutes."

Dawson grabbed Spock by the shoulder, both of them grinning. "That's good news, Control. What are we looking at?"

"A Hesco RAID-Twelve system, seven feet tall, three-and-a-half feet wide, a thousand feet long."

"Why didn't we get that thing inbound earlier?"

"There was no point earlier, Zero-One. Until you had that front loader, you'd have had to deploy and fill by hand. Now, I suggest you pick the optimal layout that uses the least amount of fencing, because I doubt you're going to have time to fill the damn thing."

"Copy that, Control. We're on it. Zero-One, out." He turned to Atlas. "Now, that's the best damn news I've heard since this started. We've got a Hesco RAID-Twelve coming in."

Atlas tossed another log onto the ground. "An FOB in a can? Where the hell did they find one of those?"

Dawson shrugged. "Who the hell cares? It's going to be here in twenty minutes." He flagged down Buhari, who jogged over to join them.

"You have news, Sergeant Major?"

"Yes, we've got a Hesco RAID being delivered in twenty minutes."

Buhari's eyes widened as a smile spread. "Thank God!"

Dawson eyed him, surprised the man was aware of what the RAID was. "Why do you not seem so surprised by this?"

Buhari jerked his head toward the massive pile of dirt outside the fence. "Do you really think we're that stupid? We wanted you guys to bring in one of the kits. We'd fill it with that sand from leveling the base, and solve two problems at once."

Dawson laughed, shaking his head as Atlas rolled his eyes. "So, just another UN peacekeeping operation."

Buhari eyed him. "What's that supposed to mean?"

Atlas shook his head. "Nothing, just that you guys are far more clever than we gave you credit for."

Buhari was about to respond when Dawson cut him off before this escalated into something he had no doubt Atlas hadn't intended. "All that matters is that we need it and it's coming. I would have requested one be sent in regardless, after my assessment was done. Now we need to prep." He pointed at the fence. "Filling this thing is going to take time, time we probably don't have, so we need to take advantage of what we already have. We'll fill the gaps in our barrier first, and then if we have time, fill the rest of it."

"How high?"

"This size barrier should require two loads. Let's get one load in each, and if we have time, top them up."

Atlas eyed the loader that continued to push back the tree line. "I've got a crazy idea that just might buy us some time."

"What's that?"

"We've got a thousand feet of barrier about to arrive. I say we wrap the camp where the buildings are, then extend it around the sand pile. At seven feet, that loader can operate inside the fencing and keep filling the barriers even if we're under attack."

Dawson nodded. "Good thinking, but something tells me there'll be an awful lot of ducking. We might want to rig some body armor around you." He turned to Buhari. "We need to project some firepower outside the wire until that chopper is safely away. Four of my men will pair up with yours so that every team has comms. Our eye in the sky will direct us toward any trouble spots."

Buhari agreed. "You'll have the men."

Dawson turned to Atlas and Niner. "I want you two to prep everything. Make sure the landing area is kept clear and that the civilians know what's about to happen. We need to make sure the perimeter is clear of debris, including around that sand pile. Remember, that helicopter coming in is a monster. We might be able to get out all of the children."

Buhari brightened at the possibility. "I'll get the children ready."

"Good. And make sure they pick out which women are going with them. I don't want some fight when the chopper arrives."

"It will be taken care of."

Dawson slapped his hands together. "Then let's get to it. This whole shit-show just might be about to turn around for us."

Boko Haram Staging Area

Outside Maiduguri, Nigeria

Ibrahim greeted several new arrivals. He had given instructions earlier to split into three staging areas, as there were simply too many warriors of Allah answering the call to arms, and the last thing he wanted was everyone gathered in one juicy target for an American drone. He had instructed his men to start marching the girls around the building in plain sight so any American spy satellites would know not to hit the building, and he had instructed other cells to bring some of their own girls to the other rallying points to act as human shields.

It was one of the many weaknesses of the infidel—they weren't willing to sacrifice the innocent for their cause, and as long as that held true, they could never win. Hundreds were assembling, and by nightfall, they would be an unopposable force. They had lost contact with their advance team, though not before he had been informed of the two choppers shot down, and that there were only six Americans on the base with barely twenty Nigerians.

This would be a glorious victory heard about around the world. Koshebe had sent a message locally and had resulted in a surge of donations to the cause, but it had led to little attention from the outside world. This was already different. They had just shot down two helicopters, a rare achievement, and when this night was through, six American soldiers would be dead, their bodies stripped naked and hung from meat hooks for the world to see. If any survived the attack, video would be taken of their beatings, and he would personally slice open their stomachs and pull out their entrails, then share with the world what happens when the infidel interferes with the will of Allah.

One of his men sprinted inside, holding up one of their handheld radios. "Imam! Another helicopter has been spotted."

"Where?"

"Coming from the east. It's American and it's big."

Ibrahim's eyes narrowed. "American? Are you sure?"

The man nodded. "That's what he's telling me. It's got American markings and it's huge, two large propellers. And it's carrying a container."

"Carrying?"

"Yes, underneath. A big shipping container."

Ibrahim cursed. It had to be a weapons shipment, and a helicopter that big could potentially carry dozens of American soldiers. If his warriors ended up going up against 40 or 50 well-equipped Americans, his men would take heavy casualties. And if this was a sign the Americans were committing to the battle, it could be the first of many choppers, and potentially air support. If that were the case, his men wouldn't stand a chance.

There was only one way to stop this, and that was to put a halt to it before it started.

"Do we know how far it is? Can we get there in time?"

"We might. But just barely."

"Then put out the call. Anyone who can reach that helicopter leaves now with RPGs. As soon as they have a shot, take it. We need to bring that thing down."

"Yes, sir!"

Ibrahim turned to the others. "You heard him! Let's get out there! Bring RPGs and any heavy weapons we've got. It's time to teach those Americans a lesson!"

Cheers erupted, cries of "Allahu Akbar" filling his ears as he headed for the weapons stockpile along with the others.

Lawan emerged from one of the entertainment rooms, zipping up his fly. "What's going on?"

Ibrahim beckoned him to follow. "We're going to kill some Americans. Care to join us?"

Lawan grinned. "I'm always up for that."

Operations Center 2, CIA Headquarters
Langley, Virginia

Leroux wasn't certain who spotted it first, but Tong was certainly the first to react. "That doesn't look good." She gestured toward the satellite image showing Boko Haram's main staging area. At least twenty motorcycles roared away from the building, heading toward the inbound Chinook and its essential cargo. He snapped his fingers over his shoulder at Child. "Give me an expanded view. I want to see what our identified targets are doing."

Child tapped at his keyboard then the image zoomed out to include the entire area. He tensed at the sight of scores of red targets moving into the flight path of the inbound chopper. He rose and pointed at Tong. "Patch me into the other OCs."

She pressed several buttons then adjusted her mic. "Stand by for priority message from OC Two Control Actual." She gave him a thumbs-up and he fit his headset in place.

"This is OC Two Control Actual. We've got a serious situation here. I need all eyeballs identifying targets that might be carrying RPGs or some other weaponry that could take down the inbound Chinook. We need to give him the most optimistic flight plan we can. Identify targets using color code purple. Control Actual, out." He tossed his headset on his workstation. "You heard the orders, people. Everyone is identifying targets. Sonya, divvy up the workload so that there's no overlap."

"I'm on it."

Leroux stood facing the displays, his hands on his hips, watching for what the teams would find as Tong split the work into quadrants. A cluster of purple targets appeared near the main staging area. He bent over and tapped at his keyboard. The display updated showing the predicted flight path of the chopper.

The door to the operations center hissed open and Morrison stepped inside, his eyes immediately on the screens. He stabbed a finger toward an image showing the helicopter. "Please tell me that the Central Intelligence Agency did not just steal a US Army helicopter and its cargo."

Leroux's chest tightened as Morrison joined him in the center of the room. "Sir, I can honestly say that the people piloting that helicopter are not employed by the CIA."

Morrison eyeballed him. "You chose your words quite carefully. Are they *paid* by the CIA?"

"No, sir."

This caught Morrison slightly off-guard, then his eyes narrowed. "Are they volunteers?"

Busted.

"Yes, sir."

"Is there anything to link us to this?"

"That depends, sir."

Morrison sighed. "Depends on what?"

"On how well Colonel Waters holds up under interrogation."

Child snickered and both Morrison and Leroux shot him the stink-eye. Child shriveled in his chair, leaning forward and hiding behind the array of monitors in front of him. A meek "sorry" was heard and Leroux continued.

"Sir, do you want the full truth or deniability?"

Morrison waved a hand at the crowded room. "Don't you think that's the kind of question you ask in private?"

Leroux's cheeks flushed. "Sorry, sir, I suppose it is." He leaned closer, lowering his voice. "Would it help if I told you that the two men involved are Aussies?"

A smile spread on Morrison's face. "No Americans?"

Leroux shook his head. "No Americans."

"Well then, if two Aussies decided to steal a helicopter and its cargo from one of our installations in Africa, then the US Army should be talking to the Australian government and not me."

"Sounds reasonable, sir, however, if we're successful, whoever is ultimately behind this will be thought of as heroes and geniuses."

"And will it work out?"

Leroux turned toward the tactical display, showing an uncomfortably large number of purple targets moving toward the red line that showed the flight path. "If you had asked me that five minutes ago, I would have said yes."

"And now?"

Leroux drew a deep breath through his nose and held it as his beautiful mind analyzed the data in front of him. He exhaled. "Fifty-fifty at best, sir."

En Route to FOB Ugurun, Nigeria

Ledger grabbed the satphone from its holder and took the call. "Go for Roo Wrangler."

A woman's voice responded, a voice so calm and soothing that he swore one day he wanted to meet her. "Roo Wrangler, this is Control. We've identified multiple targets carrying RPGs moving toward your flight path. We need you to increase altitude as much as possible and adjust your bearing ten degrees north."

Ledger cursed, wedging the phone between his ear and shoulder as he adjusted their heading and pulled up on the collective, the lumbering beast slowly gaining altitude. "Control, just how many RPGs are we talking here?"

"At least two dozen identified so far, but your adjusted flight path should put the majority of those out of range."

"Majority?"

"Affirmative. There are still at least ten along your new flight path, and more may yet arrive."

144

Ledger cursed and Clarke eyed him. "What now?"

"We've got at least ten RPGs in our path."

"Bugger off! Ten?" Clarke wagged a finger at him. "Listen, those wristy bastards trying to kill us are getting seventy-two virgins if they die. With the life I've led, I'll be lucky to get one syphilitic—"

Ledger cut him off. "Control, is there any indication they're moving on the base yet?"

"Negative. No indication. They appear to still be staging their forces."

Ledger banked slowly to the left, executing a 180, and Clarke's eyebrows shot up. "We gone walkabout because of what I said? Listen, I can be happy with one—"

"No. I'm just improving our odds." Ledger straightened out, continuing to gain altitude. "Control, tell our friends that we're going to be a few minutes late, and we're going to be dropping in like Apollo Thirteen."

"Copy that, Roo Wrangler. We'll pass on the message. New ETA?"

"Add ten minutes. Roo Wrangler, out."

Ledger ended the call and fit the phone back in its cradle. Clarke stared at the altimeter as the massive chopper dragged them higher into the sky, along with the 20,000 pounds of cargo dangling underneath.

"All right, what's the ridgey-didge? We're gaining altitude to get out of range of the RPGs, that, I understand. It's not like they're packing Stinger missiles. But what was that last bit about Apollo Thirteen? Ron Howard doesn't exactly make movies about space missions that go well."

"If we manage to avoid the RPGs on the way in, we're going to be in a dog's breakfast as we descend, and because we're descending from a higher altitude, it's going to take even longer, which could give those wankers a chance to reposition and still shoot us out of the sky."

"So, what's your plan?"

"Cut the power, drop out of the sky like a rock, and hopefully get the engines going enough to slow us down so we don't pancake."

Clarke eyed him incredulously. "What are ya? A flaming galah? That's suicide!"

"Not doing it is definitely suicide. Regardless, if we float down nice and gently to a soft landing, they're taking us out, guaranteed. And if they manage to turn us into a flaming ball of wreckage, we could land right on those civilians that are clustered in the middle of that base. I'd rather go down hard, fast, right where I intend to, and sacrifice the aircraft rather than risk the people."

"Well, ya tosser, do you plan on landing us right on top of the damn cargo? It'd make this entire shit-show a complete waste beyond giving our biographers an awesome closing chapter."

Ledger pointed at the control panel for the cargo system. "As soon as that indicator shows it's touched the ground, we cut the cable. I bank us a hundred yards to the right and Bob's your uncle."

"My Uncle Bob's dead and I hadn't planned on meeting him today."

"Uncle Bob. Was he the one who thought he had picked up those two Shielas but they turned out to be—"

"Nah, yeah, he's the one."

Ledger grinned. "I can't wait to meet him and hear how that story ended."

South of FOB Ugurun, Nigeria

Dawson had paired up with one of the trainers named Sunday, a capable young man who spoke excellent English and at least knew how to hold his weapon correctly. Dawson peered at the display of his tactical computer, half a dozen targets indicated, all rapidly moving toward their location. The latest update from Control indicated Ledger was delaying the arrival to gain altitude, but would have to do a hard insertion. The more potential RPG toting Boko Haram they could eliminate before he arrived, the better a chance he had of executing a controlled landing that would save the chopper to evac the children.

They had a slight advantage. There was only one road that led into or out of the village. With Ledger's plan to approach at high altitude, they had much less ground to cover. Unfortunately, everybody en route to this area was also on motorcycles that had little trouble traversing much of the landscape.

"Zero One, Control. We've got a group of four approaching your position from the east, three-hundred meters out, over."

"Copy that, Control. Stand by." Dawson signaled to Sunday to slow down. He spotted a nearby berm that would make perfect cover and gunned his engine, sending his motorcycle surging toward the slight rise. He squeezed the brakes, skidding to a halt, then lay the bike on the ground out of sight, Sunday doing the same. Dawson unslung his M4 and lay prone at the top of the berm. "We've got four coming in on bikes from the east."

Sunday readied his weapon. "Your orders?"

"Watch your arcs. You're on my right, so you cover the right. We've got four targets so I'll take the two on the left, you take the two on the right. When you've taken care of your two, turn your attention to mine if I haven't been able to take them out. If everyone's down, we advance on foot and make sure they're dead. A wounded man can still fire an RPG."

"Yes, Sergeant Major."

The whine of the engines grew louder and Dawson spotted the first rider come over a rise. "Here they come." He peered through his scope. "Don't shoot until all four are in sight."

"Yes, Sergeant Major."

The fourth rider appeared.

"Set?"

"Yes, Sergeant Major."

"Take them out." Dawson squeezed the trigger, the left-most rider dropping as he repositioned for the next shot. Sunday fired and his right-most target flipped over the handlebars, leaving Dawson to wonder if the motorcycle had been hit or if the man had involuntarily squeezed the

148

brakes when he was shot. It didn't matter at the moment. Dawson took out his second target cleanly then turned his attention to Sunday's remaining target, but the Nigerian took him out first.

Dawson leaped to his feet and sprinted toward what he hoped would be four bodies. Sunday was to his right, a few paces behind him, and as they neared, Dawson slowed up, raising his M4 to his shoulder. Movement to the right had him firing several shots before continuing a slower advance. "Be careful, they could be faking being wounded. And don't touch any of the bodies. One of them might have pulled a pin on a grenade before he died."

"Yes, Sergeant Major."

Dawson indicated for Sunday to break right to provide broader coverage. Dawson advanced the final ten yards, confirming all four targets were down and dead. He carefully liberated them of their RPGs, handing two to Sunday before slinging two of his own.

"Control, Zero One. We're secure here. Do we have any new hostiles approaching?"

"Affirmative, Zero One. Four more again from the east, half a klick out."

"Copy that, Control. Status report on the other teams."

"Two teams have successfully engaged hostiles. All of our people are good."

"Copy that, Control. Zero One, out." He turned to Sunday as he pointed toward the rise ahead. "We've got more coming. Same deal as before. You take them from the right, I take them from the left."

"Can't we just use one of these RPGs?"

Dawson shook his head. "We save these for when there are too many to take out with just guns. The last thing we want is a detonation. It'll warn their friends that there's trouble ahead."

"I'm afraid I've got a lot to learn," said Sunday as they sprinted toward cover, the sound of the approaching motorcycles growing.

Dawson reached out and slapped the man on the back. "You just proved you can shoot accurately in battle. That's the most important lesson. The rest will come in time."

Sunday grinned at him. "Soon I'll be Rambo."

Dawson laughed. "I suppose that makes me Colonel Trautman?"

"Yes, yes, it does."

Dawson dropped to the ground, crawling forward the final few feet. "We're going to have to pick a different movie."

"Why's that?"

"Because I know I'd make a terrible officer."

Approaching FOB Ugurun, Nigeria

Ledger's heart hammered with the adrenaline pumping through his system. It had been a long time since he was this wired, and was a little out of practice, struggling to keep his nerves under control.

Clarke pointed out the window. "There it is."

Ledger squinted as he leaned forward slightly. "Are we farther away than I think, or is that thing too small to fit two men and a dog?"

"Looks damn small to me."

An alarm sounded and an indicator flashed.

"Strewth! What the hell was that?" cried Clarke.

Ledger squinted at the indicator. "Threat alarm. Deploy countermeasures."

"How the hell do I do that?"

Ledger leaned over, pressing a button, the thump of chaff and flares launching from the defensive pods bringing him no comfort, the countermeasures designed for heat-seeking ordnance, not a basic RPG that simply hurled itself in the direction it was launched. And there were no evasive maneuvers to be performed in a chopper like this with 20,000 pounds of cargo dangling below it. It would be like telling a stationary elephant to dodge an incoming clown fired from a cannon.

He had to rely on the inverse relationship between distance and accuracy when it came to RPGs, and the fact they should be high enough for them not to be reached. That combination should protect them until they began to land, then the countermeasures would be employed as shock and awe.

A detonation that sounded distant had him removing his hand from the countermeasures that would be needed for when they landed. Clarke pointed to their left, exhaust trails from at least a dozen RPGs arcing toward them from the south. If they hadn't altered their route, they would be directly in their path, though altitude should still have hopefully saved them. "Keep shooting, ya wankers, you've only got so many of them," muttered Clarke.

Ledger agreed with the sentiment. The more desperate shots fired now, meant fewer they would have to contend with later.

Clarke pointed ahead. "Small arms fire." He pressed a set of binoculars to his eyes. "It doesn't look like they're shooting at us. Looks like ground engagements."

"Dardy. Maybe BD and the lads are projecting a little force outside the wire. Hopefully, that'll give us a smoother landing."

"Are you still planning on autorotating all the way down?"

"Unless you can think of a better idea."

"Nah, yeah, just hover over them and cut the cable."

"Perimeter fencing is only useful if it's not the height of a pancake."

Clarke shrugged. "Just a suggestion."

"Besides, if there's any way in hell I can save this beast, we can evacuate a shitload of civilians."

Clarke glanced over his shoulder at the empty cabin that could comfortably hold fifty adult males and far more children. "We might be able to get them on board, but with this level of activity in the area, there's no way in hell we'd get to altitude to actually save them. We'll be shot out of the sky."

Ledger sighed. Clarke was right. Even freed of its heavy cargo, the Chinook was a beast. It was never designed for a rapid exit under fire. But if he could save the chopper from serious damage, he would be willing to risk his life to get it back off the ground to bring in reinforcements. "Change of plans," he announced.

"We have a plan?"

"We drop this cargo and get the hell out of there and try to pick up Red's team. We can't take the risk of seventy or eighty kids back there. If we take an RPG, they're dead."

Clarke regarded him. "You know, if we take an RPG, we're done like dinner too."

"You're free to depart with the cargo."

"What, and let you take all the glory if you succeed?"

"I thought you were in it to get cashed-up?"

"You already told me there's no money, so if I have to settle for something, glory will have to do. I'll upload my story to Instagram and strike me lucky. I'll make millions."

Ledger rolled his eyes. "You've got three photographs and two followers. Something tells me you'll be lucky to get a jar of Vegemite out of this."

Clarke's eyes widened and an exaggerated smile spread. "Suddenly, this all became worth it."

Ledger roared with laughter as he cut their speed for the final approach. "I'll put that on your gravestone. 'He did it for Vegemite.'"

FOB Ugurun, Nigeria

"Zero-Seven, Control. Your chopper is on final approach now. ETA, two minutes."

Atlas turned, peering into the distance. He spotted the chopper and its massive shipping container dangling below it, lumbering toward them, RPGs streaking through the sky and falling short, small arms fire chattering in all directions around the base as Dawson and the others engaged the inbound hostiles hell-bent on taking down the helicopter. He and Niner had already cleared the landing zone, making enough room for the container and the chopper. Buhari's men had cleared where the new barrier would go, the front loader already having scraped it level before returning to its tree-clearing efforts. He whistled loudly and Buhari spun. Atlas pointed at the front loader. "Get it in position with a full load."

"Yes, Sergeant," replied Buhari, who then sprinted outside the wire through a large opening they had cut that would give them access to the pile of dirt, and space for the new barrier to pass through. Niner lit half

155

a dozen flares and began dropping them around the perimeter of the LZ as Atlas started popping smoke, tossing the canisters toward the fence line as the chopper positioned overhead. Niner joined him and they both peered up into the sky.

"So, what do you think?" Atlas asked his diminutive friend.

"I give the cargo a fifty-fifty chance."

"And them?"

Niner shrugged. "If that barrier saves these people's lives, then they'll have died heroes."

"And if it doesn't?"

"Then they'll just be two more names on a forgotten list, just like us."

Atlas frowned at his normally chipper friend. "You're pessimistic today."

Niner glanced over his shoulder at the terrified civilians. "I'm just wondering if I want to bring a child into a world where shit like this happens."

Atlas' eyes shot wide. "You and Angela are already talking children?"

Niner's eyes bulged. "Hell no! That's way too soon. But this is the first time I've been in a relationship that I could see potentially working out, so it gets you thinking. You and Vanessa have been together way longer than Angela and I. You must have had these discussions."

"We have."

"And?"

"Well, you remember her reaction when she found out what I did for a living. She's still pretty paranoid about it. So, for the moment, we've agreed that any type of family plans, including marriage, are on hold until she gets her career going."

Niner regarded him. "Do you think she'll ever come around?"

Atlas shrugged. "I hope so, because no kids is a deal-breaker for me."

"And your mama."

Atlas chuckled. "Oh yeah, if I don't give her grandbabies, she'll never speak to me again."

"Has Vanessa ever said she wants kids?"

"Oh, she definitely wants kids, that's not the problem. She's just worried about the kids growing up without a father."

They both turned as gunfire rattled nearby and another RPG launched skyward as the Chinook and its cargo positioned overhead. Atlas sighed. "Something tells me the whole question of when we're having kids could be a moot point if we don't get this barrier."

Niner slapped him on the back. "Well, if we're going to die, at least we're dying together, exactly how I always imagined it."

Atlas eyeballed him. "Really? I always imagined being there when you died, but only because I shot you for crossing the line one time too many." His comms squawked. "Zero-Seven, Control. I'm patching you through to Roo Wrangler so you can guide them in, over."

"Copy that, Control. You're a go for Roo Wrangler."

"G'day mate, is that the Wakandan Hulk's voice I'm hearing?"

Atlas laughed, as did Niner, punching his friend on the arm. "Wakandan Hulk. I'm using that."

"That's an affirmative, Roo Wrangler. Did you pick your own callsign or did Langley see a photo of your girlfriend?"

Ledger laughed. "Mate, we're going to have words when I get on the ground."

Atlas stared up at them. "And just how do you plan on doing that?"

Ledger became serious. "I'm going to cut power and autorotate her down. I'm going to be too busy trying to keep this thing under control to keep an eye on the ground, so I need you to tell me if I'm going off course and how to adjust. And the first time you see an RPG coming in that might have a chance of hitting us, we'd appreciate it if you'd give it a mention."

"Copy that, Roo Wrangler, we'll keep an eye on the skies for you."

"Appreciate it, beginning our insertion now."

Atlas flagged down Buhari. "Sergeant Major, I need four good sets of eyes that speak English perfectly."

Buhari pointed at four men, snapping orders. They rushed over to Atlas and Niner.

"Yes, Sergeant, what do you need?" asked one of them.

Atlas pointed up at the chopper. "I need eyes on the sky in all four directions. Watch for rockets that might actually reach the helicopter. If you see one, even if you're not sure, I want you to shout, 'Incoming from the north!' or whatever direction you're covering"—he pointed at each of them—"north, south, east, west. You see one that you think could hit the helicopter, you shout it loud and proud, got it?"

"Yes, Sergeant!" they echoed then broke off in their assigned directions, encircling the landing zone.

Atlas glanced at Niner. "Your head on a swivel. If one of those guys calls out a shot, make your own assessment and radio it in with your recommendation. I'm going to be too busy standing right under this twenty-thousand pounds of cargo."

"You don't plan on catching it, do you?"

"The thought had occurred to me."

"Here goes nothing," said Ledger as he cut the power to the rotors, RPGs continuing to streak below them. He pointed at the countermeasures. "The moment you hear them announce something incoming, you hit that button and leave it on. I want to make it as difficult as possible for those wankers to get a bead on us."

"Got it." Clarke tightened his belts and positioned his fingers around the panel, his index finger hovering over the button that just might save their lives.

"Control and everyone else listening in, here we go."

The chopper had already begun the drop before he informed the world, the airframe shaking as the rate of their descent increased.

Clarke glanced at him. "You do realize this is one of the dumber things we've ever done?"

Ledger gripped the controls tighter. "One of? If you can name a single other time I've done something stupider, I'm buying you a *case* of Vegemite."

South of FOB Ugurun, Nigeria

Dawson and Sunday sprinted toward the next target, a cluster of five hostiles in the opposite direction of their abandoned motorcycles. An RPG streaked skyward and Dawson glanced up over his shoulder to see the chopper behind them making its descent.

"Zero-One, Control. One hundred meters directly ahead, over."

"Copy that, Control."

"Zero One, the chopper is about to be within range and it looks like your guys have four more RPGs. Suggest you hurry, over."

Dawson rolled his eyes. It wasn't Leroux on the other end of the line, it was one of the minions. So much was going on right now, he had no doubt that Leroux and Tong, the two most experienced people in that operations center, were too busy coordinating things. "Thanks for the suggestion, Control." He glanced over at Sunday. "Our eyes in the sky suggest we hurry."

Sunday laughed as they continued to sprint forward. "Only Olusoji Fasuba could be running faster than we are now."

160

Dawson's eyes narrowed. "Who?"

"Famous Nigerian sprinter."

"Ah. Well, it wouldn't do me much good."

"Why?"

"Because I'm having a hard enough time keeping up with you, you bastard."

The younger and apparently fitter Sunday roared with laughter. "Maybe if you weren't wearing all that gear, you could keep up easier."

Dawson glanced at the flimsy fatigues his partner was wearing, not a shred of body armor to protect him. "I'd sacrifice speed over body armor any day."

"And I would prefer to be able to run away as fast as I can."

Dawson spotted their targets ahead and became all business. "Eleven o'clock. Five hostiles." He raised his weapon, as did Sunday, and they continued to sprint forward. There was no cover between them and the enemy, but at the moment, all five men were staring skyward, no one noticing their mistake was about to cost them their lives.

Another RPG streaked toward the Chinook and the man who had fired it momentarily took his eyes off his efforts as he tossed the spent launcher onto the ground. And spotted them. Dawson stopped and opened fire, squeezing the trigger on his assault rifle, single shot, left to right. Another missile launched just as Dawson took out the man responsible, and moments later, all five were down. He stared at the smoke trail streaking toward the chopper, now much lower than the last time he had looked. Ledger was bringing it down fast and hard, and unfortunately for him, it meant he was now in range.

FOB Ugurun, Nigeria

"Incoming from the south!" shouted one of the sentries.

Niner spun, spotting the trail of spent propellant and cursed as he activated his comms. "Incoming from the south," he reported. "Adjust to port. Repeat, adjust to port." There was no time for callsigns or proper protocol. Every millisecond counted.

The crackling of chaff and the hiss of flares deploying filled their ears. Niner stared up to see the brilliant display overhead as the chopper continued to drop, banking to the left slightly. The rocket continued to streak toward the chopper then blasted past, falling to the ground beyond the fence line. The warhead exploded with a brilliant flash and Niner activated his comms. "Roo Wrangler, you're all clear."

"Copy that, Ground. Requesting you have fresh underwear ready upon our landing."

Niner laughed. "Negative, Roo Wrangler, no clean underwear available. However, you're welcome to mine."

"Commando it is, but break out the hose. I think my partner here is going to need to be sprayed down. Powering up now, I recommend everyone keep a safe distance. This is going to be a shit-show."

Ledger sent as much power as he could toward the rotors, the roar of the engines growing as more horsepower was generated, but with the weight of the massive airframe and the 20,000 pounds of cargo underneath it, Sir Isaac Newton continued to drag them toward impending doom.

Clarke gripped anything he could as he white-knuckled it. "Screw the Vegemite. This is by far the *stupidest* thing you've ever done."

Ledger gripped the controls, staring at the altimeter as it wound down at far too rapid a pace. "I'm glad we're finally in agreement." As they continued to hurtle toward the ground, he closed his eyes and said a silent prayer, not for himself, not for Clarke, but for those below whom he had failed.

"Open your bloody eyes, ya tosser! What are you trying to do? Kill us?"

Ledger opened his eyes and gave his friend a look. "I've already done that."

The Chinook chose that moment to make a liar of him and he roared with glee as the rattle of the airframe smoothed out. Their descent slowed as the rotors finally had enough speed to provide them with some lift. He punched Clarke on the shoulder. "You crazy bastard! We might just survive this!"

Clarke stared at him wide-eyed. "Who the hell are you calling crazy, ya slagger? The only thing I've done that's crazy is agree to partner up with you."

"Yeah, but doesn't it make you feel alive?"

"I can feel alive sitting in my recliner in front of the idiot box and not be wondering just how many more seconds of life I have left. When this is over, you and I are having words about volunteering my arse for missions."

Ledger continued to battle the Chinook as their descent gradually slowed. "There are plenty of other airlines that I'm sure would be happy to hire someone as unqualified as you."

"Incoming from the north. Adjust to starboard," reported the ground team over the satphone now on speaker. Ledger guided them slightly to the right, sensing the resistance of the massive cargo below.

"I can't believe you still call this thing an airline. We're one bloody plane."

Ledger flashed him a grin. "One plane and a helicopter. In just one day, we doubled in size."

"You're right, I forgot. We're a two-aircraft airline with half its fleet stolen from the US Army, the other half held as collateral. And they just might send you the bill if you pancake us."

"If I pancake us, the bill is the least of our worries." Ledger jutted his chin at the altimeter. "We might just survive this. If we're arrested, I'm telling them you made me do it."

Clarke flipped him the bird as the Chinook rocked from the explosion of the RPG. "Must have caught a flare or something."

"Or something."

The voice from below crackled with a new warning. "Incoming from the east and north. Suggest adjusting forward to port and praying."

Ledger growled as he eyed the altimeter. "Perhaps I spoke too soon."

"Ya think?"

"Get ready to cut that cable then hang on. It doesn't look like Uncle Sam is getting a functional chopper back."

South of FOB Ugurun, Nigeria

Ibrahim cursed yet again as another RPG fell to the ground uselessly. "Stop wasting the rockets! We need to get closer!" he hissed, those nearer the action obviously unable to hear his critique of their efforts. The chopper was too high to hit. If his men would simply get closer while it descended, they could make them count. It was the biggest helicopter he had ever seen, two massive rotors overhead with what appeared to be a sea container dangling far below it. He had to guess at least fifty reinforcements could be in the chopper itself, and if he were to assume the container was filled with weapons and ammo, then they could be in for one hell of a fight.

They had to take it down in a ball of fire—either the chopper or the cargo. Destroy the weapons and ammo, then it didn't matter how many more men you brought in if they had nothing to shoot with. Eliminate the reinforcements, then it didn't matter how much ammo was brought in because there were only so many fingers to pull the triggers. Either would keep the odds heavily in their favor, but if they failed, it would make their attack that much more difficult, and they might need to delay until more warriors could be assembled.

Yet he couldn't delay it for long. The attack had to be finished by tonight. Reports indicated a large column of Nigerian troops were already on their way here, and the US Army markings on this helicopter indicated the Americans were committing, though apparently not fully. Any commander with access to the firepower the Americans had would have sent in gunships along with the heavy transport. Leaving it defenseless like this made no sense. Then again, a lot of what he was seeing didn't make sense. For example, why could he see those propellers rotating when they should be moving so fast, it would be a blur? Why was it dropping out of the sky so rapidly, it appeared to be out of control? Something strange was going on here, but what it was didn't matter. All that mattered was taking down that chopper.

He gunned his engine, taking the ditch around a felled tree and leaping back onto the road, the worn suspension providing little relief from the impact. But he didn't care. Discomfort mattered not in the fight against the infidel. They were at the outskirts of the village now, a village he intended to wipe from existence, and he came to a halt along with the others. Rockets continued to streak, most uselessly, but he was close enough now for a clear shot at the helicopter. Gunfire rattled around them, suggesting those on the base had sent forces outside their chain-link fence in an attempt to engage his men and protect their helicopter. It made sense. It was what he would do if he ever had access to those types of weapons.

But it also meant he had to be careful. There was no way he wanted to die here today and leave the organization in the hands of the likes of Lawan. Lawan had to die and had to die soon, but he couldn't just shoot him. He had to do something different. It had to either look like an accident, look like somebody from outside, or something justifiable. Could he perhaps frame him for something? Shoot him, then plant some evidence on him to make it appear as if he were a traitor? That would be the best way. If Lawan died an innocent man, he could become a martyr, and his supporters would rally behind a memory.

And memories could sometimes be impossible to fight.

No, he had to discredit the man so the memory left behind would be tainted, would be something not to be rallied around, and instead, those who supported him would be forced to admit they were misled, and to instead join him fully rather than tacitly.

It was something to worry about later.

He peered at the chopper, chaff and flares deploying uselessly if his understanding of how an RPG worked was correct. The weapon slung over his shoulder wasn't heat seeking. You aimed, fired, and hoped it reached the target. All the deployed countermeasures seemed to be doing was making it hard to pick out the chopper from within all the smoke.

One thing was certain. They were within range.

Lawan fired his RPG and it went wildly off course. He tossed the spent launcher. "Piece of shit! I'm getting my money back on that."

Ibrahim chuckled. "I've never met an arms dealer who offers a money-back guarantee."

"Then I'll cut out his tongue so he can never make another deal."

Ibrahim watched as another rocket failed to reach its target, this one somehow detonating close, perhaps hit by a lucky flare. He pressed the launcher against his shoulder and aimed at the chopper. He was about to squeeze the trigger when he thought better of it and instead adjusted his aim, pointing the rocket at an extremely high angle.

"What are you doing?" asked Lawan.

"Trying something different." He squeezed the trigger and the rocket launched, racing skyward, far above the chopper, and Lawan laughed.

"Have you never fired one of those before?"

Ibrahim ignored him, instead continuing to follow the upward trajectory. His heart hammered as the propellant ran out and the rocket tipped then fell back to Earth. He was about to either appear the fool or the genius, and as the warhead picked up speed in its descent, he tossed the launcher aside and stared as Lawan muttered an appreciative curse.

His gamble might just be about to pay off.

FOB Ugurun, Nigeria

Niner winced as the RPG detonated between the large Chinook and its heavy container, having dropped in from above in a high arc, someone out there employing a different tactic.

Atlas cursed. "Man, I think that one bounced off the cable."

Niner glanced at him, his best friend staring directly overhead. "I'm glad you realize that, you idiot. Now, how about you get over here so that you're not directly under it."

Atlas took a look around, reestablishing situational awareness. "Yeah, I suppose you're right," he said as he jogged over and joined Niner.

The dangling container was only a few hundred feet from the ground now, and the descent had slowed considerably. Another RPG detonated outside the wire and they both stared as smoke streamed out of the rear rotor assembly. "What the hell hit them?"

Atlas shrugged. "AK? Whatever it was, they caught some damage there."

Niner cursed. "Roo Wrangler, One-One. You've got smoke coming out of the rear rotor assembly. Repeat, smoke coming out of the rear rotor assembly."

"Thanks for the weather report, One-One, kind of busy here. We're about to cut this cable, so watch your heads. God knows where it's going to go, and it's a long mother."

"Copy that. Don't worry about us, just get your asses on the ground."

"Oh, don't you worry about that. Our arses are going to be on the ground one way or another. Just give us a count, would you?"

Niner peered up and picked a number—there was no way he could be accurate from this position. "One-hundred meters, eighty, sixty, forty…" The entire time he counted, the heavy load continued to slow. Two more RPG warnings were called by their Nigerian friends, but the countermeasures were continually deploying the entire way down, obscuring things, and hopefully spoiling the aim. There was nothing else they could do. Smoke continued to pour out of the rear engine, growing in intensity, and the entire helicopter threatened to explode if they didn't get on the ground soon and shut down.

"Twenty! Ten! Contact!" shouted Niner, and a moment later the long cable stretched overhead dropped like a rock. The helicopter banked to the right, away from the container that had just slammed into the ground, then he gasped as the downdraft from the massive rotors shoved the descending strap away from it and toward one of the Nigerians eying the sky, his back toward the danger.

"Hey West! Look out!"

The soldier, thankfully, recognized he was the one being warned and turned toward Niner, who pointed at the rapidly descending cable. The man's eyes bulged and he leaped out of the way just as the knuckle of the cable slammed into the ground, throwing up a cloud of dust.

"You okay?" asked Atlas.

The Nigerian gave a thumbs-up. "Yes, Sergeant!"

They both returned their attention to the chopper as Ledger overcompensated by banking a little too far to the left. "It's going to be ugly!" cried Atlas as Niner shielded his mouth from the dust and debris whipping up around them. The heavy-lift helicopter slammed into the ground, leaning heavily on its left side. They could hear the power cut and the tips of the rotors scrape the ground as everyone within the vicinity sprinted for safety.

Niner raced toward the container, the sturdiest cover in sight, and Atlas lumbered after him. They both hit the side and Niner peered out around the corner, wincing as the chopper continued to teeter before it finally recovered, bouncing onto all four sets of wheels. "Holy shit! I can't believe he actually landed that thing!" He stepped out from behind the container and could see through the windshield that Ledger and Clarke were going through the shutdown checklist.

Niner raced toward the chopper as the ramp dropped. He ran up inside and grabbed two of the fire extinguishers strapped to the fuselage, then jumped back outside, tossing one of them to Atlas. They both directed the spray on the smoking engine, the concern no longer whether they could fly this thing out of here, but instead the real risk of all the aviation fuel on board detonating and incinerating the entire area, including their brand-new barrier that had just been delivered. Ledger and Clarke joined them a moment later with their own extinguishers, and between the four of them, the freely billowing smoke died down then out.

Atlas smiled broadly at Ledger. "You are one crazy son of a bitch."

Ledger laughed and exchanged fist bumps with the Delta operators. "Even I have to say I'm impressed with myself." He jerked a thumb at Clarke. "This Sheila screamed the entire way down."

"I did no such thing."

"Then what was all that wailing about?"

"I was merely commenting on your piloting skills."

"Huh? I've never seen a performance report with 'Oh shit! Oh shit! Oh shit! Oh shit!' written on it."

Niner roared with laughter. "Well, you both made it and we're happy to see you." He jerked his chin toward the shipping container. "Now, how about we go unwrap that gift you just brought us?"

Ledger leaned closer, lowering his voice. "I'll be happy to help you with that, but someone mentioned being able to borrow their underwear?"

Operations Center 2, CIA Headquarters

Langley, Virginia

Cheers erupted throughout the operation center as they watched the container set down then the Aussies who had delivered it emerge alive and well from the damaged chopper. Tong beamed a smile at Leroux and he returned it.

"I'll let you do the honors. Let the rest of Bravo Team know."

Her smile broadened as she activated her headset. "Bravo Team, Control. The package has been successfully delivered and the chopper is on the ground with no casualties. I repeat, package has been delivered and chopper is on the ground, no casualties, over."

Dawson replied. "Copy that, Control. Zero-One to Bravo Team, eliminate any targets in your vicinity then return to base. Zero-One, out."

Acknowledgments were heard from the overhead speakers, all four teams outside the wire heading back toward the base. Leroux turned to his team. "Remember, it's not over yet. Make sure those guys get back safely."

Head bobs, thumbs-ups, and various other forms of acknowledgment responded to the instructions he knew he didn't need to issue. His team was the best and would do nothing to jeopardize the safety of those they were responsible for.

"Sonya, contact the Pentagon. Tell them we found their stolen chopper and equipment, and that when this is all over, they'll need to send in a repair crew."

Tong grinned. "There's no way we're getting away with this."

"If we save those people, they'll take credit and no one will care about a stolen chopper. If we don't, then we'll wear it, and frankly, I don't think I'm going to give a damn if I get demoted or fired. Hell, if I get thrown in prison because we tried to save all those people using any means necessary, then I can live with that because at least I can go to sleep at night knowing I had done everything I could."

Tong wiped a tear from the corner of her eye. "If you're going to prison then so am I."

Child snickered. "You know you two can't share a cell, right?"

Tong, who Leroux was aware had an unhealthy infatuation with him, flushed at what he had no doubt was simply an innocent joke from Child that by pure luck was a little too on the nose, and he threw her a lifeline before anyone noticed her reaction. He faced Child. "Then I guess I'm going to have to settle for you. I promise I'll be gentle."

Child's eyes shot wide and his jaw dropped. The room erupted with laughter and Marc shouted from the back, "You're going to be his bitch, Randy!"

The laughter grew despite all eyes still being glued to their screens, somebody announcing that Dawson had just crossed the wire. Leroux turned back to face his workstation to see Tong laughing with the others, though he knew her well enough to know it was forced. She made eye contact with him, her eyes conveying her thanks, and part of him wondered once again what it might be like if Sherrie weren't in his life and Tong instead was the woman he loved.

And as it always did when he had such thoughts, his stomach churned with guilt.

FOB Ugurun, Nigeria

Dawson sprinted through the gate, his eyes scanning from left to right, taking in everything that had changed. The mood was mixed among the civilians, some no doubt happy that what could help save them had arrived, but disappointed that the chopper, which judging by the foams sprayed all over the rear engine, wouldn't be taking them to safety. One end of the container was open. Ledger and Clarke already had the first segments of the HESCO RAID barrier pulled out, and the front loader with Atlas behind the controls was rumbling toward it with the bucket loaded.

The barrier was an ingenious design. The container, despite being only twenty feet long, contained over one thousand feet worth of the fully collapsible system. The principle was simple. The system itself wasn't the barrier, it was a container for it. As it was stretched out like an accordion, it left behind a honeycomb that could be filled with dirt, sand, or any other granular material, held in place by the barrier.

Bullets, RPGs, vehicles—nothing was getting through three and a half feet of sand. It provided incredible protection once set up properly. Their problem was they only had one piece of equipment that could fill it and limited time. He had no doubt the moment Boko Haram learned of what they were doing, they would advance their plans.

He jogged over to join Niner who was directing the deployment. "Status report."

Niner stepped back as Atlas emptied what appeared to be a second load in the first segment of the barrier. He pulled back then maneuvered to the opposite side of the container where Ledger and Clarke hooked straps from it onto the bucket. "The cargo arrived intact, though the frame of the container was a little twisted so we had a bit of a chore getting the door open. The cargo was undamaged though. Chopper's shot. It took some shrapnel or something to the rear rotor assembly. Nothing that can't be fixed, but certainly not by us. If Wings gets here, we'll have him take a look at it. If he thinks he can repair it here, maybe we can get an airdrop with the spare parts."

"Maybe, but something tells me coordinating all that is going to take more time than we've got."

Niner agreed. "You're probably right, but faint hope is some hope."

Dawson turned as the engine on the front loader roared, thick black smoke spewing from its exhaust pipe. "We've got the path cleared?"

"Yeah, we've picked a layout that will encompass our filler material"—Niner pointed at the pile of dirt outside the wire—"and provide enough room for the loader to work inside, as well as surround these buildings. At a minimum, they won't be able to see what we're doing, but until we can get it filled, we're still sitting ducks. It's just they won't know where we're sitting."

Atlas reversed the loader, dragging the container, the barrier slowly pulling out, the forms expanding. As the civilians realized what was happening, cheers erupted with the misunderstanding that they were already protected.

Buhari joined them, smiling broadly. "It's beautiful, is it not?"

Dawson agreed. "I'd put one around my own place if my fiancée would let me."

Buhari laughed. "Any word from your"—he pointed up—"eyes in the sky on when we can expect the attack?"

Dawson shook his head. "Last report is that they're still staging. I anticipate they'll hit us tonight, though if they hear about this, they might decide to move up their plans."

Buhari turned and watched the barrier continue to unfurl, Atlas already rounding the pile of sand at the far end. "Would they even know what this is? I mean, if they saw it, would they know it needs to be filled to be effective?"

Dawson shook his head. "I doubt it. But as soon as they see the front loader filling it, they'll figure it out pretty quickly." He pointed to the clustered civilians. "This is why we need to get this part of the barrier filled first. We can fit most of the civilians between it and the buildings. Get that filled and they stand a chance. We can position some vehicles if necessary to provide them with additional cover if we run out of time."

Atlas roared toward them on the opposite side of the encampment, rounding the first segment then coming to a halt, double-wrapping the final segment by about fifty feet, leaving a gap large enough for the loader to operate in. In a normal situation, proper entry points would be created, but this was anything but normal. They would leave the opening and treat it as a chokepoint where they would set up a kill box that would eliminate anyone who attempted to get through. Ledger and Clarke unhooked the loader and Atlas roared through the opening, heading down the far side to pick up another load of dirt.

Dawson and the others walked over to the seven-foot-high wall. He pressed his hand against it to test how high the load of dirt had filled and found it was a hair shy of full height. "It's going to take two loads per to fill each of these segments. Let's just do one load for each of the priority segments, and then if we've got time, do the second load. Three and a half feet of protection all around is better than seven feet in some and none in others."

Niner patted him on the back. "Atlas and I have it all figured out. Don't you worry your pretty little head."

Dawson rolled his eyes and activated his comms. "Control, Zero-One. Any sign the hostiles have taken notice of what we're doing?"

"Stand by, Zero-One. We have a situation."

Atlas and the loader disappeared behind the mound of dirt, blocking the roar of the engine slightly, allowing them all to hear just what that situation might be.

The revving of motorcycle engines too close for his liking.

Operations Center 2, CIA Headquarters

Langley, Virginia

Leroux stood staring at the satellite image. Three of those who had been sent in to shoot down the helicopter had taken refuge inside a barn when they had heard their comrades engaged by Dawson and the other fireteams. And while they had hidden rather than engage, they had also done something else unexpected. When the chopper had landed and the excitement was over, rather than retreat, they had instead raced toward the base, and from their vantage point had witnessed the barrier dragged from its container. They couldn't be allowed to deliver that critical piece of intel to their leadership.

"Get me Drone Control."

After some taps, Tong gave a thumbs-up.

Leroux activated his comms. "Drone Control, this is Control Actual. We're sending you coordinates now." He pointed a finger at Tong who nodded as she sent the information. "We have three hostiles on motorcycles heading south. We need you to take them out ASAP."

Child cursed and before Leroux could ask why, the young analyst had brought up a map showing the current location of the bikes and the fact there was a crossroad just ahead where they could split into three different directions. Leroux covered his mic. "ETA to that intersection?"

"Three minutes."

He removed his hand. "You have less than three minutes."

"Copy that, Control. Repositioning now," came the eerily calm voice.

"Put that Reaper up on the map. I want to see it, the hostiles, and that intersection with projections."

"You got it," said Child, three red indicators appearing on the map he had just put up, a blue indicator appearing a moment later. The General Atomics MQ-9 Reaper Unmanned Aerial Vehicle banked hard to the right, racing toward the target coordinates, the motorcycles speeding for the crossroads. Leroux's heart raced as the distance between them and the intersection rapidly shrank.

"Control, I have the targets in sight."

The door to the operations center hissed opened and Leroux caught Morrison out the corner of his eye, the Chief's eyes bulging slightly at the realization of what was going on. "Copy that, Drone Control. You're clear to take the shot as soon as you're in range."

"Copy that, Control. ETA sixty seconds."

They weren't going to make it. It was just too close. The question was how accurate was the time estimate? Was it 60 seconds? Or was it 65? Or was it 55? Seconds counted. All he knew was the mental tally in his head he had been counting down from 60 was higher than the computer's estimate for the time the first rider would reach the crossroads.

They were three seconds apart.

"Launching now," announced the voice over the speakers. The satellite image showed an AGM-114 Hellfire air-to-ground missile streak from the Reaper and toward the three riders.

"She launched too late," said Child, staring at the indicators rather than spinning in his chair. "She launched way too late."

"She can only launch when she can legally launch," explained Tong. "ROEs on a UAV require line of sight unless you have special clearance, which we don't."

The motorcycles reached the crossroads with the missile still ten seconds out according to the computer, when suddenly prayers were answered. The three motorcycles came to a halt at the intersection, a conversation held, perhaps deciding who should go where.

"Impact in three seconds," murmured Tong.

Leroux rose, leaning forward, his fingers splayed across his workstation as he prayed for the riders to stay in place. One of them turned and surged forward, taking the southern road when the missile hit. A brilliant flash briefly overwhelmed the displays. The filters adjusted and a cloud of billowing smoke appeared, completely obscuring the crossroads.

"Did we get all three?" he asked, unable to see anything. "Zoom-out. We need to see if there's anybody on those roads." Tong complied and the image adjusted, giving them a wider radius. Leroux scanned all four roads the entire length visible, but saw nothing.

Child pointed. "It's clearing now."

Leroux returned his attention to the center of the image as the breeze blowing in the area slowly cleared the bulk of the smoke from the initial explosion. He smiled at the sight of one of the motorcycles, now at the side of the road, the twisted body of its rider entangled in the wreckage.

"That's one!" cried Child. "Come on, baby, give us two more!" He rubbed his hands together eagerly, as if warming dice for the craps table. The bloodlust was understandable but inappropriate. While Leroux was praying that two more people were dead, it was important to remember what was happening here. These were still human beings no matter how vile they were. They should be treated with respect, for that's what separated us from them. Kill them? Yes. But don't dance on their corpses.

The use of the code word 'Irene' had brought back memories from when he was younger, watching the movie Black Hawk Down, and years later reviewing the news coverage of the disaster in Mogadishu and how the enemy had dragged the bodies of the American dead through the streets. It was something he couldn't imagine American troops doing, and it showed to him at an impressionable young age the difference between the civilized and the uncivilized.

Yet there were limits, and his smile spread wide as the other two terrorists were revealed, their bodies aflame. He felt no guilt about killing these people, nor in celebrating their deaths for a brief moment.

But he would never dance on their graves.

"That's three!" shouted Child, thrusting his hands in the air and spinning.

Leroux straightened, allowing the display for the moment. "Good work people. Sonya, pass my thanks on to Drone Control. Now, let's get back to work. We spotted those three, there may be more."

FOB Hadejia, Nigeria

Wings said a silent prayer then flicked the switch, a smile spreading as the engine of the old Huey roared to life, the rotors overhead beginning to turn. But he didn't declare victory yet. He monitored all the indicators, watching for anything wrong, but everything continued to show as nominal. He applied more power and the blades overhead pounded at the air, the entire craft vibrating just as it should.

Man, they sure don't make them like they used to.

He waved at his Nigerian partner to get clear, and the man scrambled out of the way as Wings lifted off, did a quick ring of the base, then landed, satisfied the repair had been successful. He powered down and hopped out. "Top off the fuel," he said to his grinning partner who gave him a high-five.

Wings walked over to his gear piled nearby as he wiped his hands on a cloth. He was filthy, covered in grease and worse, but he didn't give a shit about that. The job was done. He fit his comms back in place. "Zero-Two, this is One-Two. Come in, over."

"Go ahead, One-Two."

"Zero-Two, the Huey has a heartbeat. We're refueling her now. Estimated departure, less than ten minutes."

"Copy that, One-Two. Coordinate with Control for our current position and check with our hosts to see if they have more chainsaws. We have the manpower but not enough tools to clear this road."

"Copy that, Zero-Two. I'll check on that for you. Anything else you need me to bring?"

"Negative, One-Two. Just get your ass here as fast as you can so we can get in this fight."

"I'm on my way. One-Two, out." He headed toward the headquarters and spotted the base commander standing on the plywood steps.

"I see you got her working," said Colonel Kalgo.

Wings came to a halt in front of the man, standing at ease with his hands clasped behind his back. "Yes, sir. With the right parts and good help, anything's possible when it comes to helicopter repair."

Kalgo chuckled. "I could use a man like you in my command."

Wings smiled. "If I ever decide to switch allegiances, I'll consider it."

Kalgo roared with laughter. "Good answer, son. Good answer." He nodded toward the helicopter being refueled. "What are your intentions?"

"My second-in-command has requested as many chainsaws as you can spare to help in the clearing of the roads. With your permission, I'll deliver those, pick up the rest of my team and as many of yours that can fit in the chopper, and bring them to the FOB. And I'll repeat that journey as many times as I can until the situation is resolved."

"We've already lost two choppers. What makes you think you can make it in?"

"They were lost because they weren't prepared for what they were facing. Now we know and, frankly, sir, I have far more experience flying in combat than I suspect most of your pilots have."

"You guarantee you'll bring her back in one piece?"

Wings decided it was best not to lie to the man. "Negative, sir. I could lie to you and say yes, but I think you and I both know the risks. All I can promise you is that I will try my damnedest to help save those villagers."

"Understood, Sergeant. The Nigerian Army is pleased to grant you permission to pilot its helicopter in this matter."

Wings snapped to attention and saluted the man. "Thank you, sir."

The salute was returned and Kalgo flagged down a nearby lieutenant. "Yes, Colonel?"

"Get as many chainsaws as we have and load them on that chopper."

"Right away, sir." The lieutenant sprinted off to one of the nearby storage buildings.

Kalgo turned to reenter his command post when he paused. "Oh, and Sergeant?"

"Yes, sir?"

"Tell your people that I'm sending another one hundred men with heavy weapons and supplies within the hour. If they can hold out, we'll get to them. They just need to hold."

"Yes, sir. I'll pass it on."

Kalgo stepped inside and Wings headed for the latrine to take care of business before he flew out of here, since with what he expected ahead, he had no idea when he would get another opportunity. The sense of accomplishment he felt at getting the chopper working, and the excitement rippling through him at the mission ahead, reminded him yet again of why he loved this job. He could die tonight fighting to save hundreds of innocents, or he could be hit by a bus tomorrow buying a churro from a street vendor.

Certainly, the odds were astronomically different, but that wasn't the point. Everyone was going to die, some in their beds asleep in the winter of life, others uselessly in a car accident, killed by a drunk. And while he would prefer to grow old and meet the grandchildren that were far in his future, he was comforted in knowing that should he die today, on this mission in particular, those grandchildren would be proud to call him Pop-Pop despite never having met him. Knowing that he was fighting on the side of right, of freedom, of mercy, was how he could go into battle, prepared to die for those he loved while still fighting to live for the same reason.

And while today's cause might be a good one to die for, it was an even better one to survive for.

FOB Ugurun, Nigeria

Atlas brought the loader to a halt, dumping another load of dirt before disappearing yet again. There had been just enough fencing to do the job, and it would have been more than enough if they hadn't been forced to enclose the sand pile. But this would have to do. If they could indeed fill in the critical areas to at least half-height before any action began, they stood a chance.

Buhari jogged up to Dawson. "The villagers want to help. Is there anything they can do?"

Dawson pushed up on his toes and peered out past the barrier, the tree line having been shoved back dramatically. There was no longer a need to bring in the felled trees—it would be too much work with the barrier now in the way. But there was something that would keep them busy and potentially prove useful.

He pointed at the sandbagged positions. "The barrier is now the defensive perimeter. Let's get all these sandbags inside the new wire.

We'll use them to set up protective positions on top of the buildings so we can lay fire on the tree line."

Buhari nodded. "Consider it done." He rushed toward a group of villagers and within moments, scores of men and women headed out from behind the barrier, putting their lives at risk to save their family and friends.

It was a scene that warmed Dawson's heart, but had him questioning whether he would ever see the same back home, where his country was so divided. He feared there would be two barriers going up, one painted red, the other blue, where protection was granted based upon who you voted for and not whether you had been a good neighbor for the past twenty years. His country was in trouble, in serious trouble. He just prayed every night that the civil war potentially coming never came, because killing fellow Americans in defense of the Constitution wasn't what he had signed up for.

Niner jogged over and tapped his ear. "I take it you heard Wings is on his way?"

"Yeah, I monitored that."

"We might have some more help in less than an hour, but only if he doesn't get shot out of the sky like the others."

Dawson nodded. "Yeah, I was thinking about that. I think we need a secondary LZ."

Niner stomped his foot and threw his head back. "Argh, why do you always think of my good ideas before I get to say them?"

Dawson shrugged. "I'm older and wiser."

"And don't forget handsomer," said Spock, as he strolled up to join them. "What are we talking about?"

"Oh, just how Niner's always behind the eight ball."

"Yeah, it's a wonder he's still in the Unit."

Niner flipped them both the bird. "Anyway, as I was going to suggest but BD beat me to the punch, we should set up a secondary LZ with direct road access to here. Take two of the transports, refuel them, and they can be used to shuttle men and equipment between here and there. We have Langley monitor things from the air to make sure nobody's getting too close, and if they do, we switch the LZ. Each time they come in if we have to."

Dawson's head bobbed in agreement with Niner's plan that pretty much mirrored his own.

"What about evacuating the civilians?" asked Spock.

Dawson shook his head. "Not on the first run. We need to see what happens. If we can safely get a second run in, then we'll consider it. But we should try to get the wounded out." He swatted Niner on the chest. "It's your idea so you coordinate it."

Niner grinned. "Soon we won't need you on missions."

"I'll always be needed. If I'm not here, who's going to play referee between you and Atlas?" Dawson activated his comms. "Control, this is Zero-One. Prepare for communication from One-One. He'll be coordinating the inbound chopper, over."

"Copy that, Zero-One. Awaiting communication from One-One."

"It's all yours," said Dawson to Niner. "I'll let Sergeant Major Buhari know."

Atlas rolled by, filling another segment of the barrier, his shirt, along with his body armor, sitting in a nearby pile, his skin gleaming with sweat, his chiseled physique on full display. Niner gave the man a wolf whistle and Dawson had to chuckle as Atlas expertly reversed the loader while flipping a bird over his shoulder.

Atlas roared back toward the pile of dirt at the far end of the camp. At this pace, they would run out of time long before Boko Haram would arrive. They needed to buy some time. Every bucketful provided more desperately needed cover.

Spock regarded him. "I know that look. What's bothering you?"

"The clock. The biggest concentration of the enemy is only a twenty-minute ride from here. If they find out about this, about what we're doing, they could put almost two-hundred men around this installation inside of half an hour."

"But the fact they haven't suggests they don't know yet. There's not much we can do about it, but I would have to think if there was anybody within sight of this place with a radio, they would have already called it in."

"Agreed."

They both stood back as a line of villagers walked past with sandbags from the main gate. The spirit of these people was indomitable. Their fear was evident, but so was their determination to not just roll over and accept their fate. At the opposite end of the compound, at least twenty women were firing weapons for probably the first time in their lives, weapons they had just been trained to use, giving them a fighting chance against the horde that could be on its way at any moment. If these people were willing to fight to the death, then it was his moral obligation to do whatever he could to give them another option. He needed to give them every chance to fight to survive.

And he had an idea how he might just buy the time needed to give them that chance.

En Route to FOB Ugurun, Nigeria

Wings landed the chopper with a gentle bounce. He had flown pretty much anything imaginable during his career, including state-of-the-art Black Hawks and Apaches, and even the best America's enemies had to offer. Yet there was something about a classic that brought a smile. It brought back memories of watching movies about the Vietnam War and how the helicopter had redefined it. Classics like The Green Berets, Platoon, or even We Were Soldiers were favorites. All were stories about the same period but made in different eras, the jingoistic John Wayne classic versus the critical Platoon versus the reflective We Were Soldiers that so poignantly reminded the viewer that many of those men had families back home with wives and children. It reminded him of how, just as with the beginning of the Vietnam war when America was ill-prepared for the inevitable casualties, so too was the America of twenty years ago, when it went into Afghanistan then Iraq. No one could have imagined they would be there so long, nor the price ultimately paid by the men and women lost, and the incalculable damage done to their families and fellow comrades that survived.

Today, he was in a country most people couldn't find on a map if their life depended on it, fighting to protect those whom he had nothing in common with beyond the fact they were all human beings. And despite the overwhelming odds, he couldn't imagine anywhere else he'd rather be than right here, right now. Though, perhaps, right here, right now, in a loaded to bear gunship might be a little better.

A relieved Red, soaked in sweat, waved at him as he idled the engines. Wings opened the door and stepped out, then slid open the side door. "I've got chainsaws, courtesy Colonel Kalgo!"

Smiles broke out among the Nigerians and they rushed forward, grabbing the precious cargo, the high-pitched whines filling the air as they were quickly put to work on a large tree blocking the road. Red and the others grabbed their gear from the back of one of the transport trucks and joined him, tossing their equipment in the back.

Red glanced up at the rotors. "So, she's safe?"

Wings shrugged. "I flew her."

"That's not much of an answer, but it'll have to do. She's safe, though, for a full load?"

"I'd fly in her before I'd drive a certain British sportscar. She could probably use a complete overhaul, but what can't on this continent? She's an old girl, but she'll get us there."

"Good." Red raised a hand. "Sergeant Akintan, we've got room for six plus a few cases of ammo."

Akintan gave him a thumbs-up, barking orders, and a few minutes later a healthy load of ammo was sitting in the rear of the chopper along with eleven sweaty, stinky men.

Wings shook his head as he scrunched his nose and lifted off. "You guys stink to high heaven. We should just drop you on the enemy. They'll surrender for sure."

Red glanced at him from the copilot seat. "You're no bed of roses yourself, Sergeant."

"How the hell can you tell over your own stench?" Wings banked to the east, making a direct line for Dawson and the others.

"Zero-Two, Zero-One. Come in, over."

Red activated his comms as Wings and the others listened in on their own earpieces. "Go ahead, Zero-One."

"Status?"

"We're on the chopper. All six of my team plus six Nigerians with weapons and three cases of ammo."

"Good. I've got new orders for you."

"Am I going to like them?"

Wings turned back and grinned at the others. "My money is on no."

"I can tell you the Colonel will hate them," said Dawson.

Red smiled. "Those are just the kind of orders I love."

Operations Center 2, CIA Headquarters
Langley, Virginia

Leroux's eyes narrowed as he exchanged a puzzled look with Tong. "Can you repeat your last, Zero-One?"

Dawson complied, confirming they had all heard his request properly. "I want you to take that Reaper and fly it around their primary staging area, low enough that they can all see it."

"To what end?"

"I'm redirecting Team Two and the chopper south of the primary staging area. We need to buy some time, so I intend to toy with them. We'll need to time this perfectly so I'll need your people to be sharp. I don't want to lose another chopper full of good people if it can be avoided."

"Understood, Zero-One, we'll be ready."

"Copy that. I'll provide you with the full details shortly. Zero-One, out."

Child spun in his chair, staring at the ceiling. "My God, if he doesn't want to lose another chopper full of men, why in the hell is he putting them in the middle of ground zero? And what does he think a dozen guys can do against what, the two-hundred-fifty that are there now?"

Leroux scratched his chin as he puzzled out Dawson's thinking. Right now, the terrorists assumed they had the upper hand simply through numbers. They had taken down two choppers in spectacular fashion, and while the third had landed, it wasn't going anywhere. Not to mention the fact the roads were still out. In Boko Haram's mind, everyone that was a threat was trapped on the base. Minor projections of force in the immediate vicinity wouldn't have been a surprise to them, and he had found over the years that fundamentalists valued life in a very different way, so losing men to the cause in an attempt to kill their so-called enemy was acceptable. They would move in with overwhelming force and simply keep firing until everyone was dead, and if that included themselves, most of them wouldn't mind, their twisted and deluded version of Heaven enough to excuse the fact they had failed.

If things remained the way they were, Boko Haram would continue to muster their men in the three staging areas they had now identified, all protected by children acting as human shields. But a dozen men, brought in by helicopter, with a Reaper circling overhead might be enough to give them pause should they get it in their heads to move early. The barrier was in place, but it was still only a hollow shell. Yes, the enemy couldn't see inside to find their targets or spy on what they were doing, but they could shoot through the barrier with impunity, for it went both ways.

Those inside couldn't see out.

Dawson wisely had gun nests being assembled on top of the roofs of the buildings. They might be sitting ducks against a well-aimed RPG, but from what they had seen so far, their opponents didn't grasp the capabilities, and, more importantly, the limitations of the weapon. Atlas was rapidly filling the barrier cells, and with each one, more civilians were better protected. They just needed time, and Dawson's insane plan might just buy it for them.

The sad thing was that there was a real solution to this problem, only politics was preventing it from being implemented. It disgusted him how innocent civilians were merely a variable in a large algebraic equation used by the bean counters that advised the leaders of the world. It was why they could never win the war on terrorism, and why those who ruled from the capitals of the nation-states made the lives of people like him so much more difficult than they should be.

The door hissed open and Leroux looked to see Morrison beckoning him. Apparently, whatever needed to be said was something that couldn't be overheard. Leroux joined him in the corridor.

"It's a no-go. The Nigerians are hopping mad about the Chinook. They consider it a violation of their sovereignty."

Leroux held his tongue. There was no need to verbalize the anger he could see his boss shared.

Morrison leaned in closer. "I've got an idea, but it can't come from me, and frankly, it can't even come from you."

"I don't understand."

"You will when I explain it to you."

Amman Rotana Hotel

Amman, Hashemite Kingdom of Jordan

Kane groaned in ecstasy as Lailan, a Jordanian masseuse he had been acquainted with for some years, worked her magic on his sciatic nerve. It had been a long, uncomfortable, thankless mission in Syria, but well worth it in the end. The leader of ISIS was dead, in part thanks to intel he had provided—confirmation of the bastard's location, verified after days of posing as a rock on the outside of a shithole of a town.

The man was dead, and in the chaos of the attack that had killed him, Kane had managed to slip away and make his way to Jordan. Normally, he would be heading back stateside where Fang's magic fingers would take care of his pain, but his handler had already indicated he was needed elsewhere in this part of the world, so sending him home made no sense. As a result, Lailan now tended to him.

"Do you want the full package like last time?" she asked as her hands slid under the towel, caressing his buttocks.

He reached back and moved her hands up a little higher. "Not this time. I'm practically a married man now."

"I'm insanely jealous."

"Yeah, I've been hearing that all over the world."

She smacked his ass. "I thought I was special!"

He chuckled. "You know better than that, though I will tell you this. Whenever I come to Jordan, you're the only girl I want to see."

Both cheeks got another squeeze.

He wagged a finger. "Remember, no hanky panky. I've got a bad back. I'm here to have it worked out by somebody I trust. Is that going to be you?"

She sighed and he could almost hear her pout. "Fine, but I was looking forward to tonight. You always take me to the nicest places."

"You don't have a boyfriend, a pretty girl like you?"

"Oh, I do, but life is so boring. We can't afford to do anything."

"Does he know what you do here?"

"What? Physiotherapy on foreigners?"

Kane laughed. "That poor bastard, he has no clue what he's gotten himself into, does he?"

"What he doesn't know can't hurt him, and he enjoys the money I bring home."

Kane frowned. He felt sorry for these women, and in his old heavy drinking, heavy partying days, he was ashamed to say he was guilty of taking advantage of what they were forced to offer out of desperation. He was always careful to avoid any form of human trafficking—he only associated with women who worked for themselves. And he always treated them well, always paid them extremely well, and always cared for them as if they were his girlfriend, even if it were only for the night. A guaranteed one-night stand.

His CIA-customized TAG Heuer watch fired an electric pulse into his wrist in a pattern that indicated he had a high-priority message that couldn't be ignored. "What time is it?" he asked.

She lifted his wrist above him. "Ten to seven."

He sighed. "I forgot, I've got somewhere I need to be at 7:30." He rolled off the table and she toweled him down, rubbing the oil off, and as she kneeled in front of him, paying particular attention to his most favorite body part, she stared up at him mischievously.

"Are you sure you have to be there at 7:30?"

He smiled down at her. "Yes."

She sighed and gave Dylan Jr. a kiss. "Maybe next time." She stood and he walked over to the table, grabbing his wallet. He fished out five times what he owed her and handed the wad over.

Her eyes shot wide. "So, we *are* going out?"

He shook his head. "No, *you* are going out. Take that boyfriend of yours and go have a good time, dinner, dancing, the works."

She stared at the money then back at him. "You're sure you don't want me to do anything special for you?"

Kane again wagged his finger at her. "Nothing. Take the money, enjoy yourself."

She shrugged and smiled. "All right, I will." She leaned in and kissed his cheek, her hot breath tickling his ear. "If you change your mind, you know how to reach me."

The sensual whisper sent a shiver down his spine, and a weaker man might have given in. But he loved Fang, and he had no intention of cheating on her outside of the job, and this was definitely outside of the job. She left the room, a bounce in her step, and he quickly dressed then entered a coded sequence by pressing buttons around the watch face. A message scrolled, indicating he had a priority communique through his private network. He pulled out his phone and logged in to his secure messenger, surprised to see it was from his best friend, Leroux.

Now, why aren't you using regular channels?

He brought up the message and his eyebrows shot up. "Holy shit!" They rose even more as he read the proposed solution to helping Bravo Team. If there was a way to make it happen, it could very well work.

But there was no way in hell he could see them going for it.

Saint-Raphael, France

Alex West smiled at his daughter, Alexis Bertrand, bringing a new round of drinks. He didn't get to see her very much, which he wasn't pleased about since he had missed out on the bulk of her life, not even aware she existed until recently. By the time he met her, she was an accomplished woman, having followed in her mother's footsteps into the French General Directorate for External Security, France's CIA.

His daughter was a spy, just like he had been, just as her mother had been, Alexis conceived in a night of passion in Moscow years ago. Her mother, Adelle Bertrand, and he had rekindled their relationship recently, and he could honestly say he had never been happier in his life, and wanted to make the most of what few years he might have left.

And a family beach vacation on the French Riviera was his idea of paradise.

Warm sun, a gentle breeze, the Mediterranean lapping at the beach, the laughter of children—it all mixed perfectly, and he wouldn't change a thing.

"Thank you, my dear," he said, as he took his drink. Alexis smiled at him and sat on the lounge chair to his left. He sighed. "It doesn't get any better than this, does it?"

Adelle agreed. "How much longer will the repairs to your place in the Black Forest take?"

West frowned as he pictured the disaster they had left behind after the Russians had paid a visit. "Months."

Alexis' eyes narrowed. "Why so long? I thought it was just damage from gunfire, grenades, and rockets."

He gave her a look and she giggled at her own joke.

"I know, I know, but still, it's already been a couple of months, and it's going to be months more?"

"Well, it's not just replacing drywall and installing a new door. I'm having all the armor built into the walls beefed up. It's going to take a hell of a lot more than an RPG to punch a hole through it next time. Plus, I'm getting everything EMP protected so we don't have a repeat. It's expensive custom work. You can't exactly have your local contractor come in. He'll be at the bar the next day, telling everybody what he saw. These are all professional contractors hired through the Gray Network. They can be trusted to keep their mouths shut and to do the work properly."

"It sounds expensive."

"You have no idea. But I have benefactors, and the network has what you might call 'insurance.'"

"How is this Gray Network funded?"

West smiled. "You need gray hair to be privy to that information, my dear. Let's just say most of it comes from sub-contracting work. If you survive long enough in the profession you've chosen, and earned the respect of your elders, you just might be invited in like your mother and I were."

Alexis took a sip of her drink. "Well, I'm back in the field now, so who knows what's going to happen."

Adelle reached across him and their daughter took her hand. Adelle squeezed it. "You be careful out there. The code of honor we operated under is no longer respected. I can't tell you how many times your father and I could have been killed, but instead were captured and released, or given a pass."

West cleared his throat. "Well, I don't know about you, but they almost never caught me."

Adelle swatted him. "This is serious. This is your daughter's life we're talking about."

"You're right. Just remember, treat your opponents with respect whenever possible, because you might be sitting in that interrogation chair the next time, and they'll remember how you treated them." West groaned as he spotted someone approaching. "Like this crusty old bastard. I don't know how many times we could have killed each other, but we didn't."

Viktor Zorkin, former KGB, walked up with a smile and a wave. "Fancy finding you on my favorite beach."

West gave him a look. "*I* told *you* about it."

"That's not how I remember it. Typical American spy, always taking credit for other people's work."

"Funny, that's not how I remember it."

"What are you doing here, Viktor?" asked Adelle. She smiled. "Not that you're not welcome, of course."

West's old rival from the Cold War chuckled. "Don't worry, I'm not here to ruin your vacation. I'm actually here for your daughter."

Both West and Adelle's eyebrows shot up, and Alexis smiled coyly at the elderly Zorkin. "While I'm flattered, sir, aren't I a little out of your league?"

Zorkin tossed his head back and laughed heartily. "Oh, my dear, we Russian men never get old in that department." He grinned at West and winked at Adelle. "However, not to bruise your delicate French ego, I'm here for you in a professional capacity. Old friends need help that you might be able to provide."

West's ears immediately perked. "What's going on?"

Zorkin grunted and groaned as he sat in a flimsy beach chair, and Adelle eyeballed him. "Is that the kind of grunting and groaning a lady can expect when spending an evening with you?"

Zorkin gave her the stink-eye. "I'll have you know it's why I always pair my Viagra with two extra-strength Tylenol Arthritis."

West chuckled and Adelle swatted him. "Our daughter's sitting right beside us listening to this pig."

West patted Adelle's leg. "My dear, if she blushes over that, she'll never make it in the spy game."

Alexis ignored them. "So, why do you need me? Who are these friends?"

"Bravo Team is in a world of hurt right now. They're trapped on a Forward Operating Base in Nigeria, outnumbered about twenty to one, with Boko Haram about to attack and governments playing politics. Now, some favors are owed, and you're just the person to call in those favors. But it means leaving right now."

Alexis rose. "I'll do whatever it takes. They saved my parents' lives."

"More than once," added West.

Approaching Boko Haram Staging Area

Outside Maiduguri, Nigeria

The dusk sun drew long shadows over the landscape as Wings expertly guided them into the heart of enemy territory. Red's eyes, like everyone else's, were keeping a watch for RPGs—there was no surprising anyone with a Huey. Everybody within miles probably knew they were coming, but one good thing about being so loud, and this time of day, was it was difficult to tell from exactly what direction they were coming. If it weren't for the risk of RPGs, Dawson's mission was actually rather simple and brilliant.

But they had to get there first.

And then on top of that, get out.

If they succeeded, they could buy the time needed to reinforce the barrier. It might cost them their lives, but potentially save hundreds of others, and if they didn't undertake this mission, they would die regardless. At least this way, they could be buying priceless time.

A muzzle flashed to his right. "Small arms fire, three o'clock."

Wings banked them away and glanced at him. "You do realize that I can probably get us there, but getting out is going to be next to impossible."

Red shrugged. "Not my problem. The after-action report will indicate you failed, not me."

"You're an asshole."

Red grinned. "You're just figuring that out now?"

"Oh, I've always known it. Luckily, I'm an asshole too, so we get along just fine. If the two of us are such big assholes, then why aren't we—" Wings was cut off with the squawking of the comms and Red's raised finger.

"Zero-Two, this is Control, come in, over."

"Go ahead, Control."

"We show you two minutes out. It's important this be timed perfectly. Should visuals fail, we need you to report the moment you touch down the second time."

"Roger that, Control, we'll notify you the moment the skids hit the ground. Zero-Two, out." Red opened his tactical computer, their current location plus the two touchdown points indicated, points so carefully chosen there was no margin for error if they hoped to survive this.

Ibrahim stared up at the drone that continued to circle overhead. It was obviously American, but he wasn't certain why it was there. He would have thought the Americans would have a satellite overhead to give them all the images they could possibly want. Why they would need drone footage in addition to satellite, he wasn't sure, but the one thing he was certain of was that his men were wasting ammo shooting at it.

"Cease fire!" he ordered. "Every bullet you waste on that thing is a bullet that can't be used to kill the infidel later tonight."

The chatter of the weapons quickly dwindled then fell silent. With the guns quiet, all he could hear was the breathing of his men and the whimpering of the girls used as human shields.

And the pounding of a helicopter as it approached.

It was then that he realized why the Americans had sent the drone. It was to disguise the approach of the helicopter. His men had been firing for at least ten minutes. Had there been other helicopters before? Had they inserted troops already? If so, how many?

"We're under attack!" he shouted. "Get the RPGs! We've got to shoot that thing down."

One of his men pointed to the west. "There it is!"

Ibrahim spun and cursed at the sight of a helicopter touching down behind a grove of trees. He couldn't see what was happening, but there was only one reason for it to land, and that was to unload troops. The sound of the rotors changed and the helicopter rose from behind the trees and banked sharply to his right. "Open fire!" he yelled, despite knowing they were out of range.

Gunfire erupted around him, then the first of half a dozen RPGs screamed toward the target, all aimed in haste, none effective. The chopper touched down again, perhaps half a mile farther to his right, inserting even more of the enemy. He pointed at both landing areas. "Two teams! Let's get them!"

Scores of men around him sprinted toward the enemy. The helicopter rose into the sky as RPGs streaked toward it, and Ibrahim was about to order them to stop firing when a massive fireball erupted. He cheered with the others at the successful downing of yet another helicopter, but the celebration was short-lived as they now had enemy troops on the ground that had to be dealt with. He kept waving his arm as more men poured from the building, directing them toward the two landing zones, and as he heard the gunfire ahead as his men engaged what he assumed were American soldiers, it had him rethinking his plan. If the Americans had enough troops to insert here, what had been happening at the base since they had last seen it?

Another massive explosion, much like the first, erupted uncomfortably close, and he cringed at the cries of dozens of his men delivered into the loving arms of Allah. His eyes narrowed. Something wasn't right. He spotted something overhead and stared up to see a missile streak from the drone circling them. Another explosion tore apart the second group of his men heading to engage the enemy, and rage gripped him.

They had been tricked.

The helicopter hadn't exploded at all, and now it had made its escape, though it still left the soldiers on the ground. Anger consumed him at the deception and the fact so many of his men had just been murdered. But there was nothing he could do about that now. All he could do was find and kill the soldiers that had just been inserted by that helicopter, and make sure they died horribly painful deaths.

213

But there was something he had to do first. He headed inside to grab a radio so he could put out the call that a significant reward would be paid to anyone who took down that helicopter.

Secondary LZ

North of FOB Ugurun, Nigeria

Wings waved at a grinning Niner as his friend gripped two glow sticks, guiding him into the LZ. The sun had set now, just a glow on the horizon, the dark obscuring them on the short hop from the Boko Haram staging area to this temporary landing zone set up in hopes they might avoid any opponents watching over the FOB. They had taken a few potshots along the way, none thankfully connecting, though he had a sense leaving might be more difficult than arriving.

He put her down with a bounce and his passengers unloaded the cargo and themselves. He eyed the three wounded Nigerians that were now loaded on board and turned to Red, standing on the skid, his door still open. "Do you think this is wise?"

"What?"

"Taking them. I'm expecting to come under a lot more fire than we did coming in."

"What about you? Are you willing to risk the flight? We can leave the chopper and just head to the base."

Wings shook his head. "No, it's our only lifeline at the moment. I don't mind dying for the cause, but they might."

Red jerked a thumb at the new passengers. "Do they look scared or relieved to you?"

Wings glanced at them, acknowledging Red's point. "Relieved, though perhaps relieved out of ignorance."

"It is bliss, they say." Red leaned in and slapped him on the arm. "Say the word and we abort."

Wings shook his head. "No, I'm good to go." He tapped his earpiece. "Let's just hope the eyes in the sky can find me the Northwest Passage out of here."

Red gave him a thumbs-up and shut the door. Niner signaled the LZ was clear and Wings powered up and lifted off. He activated his comms. "Control, One-Two. I'd appreciate it if you'd thread this needle, over."

"Copy that, One-Two. Proceed west, bearing two-seven-zero. The Reaper is overhead and we're showing no heat signatures in your direct path, over."

Wings adjusted his heading and applied more power, gaining altitude as he put some distance between him and the LZ. As he picked up more speed and height, he breathed a little easier as things remained calm.

Looks like I made the right call.

He glanced back at his passengers. "Just hang tight, guys, I'll have you in a comfy infirmary in no time."

Smiles were exchanged, including a couple of weak thumbs-up. He redirected his attention forward, his eyes scanning the ground ahead for muzzle flashes or any other indication he was under fire, but spotted nothing. There were scattered lights from homes as he passed over the farmland, likely candles or fires, and he wondered if they were untended, their owners taking cover at the FOB, or perhaps his enemy, waiting for an opportunity to use a weapon long stored.

"One-Two, RPG coming in from your six-o'clock! Take evasive action immediately. Say again—"

Wings didn't bother listening, instead banking them hard to the left and pushing them into a dive. He caught sight of the propellant trail against the dim sky and cursed as he realized he had put them directly in the path of the incoming warhead. He jerked them to the right, continuing the dive to the ground. "Everybody hang on! If we get hit and we aren't in a million pieces, be prepared to jump!"

He had no time to check if his passengers were listening, but as the rocket ripped toward them, he said a silent prayer to get him out of this. "Control, tell my family—"

The impact was sudden and the entire airframe was thrown counterclockwise. He struggled to compensate, counting off in his head how many seconds it was from the initial impact as every alarm in the chopper lit up in protest. He figured if he were still alive after five seconds, then the fuel might not be about to erupt.

He reached five.

But they were falling out of the sky like a rock, though perhaps that was an exaggeration. He killed the power to his engines, reducing the risk of igniting the torch, and autorotated them toward the ground. "Get ready! This is gonna hurt!"

And it did. He slammed into the ground with a spine-shuddering thud, then threw his door open. He leaped out and slid aside the rear door, helping the first Nigerian down, then the two of them assisted the others.

"Let's go!" he shouted as he half dragged, half carried his man from the wreckage as the rotors continued to pound overhead. He lay the wounded soldier on the ground, just past a low berm, then turned to see smoke billowing from the tail and flames starting to flicker. "It's going to blow!" he cried as he sprinted toward the others struggling to reach cover.

Hell's gates opened and tore toward them. The two Nigerians were caught in the initial eruption and he squeezed his eyes shut, twisting around and dropping to the ground as the flames rolled over him.

And he prayed for God's forgiveness, his arrogance having killed them all.

Operations Center 2, CIA Headquarters
Langley, Virginia

Leroux stared at the display, his mouth agape. The hostile that had fired the RPG had emerged from a farmhouse only moments after Wings had passed over. There was no warning, no way to predict what had happened. Yet it didn't change how he felt. He snapped his fingers as he rose from his station, stepping closer to the screens. "Check for survivors. We saw them escape before the detonation. Did they survive the blast?"

"I'm on it," replied Tong, furiously working her station as satellite and drone footage was isolated, images frozen and zoomed, and within moments they had their answer.

Sort of.

Nobody was moving.

"Are there any indications they're alive?"

Tong isolated the four men, the satellite footage merely showing dark forms on the ground, lit by the fire still burning from the chopper, and infrared images from the drone.

"Watch for movement, people."

"Number one just sat up!" cried Child, the excitement in his voice palpable, despite pointing out what was obvious to everyone.

"Marc, see if you can identify him."

"On it!"

"Number two just moved his foot," reported Tong.

"Zoom in."

She did, and the footage grew of the man between the two clustered closest to the chopper and the one who had just sat up. This was the man Leroux was certain was Wings, yet they had to be sure.

The man's foot twitched.

Leroux returned to his workstation and jacked in. "One-Two, this is Control. Come in, over."

The room collectively held its breath, desperate for a response from a man many had worked with for years.

But none came.

"One-Two, this is Control Actual. Come in, over."

And again, no response.

An arm moved.

And a cheer erupted.

Leroux held up a hand, quieting his team. "One-Two, if you're responding, we can't hear you, but we can see you. Wave if you're receiving, over."

The hand slowly waved and Leroux sighed with relief. "We see you, One-Two. Stand by." He glanced at the tactical map, showing the location of the chopper and the LZ. Only a few miles separated them. "One-One, this is Control. We've confirmed at least two survivors, including One-Two. Are you in a position to render aid?"

"Affirmative, Control. We're already on our way. ETA less than five minutes."

"Copy that, One-One. We'll monitor from here, however be advised, the shooter came out of a farmhouse near your position. There may be more hostiles in your area."

"Understood, Control. One-One, out."

Leroux returned his attention to the images on the screen. "Any movement from the other two?"

Tong shook her head. "Not that I've seen." She turned to the rest of the room. "Anyone?"

More head shakes.

Leroux cursed. Two good men who had survived the battle to save the schoolchildren, lost to a bloodthirsty farmer. If he could be certain the man lived alone, he would use one of the Reaper's remaining bombs to take him out. Fortunately for that man, and the family he likely lived with, the one who held the murderer's life in his hands had morals.

North of FOB Ugurun, Nigeria

Niner forced himself to slow down, though only slightly. The road was a wreck, and back home would have barely been called a trail. The ruts and holes had the unforgiving suspension abusing their bodies as they closed in on the burning wreckage just ahead. Red sat beside him, and four Nigerians were in the back. The rest of Bravo Team and the Nigerians had taken the second truck and returned to the base with the ammo, keeping the mission at least a partial success.

Yet at what cost?

He had monitored the communications between Control and Wings, and it could mean anything. Their friend might merely have lost his mic, or his face could be seared shut. He could be alive and well, or he could be near death. There was no way to know from where he sat, and it frustrated him to no end. The secondary LZ was his idea. Maybe if they had landed at the base, Wings might have gained more altitude before heading over the farmer who had shot him down.

But second-guessing was for after the mission. Right now, they had to deal with the consequences of their actions, and that meant reaching their friend and the others, assessing their condition, rendering emergency aid if necessary, then evac'ing back to the base.

"Control, Zero-Two. Any update on our man, over?"

Red was clearly as anxious as he was.

"Negative, Zero-Two. The surviving Nigerian is at his side. The other two still show no movement, over."

"Copy that, Control. Zero-Two, out." Red turned to Niner. "I never should have let him go."

Niner frowned. "Bullshit. We all knew the mission. It had to be tried." He turned them off the road, and drove across a field toward the flaming wreck. "There they are," he said, lifting a finger from the steering wheel and pointing. He could make out the shadows of the Nigerian tending to Wings, and the other two, closer to the chopper, piled atop each other. He brought them to a halt and everyone jumped out, sprinting toward their comrades.

Red reached Wings first, but Niner was a close second, dropping to his knees with the medkit. The Nigerian tending to Wings stepped back to let him work. "Hey, buddy, how ya doing?"

Wings stared up at him, his face black, but his eyes a bright white. "I think I finally understand what it feels like to be hit by a ton of bricks."

Niner chuckled, relieved his friend could speak. "Tell me where it hurts, little one."

Wings raised a finger. "Don't start with me. Atlas may put up with your shit, but I'll deck you."

Niner grinned at Red. "I think he just might live." He stared down at Wings. "I'm going to check you out. It's nothing sexual, you're not my type."

Wings grunted. "Get it over with. My own self-assessment suggests nothing broken."

Niner started at the toes and worked his way up, feeling for anything out of the ordinary, while also listening for any sudden inhalations or wincing from his patient indicating pain. There was plenty, but he agreed with his friend's assessment—nothing broken.

"Well, Doctor?"

"I think you're going to be black and blue by the morning. I want to check you out with your clothes off back at the base. I need to see if you've got any internal bleeding, but you're safe to move."

Red, his M4 at the ready as he covered them, glanced over. "Okay then, let's get the hell out of here before more farmers decide to pay us a visit." He turned to the Nigerians, huddled around their two fallen comrades. "What's their status?"

One of the men that had accompanied them shook his head. "They're both dead."

"I'm sorry for your loss. They were good men. Let's get them in the truck so they can be buried with respect."

Niner helped Wings to his feet and they hobbled slowly to the truck as the Nigerians loaded their dead on stretchers retrieved from the vehicle, the same stretchers used to carry them from the base. Red fired up the engine and they were soon underway as Niner rode in the back, checking on the other wounded man, all the while keeping a wary eye on his friend, who by all outward appearances was fine.

But could be dying a slow death on the inside.

Boko Haram Staging Area

Outside Maiduguri, Nigeria

Ibrahim cursed as he pushed through the brush. They had been searching for over an hour, yet had found no one. He had watched the helicopter touch down twice, yet they could find no one. Yes, it was now dark, but even so, with the number of men he had at his disposal, they should have encountered at least someone.

Yet they hadn't.

It made no sense.

Maduka ran up, waving a radio, excitement evident on his moonlit face. "Imam, we just received word that the helicopter was shot down near the base in Ugurun!"

Normally this would have pleased him, but not today. Not tonight. They were already behind schedule searching for what appeared to be ghosts. The chopper being shot down was good news in that it meant no one else would be brought in, though it assumed a single helicopter had been used.

226

Yet it had to be a single helicopter. If there had been more, then this place should be crawling with the enemy, though still not a single one had been found.

"Any details? How many were on board? Was it alone?"

Maduka shook his head. "None. One of our supporters heard your call and when it flew over, he shot it down then returned to his pipe."

Ibrahim cursed. A single chopper had landed twice while a drone circled overhead. To hide their escape, the drone fired a missile between them and the helicopter, making it look as if his men had shot it down with an RPG. The drone then killed more of his men sent to engage the infiltrators, then left. He had sent more men out, and there was no way the enemy would have had time to escape.

And why would they? Why insert troops for them to just run away?

It made no sense.

Then he checked his watch and it did.

"They tricked us."

Maduka's eyes narrowed. "What do you mean?"

"They were never here." Ibrahim growled in anger. "They never left any troops behind. It was all a trick to delay us!" He roared in rage at being made the fool. "Everyone! Back to the warehouse! It's time to teach these Americans a lesson!"

He marched back toward their base of operations, his chest heaving with anger, and out of the corner of his eye he spotted Lawan with several of his men, laughing and glancing his way.

Keep laughing, for tonight you die.

FOB Ugurun, Nigeria

Dawson entered the infirmary, if it could be called that, to see Wings sitting on the edge of a bed in nothing but his underwear, and Niner examining him carefully. Dawson smiled. "Should I leave you two lovebirds alone?"

Wings reached out a hand. "Please, don't leave me alone with him. If I hear one more crack about my abs or sexy ass, I'm going to break his neck. I don't know how Atlas puts up with it."

Niner grinned at him. "He loves me."

"What's the prognosis?" asked Dawson.

Niner stood back, frowning. "I'll give it to you both straight. You need a hospital, and you need it soon. I'm pretty sure you've got internal bleeding, and it's something I can't deal with here."

"But I feel fine," protested Wings. "I'm sore, but that's to be expected."

Niner pointed to some discoloration under Wings' ribcage, near his liver. "I'm concerned you may have lacerated your liver. That's bleeding beneath the surface. The good news is that it doesn't seem to be spreading fast, so it could be a slow bleed, but it's a bleed nonetheless."

"What do we do?" asked Dawson.

"We need to get him medevac'd somehow."

Wings grunted. "No chance of that. How long do I have?"

"No idea. I mean—"

"Worst case scenario."

"You could be dead by morning."

Dawson tensed. This was horrendous news, and if there were any balls in Washington, it wouldn't be an issue. A chopper could be sent in under heavy escort, and they could evac him out. But that wasn't going to happen. Even if the Nigerians arrived in force, they were arriving by truck. An evac to the nearest hospital could take another eight hours.

Wings sighed, his shoulders slumping. "Well, if I'm going to be dead by morning, let me get dressed so I can get in this fight. If we lose, I'm dead anyway."

Niner shook his head. "Buddy, if you try to move around too much, especially fight, you *will* be dead by morning. Probably by midnight."

Wings cursed. "This is bullshit."

Dawson put on the brave face. "This is life. Consider yourself lucky. You should have died in that crash, but you didn't. Now at least you've got a chance. Remember, Niner here said it was a worst-case scenario. He could be wrong."

Niner shrugged. "It's been known to happen."

Wings frowned. "Can I get dressed now?"

"Go ahead." Niner turned to Dawson. "This building is one of the innermost, so he should be safe in here. I want him lying down the entire time. The least amount of movement the better. I'll try to check on him, but if we're in the thick of it…"

Dawson chewed his cheek for a moment. "What kind of care does he need?"

"He needs plenty of water, should try to eat something to keep his strength up, and needs to stay put. Also, the bruising needs to be monitored, though like I said, even if it gets significantly worse, there's nothing I can really do here."

"So, he needs a babysitter."

Niner laughed. "Yeah, I suppose he does."

"I'll be back." Dawson left the infirmary and headed outside. He flagged down Buhari, directing the final touches on their rooftop sandbagged positions.

"What do you need, Sergeant Major?"

"I need two nurses."

Buhari's eyebrows shot up. "Nurses?"

"To watch Wings. He needs to stay lying down, plenty of water and food, and a bruise monitored. Niner can explain it all. Check with the villagers and see if you can get a couple of volunteers."

Buhari nodded. "You've got it." He headed into the thick of the civilians, huddled behind a segment of completed barrier. Atlas had been working nonstop, and the time they had bought by tricking the enemy had proved invaluable. They now had enough of the barrier filled that as long as they could keep Boko Haram on the other side of it, they might just hold out. His concern was grenades. They had found a few in the weapons caches they had confiscated, which suggested their foes had access to them. They would need to keep the enemy as far back as possible, and pray they had poor throwing arms.

Dawson joined Red, confabbing nearby with the others. He indicated the rooftop gun nests. "I want you to inspect those positions. Make sure our friends have done the job right, then I want one of our guys in each nest with two MP4s just in case one fails, and plenty of ammo. Anybody who gets too close needs to be taken out, just in case they have a grenade. We can protect these people against anything fired horizontally, but if it's tossed over, we're screwed."

Red agreed. "With the tree line pushed back as far as you got it, that should help. We were just discussing tactics. Do you have a moment?"

"Yes."

"Well, with ammo at a premium, and with Langley now estimating we could be facing over four hundred, I was thinking there's almost no way we can hold them off. If they weren't firing back, sure, half a dozen of our guys on the rooftop could pick them off one-by-one pretty quickly, but as soon as they start returning fire, we'll be spending most of our time keeping our heads down."

"True. What has the brain trust come up with?"

Spock cocked an eyebrow. "Were we just insulted?"

Dawson chuckled. "Never."

Red pointed at one of the barrier segments that hadn't been filled yet. "We've got those fifty cals that the Nigerians had ringing the base, and they had plenty of ammo. I'm thinking we put those to use, but in a little bit of an unconventional way."

And as Dawson listened, a smile slowly spread. The idea was definitely unconventional, but if it worked, and that was a big 'if,' it could catch Boko Haram by surprise, and significantly thin their numbers in short order.

If it worked.

Operations Center 2, CIA Headquarters
Langley, Virginia

"We've got movement!" announced Tong, and the entire operations center paused what they were doing, staring up at the screen. Scores of motorcycles, most doubled-up, were racing from all three rally points. The latest estimates were that almost 500 hostiles had gathered, a small portion of the thousands upon thousands in the extended region.

But this was going down tonight.

If it extended into several days, those thousands might make it into the fray, but Leroux was convinced this would be over by morning—everyone in that camp and in that village would be dead by then.

The Hail Mary initiated by Morrison had produced nothing, at least not yet. It was out of his hands, and there was no way for him to even ask for an update. Kane wouldn't know. Couldn't know. It was in the hands of the fabled Gray Network, an association of retired spies from various countries, allied to maintain peace when governments couldn't.

A noble idea, and from what he had seen of them, effective.

But so far, not tonight.

The front loader was still racing up and down the length of the FOB, Atlas now putting second loads in many of the key segments, and something was happening in half a dozen of the empty segments that had him curious, the lack of light making it difficult to discern what was going on. He didn't bother asking, as he was well aware Dawson and the others all had their hands full, though they had to be made aware of what was now happening.

He fit his headset in place and activated the link. "Zero-One, Control Actual. Come in, over."

"This is Zero-One. Go ahead, Control."

"I've got bad news, Zero-One. Boko Haram is on the move from all three rally points. We are estimating over five-hundred hostiles, all armed, most riding tandem on motorcycles."

"ETA?"

Leroux stared at the screens showing the bottleneck on the roads. "The lead riders will be arriving within twenty minutes. It will take time for them all to arrive. Perhaps an hour. Depending on their plan, if they have one, they may attack when they arrive, or they may wait for all their forces. If that's the case, you may have almost an hour, but I'd plan for the worst."

"Copy that, Control. ETA on the Nigerian column?"

Leroux glanced at Tong who held up four fingers. "Our latest estimate is four hours at the earliest. They're making good progress. But they're only two hundred men."

"Well, I'll leave it in your capable hands whether you tell the Nigerians they're sending two hundred men into a battle against five hundred Boko Haram."

Leroux smiled slightly, catching the less than subtle implication. If the Nigerians knew they were going in, hopelessly outnumbered, they might call back their troops, or they might commit even more. There was no way to know which. "Understood, Zero-One. Either way, can you hold out for four hours?"

"We have some tricks up our sleeves, Control, but I doubt it. Tell the president and whoever else might listen to this that this can be solved with a single Ghostrider. They don't need to put a boot on the ground if they don't want to, but if they don't want twelve operators, thirty-plus Nigerian regulars, and over two-hundred men, women, and children to die here tonight, then grow some damn balls and make the call!"

Leroux glanced around the room, everyone stunned at the uncharacteristically frank words from Dawson, someone who normally remained level-headed under any circumstance. It was clear the situation was getting to the man, and Leroux didn't blame him. He would have likely fallen to pieces long ago if their roles were reversed. "Acknowledged, Zero-One. Permission to send your comments up the line? It might have more effect."

"Post it on TikTok for all I care. If we don't get the help we need, we're all dead, and my career is over regardless. In fact, I'll do you one better. Mr. President, if you're listening to this, we need your help. We are American soldiers sent on a mission by our commanding officers. We are attempting to protect hundreds of innocents from Boko Haram.

A single aircraft can save us all. If the Nigerians won't give you permission to enter their airspace, then tell them to go to Hell and do your job. Protect your soldiers, and protect the innocents whose lives are at stake here. We will all be dead in a matter of hours unless you act now. I witnessed good Nigerian soldiers laying down their lives today, I held a dying girl in my arms who begged me not to let Boko Haram take her. She knew what they would do to her, they all do. This isn't about borders, this isn't about sovereignty, this is about human beings helping other human beings. Do the right thing and send in that gunship, or the blood of all of us is on your hands tomorrow." There was a pause, whoops and cheers heard on the other end as what was likely members of Bravo Team applauded their commander for telling it like it was. "Did you get that?"

Tong gave a thumbs-up.

"We got it. And I promise you this, I'm sending it to everyone I can that might be able to help."

"Copy that, Control. Zero-One, out."

Leroux tossed his headset on the desk and gripped the arms of his chair as he calmed himself. He had heard desperation before, but never from Dawson, or the likes of him. It wasn't fear in his voice, but concern, concern for his men, but more importantly, concern for those civilians they were willing to sacrifice themselves for, in order to give the innocent a fighting chance.

And he was right. Without that gunship, there was no way they could hold out for long.

"I'll need that conversation on tape."

Tong held up a memory stick. "Way ahead of you."

He smiled and rose. "I'm going to see the Chief." He took the stick and leaned in, lowering his voice. "Send a copy of that to Dylan. He can send it places I can't without compromising the Agency."

"Consider it done."

He headed for the door. "Oh, and find me a gunship in the region, just in case someone in Washington says none are available."

FOB Ugurun, Nigeria

Red stared at Dawson, his jaw square, admiration in his eyes. "Well said, BD. Very well said."

Dawson grunted. "It's a career-ender for sure, but there's no time to admire my obvious need of Toast Masters." He held up his arms. "Listen up, everyone! Boko Haram is on their way now. We expect the front edge to arrive in twenty minutes, with the rest of them within an hour. We don't know what they plan on doing, but let's hope they decide to wait for all their forces to arrive."

"How many are we facing?" asked one of the civilians in the gathering crowd.

Dawson regarded him. "I'm not going to lie to you. The estimate is five-hundred."

Gasps and cries swept through those gathered.

"Listen, I know that sounds like a big number, and it is. But you have twelve highly trained men from my team, over thirty of your own brave soldiers, plus we've shown almost forty of you how to shoot, and you all have guns. This will be a brutal battle, and we may not make it through the night, but if we die, we die protecting husbands, wives, brothers, sisters, and most importantly, children. If we can keep them on the other side of this barrier"—he patted one of the filled segments—"then we stand a chance. The risk will be from grenades." He pointed at foxholes that had been dug throughout the compound. "If you see a grenade, get in a hole. Don't be a hero and try to grab it and throw it back out. You'll just blow yourself to bits. Now, you all have your assignments. We've got less than twenty minutes, so let's get moving!"

Everyone broke as Atlas roared by with another load of dirt, peering through a sliver of an opening in the spare body armor encircling him, tied to the frame of the windowless cab that would hopefully allow him to continue to work during the battle. The man must be exhausted, but had refused relief when offered. "I'm in the zone, BD, just leave me be!"

So he had.

Dawson walked the inside perimeter, pointing out problems, whoever was responsible fixing it. The gun nests atop the buildings were ready, equipped, and manned by six of his team. They were far enough inside the barrier that it would take a good throwing arm to reach them with a grenade, and they had full coverage of the entire area to the tree line. Their only vulnerability would be from RPGs, but the corrugated metal from the sides of the buildings had been repurposed as pre-detonation screens that should provide some protection.

The biggest vulnerability to the civilians were grenades tossed over the barrier. They were keeping as many as they could inside the buildings and away from the walls. It should protect them, but it also meant they would be trapped if the enemy made it inside the wire. A kill box manned by Ledger and Clarke, along with half a dozen of the Nigerians, had been set up in the opening of the barrier, designed to funnel the enemy directly into a wall of lead, with several fallback positions should it become necessary.

They would put up one hell of a fight, they would take out a lot of the enemy, but with every lucky shot, every tossed grenade that wounded or killed, their numbers would continue to dwindle until there wouldn't be enough to hold.

That was why Red's Hail Mary had to thin the herd dramatically.

Buhari jogged up. "All six positions are ready."

Dawson eyed one of the openings they had cut in the unfilled barrier segments. "Your men know what to do?"

"Absolutely. They'll do their jobs, don't you worry."

"And the civilians?"

"They're frightened, but they know what's at stake."

Dawson slapped him on the back with a smile. "Then let's get some chow while we can. Something tells me we won't be eating again until this is over."

Or never again.

Director Morrison's Office, CIA Headquarters
Langley, Virginia

Morrison's chest tightened as he listened to the recording. It was as moving a speech as he had ever heard, and it wasn't delivered by a professional reading from a script written by another professional. It was a soldier, in the middle of nowhere, who knew he was going to die, and was doing so willingly.

And who had to be saved.

"Any word on my idea?" he asked Leroux, sitting impatiently in front of him.

Leroux shook his head. "I sent it to Kane, he acknowledged receipt, and that's it. All he could do was pass it on. I'm sure it's reached its intended recipient by now, but whether anything can be done, who knows?"

Morrison cursed. "Politics."

"Is it?"

Morrison's eyes narrowed. "What?"

"I mean, is it just politics? We've helped the Nigerians before, and hell, we were invited in. If they showed some balls and sent in more choppers, we could bring in reinforcements."

"How many choppers have they lost today?"

"Three."

"Are you aware that they only have about twenty functional helicopters in their entire fleet?"

Leroux sighed. He was aware, though had forgotten that fact. "Yes."

"So, you can see how they might be reluctant to send more. RPGs are difficult to defend against. Even we lost a lot of good men to them in Iraq and Afghanistan. Their president is also in a political battle for his future, and has to deal with a large Muslim population that does not like us."

"So, politics."

Morrison grunted. "I'll give you that one."

"Then I say to hell with them. Just like BD said. Get a gunship in there, end this, then apologize later for saving hundreds of their civilians and soldiers."

Morrison tapped his phone. "I already have a meeting scheduled with the president in ten minutes on another matter. I'll be bringing this up, trust me." He flicked a finger toward the door. "Now get out of here so I can get this added to the agenda."

Leroux rose and headed for the door, then paused, looking back at his boss. "Chief?"

"Yes?"

"Do you think he'll say yes?"

Morrison held up the memory stick containing the recorded plea from Dawson. "Son, if this doesn't convince him, nothing will."

Approaching FOB Ugurun, Nigeria

Ibrahim raced near the head of the pack, his eyes peeled on the unreliable road ahead. He had half a dozen riders out front in case something was blocking the road—he wasn't about to sacrifice himself to a felled tree in the night. He had no doubt the Americans were watching with their drones and their satellites, but it didn't matter. If they hadn't sent in more help by now, they never were.

Three Nigerian choppers, and one very expensive American one, were down. No one else was arriving except by land, and the last update he had received was that they were three and a half hours away at best. This battle would be finished long before that. A compact area, surrounded by useless chain-link fence, with a few shacks to provide cover, was no defense against five hundred guns with jihad in their hearts.

This would be a bloody, brutal victory, and he prayed at least some of the Americans survived for him to skin alive.

When this night was through, nothing would be alive at that camp, nor in the surrounding village.

Nobody defied Boko Haram, and tonight would make certain no one ever forgot that.

The riders ahead slowed as they approached the village. The farmhouses had been dark, no evening candles or fires lit, meaning they were all either taking shelter at the base, or attempting to appear not to be at home. It didn't matter. All would be searched once the base was taken.

The only light was from Allah himself, the clear sky and nearly full moon providing them with all the illumination they would need to succeed in their task. He glanced over his shoulder and smiled at the long line of single lights stretching as far as the eye could see. It would take quite some time for all his forces to converge, and the entire ride here he had debated what to do. They could set up around the camp and simply begin firing, and perhaps be done with this before all of his warriors had arrived. After all, chain-link might as well be plastic wrap—it didn't stop bullets, and it concealed nothing.

The shacks would be where most would be hiding, either inside or behind them, and a few well-placed RPGs would have them ablaze in no time. He sneered. This was his battle. This was his victory. He had brought together this massive force to kill the Americans and those who would collaborate with them. Why should he share the glory?

When they arrived, they would immediately attack.

He took the lead, gunning toward the base, his heart hammering with the religious fervor that swept over him before every battle. Tonight he might die, and receive his rewards for dying in Allah's name, or he might survive, cementing himself as the greatest leader Boko Haram had ever had.

Either way, he was content.

He spotted the camp ahead, only by the shadows, for there wasn't a single light visible. But something was wrong, something was different. He had been told there was a large open area with a chain-link fence and a collection of buildings at the center. Instead, he was approaching what appeared to be a wall taller than a man, surrounding the entire base.

Just what the hell was in that container?

Amman Rotana Hotel

Amman, Hashemite Kingdom of Jordan

Kane paced in front of the bed of his hotel room, waiting for word on what was going on. He had delivered Leroux's message to the Gray Network through Zorkin, but had heard nothing since. That wasn't necessarily unexpected, though if the request had been approved, he should have heard something through the grapevine, especially if the request had been actioned.

Yet nothing.

His watch signaled a new message and he dove for his phone sitting on the nightstand. He logged in and listened to the heartbreaking plea from Dawson to the president. He had known the man for years, and Dawson didn't fear death. He never embraced it. No good soldier did. Dawson wasn't scared of dying, and would go down fighting to the bitter end if he had to, but Kane had no doubt the plea wasn't for himself or his men, it was for those they were willing to die for to protect.

Unfortunately, too many politicians didn't care about the civilians in some poor African country. They weren't voters. But if the recording of a soldier, pleading to his president for a single aircraft that could save a dozen American soldiers were to ever be released to the public, it would sink any politician's career. America loved its soldiers and wouldn't stand for a repeat of Benghazi. One plane could save them all, could buy them the time to hold out for the Nigerian troops to arrive and secure the area.

All that was needed was a nod of the head.

And he swore, if that nod weren't given and his friends died, there wouldn't be a corner of the world where you wouldn't find someone listening to the last words of a dead hero.

FOB Ugurun, Nigeria

Dawson cocked an ear and tensed slightly at the sound of motorcycles approaching. A lot of motorcycles. He scrambled up the first few rungs of a ladder positioned against one of the buildings and cursed at the long line of headlights stretching into the distance, coming from both directions of the lone road that ran through the village.

This was it. This was the Alamo, and Santa Anna had just arrived. If they ever made a movie out of this someday, he wanted the equivalent of John Wayne playing him.

Though he wasn't dead yet.

He hopped down. "This is it people! Remember, no matter how scared you get, nobody fires a single shot until I give the order!"

"And what if you're dead, mate?" asked Ledger from his post in the kill box.

"He's too pretty to die!" shouted Niner, to which everyone began to laugh, the nervous tension relieved slightly.

"He's right. I'm too pretty and too stubborn to die. But, if I can't give it, Red will, then whoever. If we're that far down the chain of command, our little plan probably failed, so just shoot the shit out of everything you can."

The whine of the motorcycles changed and Dawson climbed back up to see the columns were holding position at either end of the road, one group at the schoolhouse to the south, the other closer to Niner's secondary LZ.

"What do you think they're doing?" asked Red from his own perch.

"Probably wondering what the hell happened to the chain-link fence."

"It's still there."

Dawson chuckled. "Yeah, along with this beast of a new wall."

Atlas drove by, filling another segment, the pile of dirt at the far end much smaller now. He paused in front of him. "Orders?"

"Keep doing what you're doing until it's no longer safe to be doing it."

"You got it." Atlas bounced away and Dawson surveyed the barrier. The key areas were all filled to full height, and the rest had a half load. Bullets weren't going to be their downfall unless the enemy made it over the wall, and RPGs were only a threat to his men on the rooftops. It was grenades. They had no way to defend well against those, which was why you pushed your tree lines back and shot anyone that came within throwing distance. That wasn't an option here if they sent in everyone at once.

A single motorcycle raced down the road then stopped at the old front gate. It was tempting to shoot the bastard, just to send a message, but it would serve no purpose. They were in a delaying action. They had to hold out 3.5 hours, assuming the roads were clear enough. The locals had had the entire day to do their own work clearing, so if they were lucky, the column on its way here would encounter far fewer delays than when they had started out this afternoon.

A day away.

It was a worst-case scenario estimate that ignored the industriousness of the local population, and the determination of the brave Nigerian soldiers to save their countrymen.

Eight hours on a good day.

Let's just pray it's a good day.

"I can take him," called Mickey from his position.

"Negative. Let's just see what they do when we don't react."

The engine revved slightly as the rider turned through the gate then gunned as he raced around the entire perimeter. Dawson held his breath, begging any itchy trigger fingers to remain calm, then sighed heavily as the rider returned to the road and rejoined the southern group.

"Is anybody else's heart beating a little faster?" asked Red.

Ledger batted Clarke. "I think my wristy friend here filled his drawers."

Clarke grunted. "Shows what you know. I don't wear any."

"That's the last time you ever borrow any of my trousers."

Dawson activated his comms. "Control, Zero-One. Come in, over."

"This is Control. Go ahead."

"I think now is as good a time as any."

"Copy that, Zero-One. Reaper inbound. Control, out."

Now the show begins.

Operations Center 2, CIA Headquarters

Langley, Virginia

"Target One in sight. Stand by."

Leroux stared at the display showing a computer-enhanced version of the situation. Two large clusters of riders had converged to the north and south of the FOB. Hundreds of motorcycles now idled as the leadership no doubt debated what to do now that they had discovered the Hesco barrier in their way. There was little chance they were even aware of what it was, which was good. If they thought it was a seven-foot wall of concrete, they might change their plans and perhaps leave, though that was wishful thinking, he was sure.

Yet the longer they debated, the stronger that wall became, every minute giving Atlas a chance to fill yet another segment. Enhanced imagery from the Reaper had given them a detailed look at the prepared defenses, and they were impressive for such a compressed timeframe. It showed what could be done with willpower and manpower. The barrier was in place, the essential areas filled to the full seven-foot height, most of the rest to half that. Gun nests were ready, pre-detonation screens installed, foxholes dug, tree lines pushed back, a kill box set up. So much had been accomplished, and yet it would be for naught if they couldn't hold out.

"Taking the shot."

He redirected his attention to the display split between the Reaper's camera, the missile's, and a bird's eye view from the satellite. A massive explosion erupted from the center of the northern cluster of hostiles, but he had already moved on from that, turning his attention to the southern group that had originated from the main stronghold.

The cluster that likely contained the leadership.

He just prayed the drone pilot was on her game.

South of FOB Ugurun, Nigeria

Ibrahim gasped as a massive fireball erupted down the road, the screams and cries of those who had joined them from the north filling his ears. He gunned his engine and surged forward into the ditch then out the other side, hunched over against what he was certain was coming.

And he was right.

A second explosion blasted the ground behind him, the shockwave knocking him off his bike. He tumbled forward, over the handlebars, then hit the ground hard, crying out in agony as the rear of the bike flipped over him and slammed into his shoulder. He rolled to the side and lay in the dirt, facedown, catching his breath and gingerly testing his shoulder.

Wails from the wounded finally pierced his own fog of pain, and he pushed to his knees then his feet, turning to witness the carnage left behind by the American drone. Dozens of his men were dead or dying, and he was certain the same could be said at the other end of the road. He stared up to see the drone circling back.

There was no escape.

He glared at the encampment, still silent, still dark, its new wall taunting him.

And he realized the only safe place was the most dangerous. He grabbed his bike and restarted it, smiling as the engine roared. "To the base! We can't stay on the roads!" He twisted the throttle, his rear tire spitting dirt as he turned, then released the front brake as he surged back onto the road and raced toward the gate to the base, entering the grounds unopposed. He did a complete circuit, confirming what his scout had reported, spotting the inexplicable opening in the wall, and again questioning it.

They must not have had time to finish.

And his thought was confirmed as he spotted a piece of heavy equipment working inside, dumping dirt into the wall.

And his jaw dropped.

It's just a big dirt holder!

It explained how it fit in the container delivered earlier, and why there had been a large pile of dirt left at one end of the cleared area. This was the intent all along—he had simply moved up their plans. Which meant they weren't ready. They had a tremendous vulnerability with that opening. If he could put a couple of hundred men at that entrance, he could overwhelm any defenses the enemy might have.

And the walls? For all he knew they were simply canvas. Little to none of it might be filled, for if it were complete, the loader wouldn't still be working.

They had weaknesses.

Weaknesses that could be used against them.

He continued to circle the base, unchallenged, now joined by scores of his warriors, more entering the gate with each passing moment, the enemy cowering in fear behind their wall of canvas and dirt. His men poured lead on the compound, the night air filling with the rattle of Kalashnikovs, and he smiled as his heart hammered with what was to come. He had hundreds and they had few. Every stray bullet that caught one of them was like killing ten of his own.

The night would be theirs.

The night would be his.

FOB Ugurun, Nigeria

Dawson, hunched over, made a circuit of the wall, checking on everything and everyone as he shouted orders to Red to fix whatever he found amiss, though it was little. He stepped aside as Atlas roared up, dumping another load of dirt. "Status?"

Atlas leaned over, poking his head out from the dangling body armor. "I've dumped a load at each of the fifty cal openings. I can keep filling the rear around the dirt pile, but I've already got it all to half-height. The only way they're coming over is on foot, then we've got a nice shooting range for them set up with fortified positions."

"Good. Park that thing inside our entrance, as close to the opening as you can. I want them on foot, not bike, if they make it through."

"You got it."

"Oh, and Atlas?"

"Yup?"

"Don't leave the keys in it."

Atlas grinned then roared away as Dawson continued his rounds. Women and children inside the buildings he passed were crying and screaming, and he didn't blame them. The sound was intense, and a stray round would occasionally catch the top of the buildings, likely fired by someone holding their gun over their head at a sharp angle—unaimed and more likely to hit one of their own than anyone inside.

He reached the last of their Hail Mary positions and patted the Nigerian manning it on the back. "You good?"

"Yes, Sergeant Major," was the response from the wide-eyed man, terrified but determined. "Your plan looks like it might work."

Dawson smiled. "From your lips to God's ears. Get ready." He stepped away and joined Red. "Report."

"Everything looks good. The barrier is holding, and so are the nerves so far."

"So far." Dawson activated his comms. "Control, Zero-One. Report."

"Zero-One, it looks like it's working. The longer you guys hold your fire, the more that are taking the plunge and entering the compound."

"Damage assessment?"

"We believe we took out over twenty north and south. Congratulations, you're only facing about four-hundred-fifty now."

Dawson chuckled. "Yay for us. What's your assessment on our Hail Mary?"

"It's pretty crowded. I doubt they'll get much more in there, and there are signs of the passengers getting off their bikes and taking up position. I think now is as good a time as any."

"Copy that, Control. Throwing the pass. Zero-One, out." Dawson gave Red a look. "Well, here goes nothing." He drew a flare gun from his hip and raised it over his head, squeezing the trigger. The flare shot into the air and burst, bathing the entire area in a dull red glow. "Open fire!"

The ground shuddered with the firepower instantly unleashed, and a rush of endorphins raced through him as he exchanged a smile with Red. Six positions cut into half-height portions of the walls had been manned by Nigerian crews with their own .50 cals that were once at the chain-link. They now belched lead on the hostiles circling the camp through slits opened in the other side of the barrier, barely visible to those outside. Six positions on the rooftops, manned by his own team, used the confusion to pick off the riders with disciplined shots, while the rest of his men tossed grenades over the wall into the thick cluster of targets.

Boko Haram, in its arrogance, had forgotten that numbers meant nothing against a well-prepared position.

He just prayed they killed enough of them in the initial attack to make them think twice about a counterattack.

Niner squeezed the trigger, taking out yet another of the surprised enemy. Dawson's plan had been brilliant, and it was so far working like a charm. He picked his next target and took him out. It was a smorgasbord of fanatics, and he had already eliminated ten himself, and between the others, the .50s, and the grenades, they had to have eliminated at least one hundred by now.

"They're figuring it out!" shouted Mickey from his left. "They're starting to bug out!"

"Just keep firing! Whoever's got a bead on that gate, shoot as many as you can. Maybe we can clog it up!" Niner fired another shot, his position covering the southern flank.

"RPG!" announced Sweets as he rose and fired one of their confiscated weapons at the gate. An explosion sent a shudder through the ground and up the supports holding the roof in place.

Niner spotted activity at the far end, around where what remained of the dirt pile was. They had opened the chain-link fence so they could give the loader room to work, and also to extend the barrier around the pile. The hostiles were now using that opening to escape the carnage inside the wire. "They found the opening!"

Jagger cursed. "Well, it was just a matter of time. Keep firing. There are plenty here who haven't figured it out yet."

The .50s continued to pound, as did the M4s, the wails of the dying and the shrieks of the terrified dwindling as more escaped, but even more lost the battle. Niner reloaded, another mag spent, another thirty dead.

He rarely missed.

And tonight, every bullet counted.

Ledger sat in his sandbagged position with Clarke, his favorite weapon, Ginger, an F88 Austeyr assault rifle, held at the ready as they, along with half a dozen Nigerians, covered the only gap in the barrier. At the far end, Atlas had parked the loader with the bucket at half height. Anyone coming in would have to abandon their bike and enter on foot, at a crouch, or a crawl.

As long as he and the others hadn't plugged the gaps with bodies.

His biggest concern wasn't holding this position. He was confident they could as long as they survived any grenades lobbed over the barrier. It was the enemy figuring out their weakness—once at the wall, they were safe. Nobody had an angle on them. They could boost each other over the seven-foot barrier, then be inside to create havoc. They had fire teams made up of Nigerians and Delta, roaming the compound, watching for just this, but throw enough men at it, and they could overwhelm them in short order.

The key was keeping them back from the wall so they couldn't figure that out.

The sound of motorcycle engines died down and the gunfire dwindled then eventually stopped. He had no idea how long the battle had lasted, though it couldn't have been the half-hour his watch suggested. Then again, perhaps it had.

A voice sounded on the other side of the barrier and he cocked an ear. "What the hell was that?"

Clarke listened as the voice continued. "Sounds like a radio."

Ledger smiled and jumped from his position, racing toward the gap. "Cover me!"

Clarke cursed and Ledger glanced back to see his friend climb up atop the sandbags so he could see over the wall. Ledger reached the end of the barrier, peering out into the carnage, and it was impressive. Twisted wrecks of motorcycles were mixed with the bloodied corpses of their riders and the still dying.

Yet it didn't affect him. He had no sympathy for these bastards, and hoped they died slowly and painfully, for however they did die would be far more merciful than what they had planned for those taking refuge inside. Though despite his lack of concern for their wellbeing, he was concerned with the fact some could still potentially fire a weapon.

The radio crackled again, perhaps fifty feet from his position. He hugged the barrier, staying low and silent, praying he didn't draw any attention. The radio sounded again and he realized he was hearing the general communications among the leadership of what so far was a fiasco on their part. If he could get his hands on that radio, they could listen in on everything the enemy was saying.

It could prove invaluable.

But they needed the radio first.

A man groaned to his right, spotting him, and struggled to raise his weapon. Ledger scurried over and pressed a boot on the man's neck, freeing him of his gun before his breathing became labored then stopped. The radio continued to relay the chatter. It was only paces away now, but there were so many bodies and wrecked bikes, he couldn't be certain who was carrying it. He slung Ginger and drew his Glock. He would need to react quickly, and at close quarters, an assault rifle wouldn't cut it.

He inched forward, his head on a swivel as he watched for threats, all the while listening for the precious device. It fell silent and he cursed to himself, continuing forward. It squawked behind him and to his left. He dropped to a knee and turned.

Then smiled.

The radio lay in the mud, under a riderless motorcycle, its owner perhaps one of the three dead around him. He watched the corpses for a moment, searching for any evidence one might be alive, perhaps faking his death to get the drop on him.

But nothing.

He reached forward and grabbed the radio, then sprinted back toward the opening. Somebody yelled and two shots rang out from Clarke's position.

"Git yer arse in here, ya wanker!"

Ledger blew past the barrier and into the funnel leading to the kill box. He pressed his back against the wall, his chest heaving, not from the physical exertion, but from the excitement of it all.

Why did I ever retire?

He grunted as he made his way past the loader.

Because you're too old, ya bastard!

He held up the radio with a grin. "Looky what I found!"

Ibrahim surged through the opening in the fence, racing across the rugged landscape, dodging between the trees and putting as much distance as he could between him and the carnage he had left behind. He turned toward the road and stopped at the north end where scores of Allah's warriors stared in shock and silence as the slaughter continued.

This was never supposed to happen. This was supposed to be an easy victory where they would ride in, kill everyone, and send their message. Instead, this was turning into a disaster. He had no idea how many were dead, but it had to be at least 100, if not 200. It was unacceptable, especially with the likely fact that not a single soul on the other side had been hurt.

This was making him look bad.

The drone flew past and everyone surrounding him cringed, waiting for another missile, but none came. He stared down the road at the scores of motorcycles still arriving, creating an even more tempting target. Were the Americans waiting, or were they out of missiles? And if they were, when would a fresh drone arrive with more?

They had to regroup and act fast.

"Ibrahim, my friend, did you survive?"

It was Lawan. If there was anyone he would want to have die today, it was his rival. And the voice on the other end of the radio dripped with joy, as if the man knew this would be Ibrahim's downfall.

He grabbed his radio off his hip. "Of course I survived. I'm pleased to hear you did as well."

"It's not difficult when one spots a trap. We lost a lot of good men. What do you intend to do?"

Ibrahim smirked slightly. Lawan had just slipped up. "I pray, my friend, that you are not suggesting we give up in Allah's work."

There was a pause and murmured conversations took place around him from men he knew little about.

"I suggested nothing of the sort." The reply was subdued, the tone not as disrespectful.

Ibrahim stood tall on his bike, gripping his radio to his mouth. "For all of you within the sound of my voice, I say this. Every single one of our brothers that has died is already being welcomed into Jannah by Allah and the Prophet Muhammad, peace and blessings be upon him. Mourn not for them, for they now enjoy the spoils of dying as a warrior of Allah in the jihad against the infidel. More of you will die tonight, I may even die tonight, but I fear not the death that may face me, as you should not fear the death that may await you. Every single warrior who falls here tonight will experience an eternity of unimaginable bliss in Jannah, surrounded by your rewards, as well as your loved ones. Even if we all die here tonight, we will be reunited moments later in paradise.

"I intend to fight on! Our enemy may have surprised us, but now we know what he is capable of, and we will treat him with more respect. If you are with me, then let me hear you. But if you are not, then follow the cowards home now, and leave Jannah and victory to those of us who truly believe." He raised a fist in the air. "What say you?"

The roar of support surrounding him exhilarated him, and he kept the button pressed so that should there not be a similar response from the southern group where Lawan was, the man and those with him could hear it.

But he needn't have worried, for he could hear them in the background of Lawan's response.

"We are with you, brother."

Wings lay on his hospital bed, itching to get in the fight, but unable. Niner had been right to be concerned. He was getting weaker, and the pain was growing, the bruise slowly spreading where his liver was. His nurses continued to tend to him, and he was impressed with their poise under fire. The battle had lasted for the better part of twenty minutes, and had been thunderously loud, with far too many bullets pinging off the steel pre-detonation screen mounted around the rooftops to protect the snipers.

He had replayed the crash repeatedly in his head, and while it could have been avoided if he had banked right instead of left, there was no way he could have known exactly where the warhead had been coming from. It was the luck of the draw. Fifty-fifty chance, and he had bet wrong. Two good men had died, and while his conscience demanded he carry that burden, his trained mind dismissed it.

This was war.

People died, and sometimes nobody was to blame. In this case, there was someone. A farmer he had no doubt would die tomorrow if they survived the day. What pissed him off was that he might die here tonight, pampered by two women while his comrades died around him. It wasn't how he had pictured going. He had figured old age or a blaze of glory.

Never a slow bleed from inside.

The chances of him surviving were slim to none, he would guess, though he was clinging to slim. Even if they survived long enough for the Nigerians to arrive in three hours, it was another eight hours to a hospital. When the bastards came for him, he would fight them to the last bullet, then the last slice of his knife, the final swing of a punch. He had to die fighting them, for he knew what they would do to him should he be captured alive.

Mogadishu would seem civilized compared to what Boko Haram would do.

The door opened and Dawson stepped inside holding a beat-up walkie-talkie. "Feel like doing something useful?"

Wings smiled. "You have no idea."

Dawson handed over the walkie. "Ledger found this outside the wire. It's still active." He handed a pen and some paper over. "Take notes of anything they say that might be important. Relay anything I need to hear over comms. If we're lucky, we might get something juicy that could help us out."

"You got it."

Dawson gave him a fist bump, but was unable to hide the frown when his eyes darted down to the bruise. "How are you holding up?"

"I'll live long enough to fulfill my orders."

"You better. I don't want to have to kill you twice."

Operations Center 2, CIA Headquarters
Langley, Virginia

"They're on the move again," reported Tong as Leroux read the updates rolling in. The Reaper's two 500-pound bombs had proven immensely effective, and Dawson's plan to lure them in had been even more so if the battlefield assessments compiled by his people were any indication. The latest numbers showed that almost 200 hostiles were dead or soon to be dead, without a single friendly casualty.

The Reaper was out of weapons, but with 27 hours of flight time, she could hang in for a while to provide them with valuable intel. And now that they had one of the enemy's radios, they were listening in on their comms through Wings. If he didn't know better, things were going exceedingly well. The Nigerian column was three hours out now, and he had to believe that the president, after hearing Dawson's plea, would dispatch the AC-130J Ghostrider gunship they had located only an hour away.

But he knew better. An hour could be an eternity. So far, everything they had accomplished was by surprise. Boko Haram wasn't accustomed to dealing with the full power of the CIA—satellites, armed drones, a dedicated ops center, and a Special Forces team second to none, fully trained for situations like this. But they still had the numbers, and more were continually arriving. The team members assigned to keep track of the participants had indicated just minutes ago that more forces, beyond the initial 500, were still entering the area, answering the call.

If they couldn't eliminate the bulk of the forces now, Dawson's people didn't stand a chance. Eliminate them before they made it inside the wire, then the stragglers that arrived could be dealt with easily enough if there were enough survivors inside. When the Nigerian column arrived with 200 well-armed troops, they could secure the area against those late to the party.

But there were an awful lot of ifs in his scenario, and it all hinged on getting that gunship, otherwise there was no way three more hours was possible, not if what he was staring at were any indication—hundreds of Boko Haram, on foot, spreading around all sides of the FOB, keeping their distance.

They weren't going to be caught again with their pants down.

He activated his comms. "Zero-One, Control. Come in, over."

"Go ahead, Control."

"We have hostiles moving in on foot from all directions. Our current estimates are approximately two-hundred with another hundred arriving within the next fifteen minutes."

"Any word on that Ghostrider?"

Leroux checked his messages yet again, praying for something from Morrison, who had been videoconferencing with the president for over an hour. "Negative, Zero-One. No word."

"Understood, Control. We're on our own. Zero-One, out."

Leroux closed his eyes, his shoulders sagging in defeat. While it wasn't true, it felt like his failure. Part of him still blamed himself for having convinced the powers-that-be to reclassify the mission as CIA, thus allowing Bravo Team to intervene at the schoolhouse. If they hadn't, none of this would be happening.

But if they hadn't, how many little girls would be getting raped right now?

His phone pinged with a message and he brought it up, tapping the link to bring him into Kane's secure app.

And he smiled, his shoulders heaving in relief.

Single sortie authorized. ETA 20 minutes. Vive la France!

US AFRICOM Base Camp N'Djamena

Outside N'Djamena, Chad

Colonel Waters' eyes narrowed as she read the message from the French commander at their nearby base, this area a hub of foreign activity to combat terrorism and insurrection in the entire region. France, a former colonial power that controlled much of Africa back in the day, felt a responsibility toward its former colonies, and provided assistance regularly.

But this was something different. All ops were coordinated between the commands so no one stepped on anyone else's toes. They were usually carefully planned, and unless there was some emergency situation, notice was never given only minutes before.

The entire building vibrated then shook. She rushed out of her office and down the corridor, sprinting outside and staring up at the night sky as half a dozen French Eurocopter Tiger HAD attack helicopters blasted past overhead, their rotors kicking up dust as they hugged the ground, no doubt on purpose based upon the message she had received.

We're going to do your job. Vive la France, Irene.

There was only one job she was aware of in the region that she wasn't doing due to bullshit orders, and that was helping those poor souls in Nigeria.

At least someone is doing something.

She headed back inside and entered the command center. "Get me AFRICOM."

FOB Ugurun, Nigeria

It wasn't that Dawson was giddy, but he was, for the first time, feeling like they just might get out of this alive. Leroux had just informed him that favors had been called in and French attack helicopters were inbound, authorized for a single sortie.

ETA twenty minutes.

Less than that, assuming some delays in communications.

If they could hold out for just twenty minutes, the French choppers could tear apart their enemy in a single pass, greatly reducing their numbers to a far more manageable amount, perhaps low enough for them to back off and give up. The Nigerians were less than three hours out, and if they could last twenty minutes, have the enemy ducking for ten or fifteen of them, then regrouping for at least half an hour, the Nigerian column might only be two hours out.

There was hope.

Thanks to favors.

He wasn't sure who was behind it, but he was kissing the man or woman if he ever found out and met them. If he didn't, he was singing La Marseillaise the next time he saw the blue, white, and red of the French flag.

But they had to last twenty minutes. This time, Boko Haram weren't playing the fools. Unfortunately, they had learned their lesson, and now had them surrounded on all sides, well back at the tree line. The question was, how to engage them? The .50s weren't accurate enough, and he wanted to save the limited ammo they had left in the event there was another mass attack. He could order his rooftop team to start picking them off, but every minute Boko Haram remained quiet, was another minute closer to the French arriving.

He activated his comms. "Bravo Team, this is Zero-One. As you heard from Control, the French are on the way. Quietly pass the news along to the others if you haven't already. We need to hold out for less than twenty minutes. Hold your fire until I give the order. We want to draw them in like last time. Anything they fire from the tree line is wasted ammo. Zero-One, out."

He walked over to Ledger and Clarke, no other member of Bravo Team near them to pass on the good news. "The French are coming. Twenty minutes. Langley thinks it's a single pass with attack helicopters."

Ledger high-fived Clarke. "Well, that's bloody good news, assuming those wankers out there stay put and scratch their arses for a while."

"I doubt they'll be doing that, but if we can keep them on the other side of the wire until the French arrive, they should be able to poke a few holes in them."

275

"Aren't you the downer. I'm holding out hope that they're playing with each other's—"

Gunfire erupted from every direction, the order Wings had warned them about having been given.

Boko Haram was attacking, and this time they knew what they were facing.

Ibrahim fired his AK-47, the butt vibrating against his shoulder as all around him muzzle flashes indicated his order was being followed. Yet there was no response. Behind the strange wall of sand, he couldn't see anything, and it was frustrating. There was no indication that a single shot was being fired from inside, and it took him a moment to realize why.

His men were no threat to them. If that wall was indeed as high as he thought it was, and as thick, and it was filled with dirt, no bullets were getting through, not even RPGs. There was only one way inside and that was through the opening he had spotted earlier, but he had no doubt the enemy had it extremely well guarded. He eyed the sandbagged positions on the rooftops of the buildings. If he were the American commander, that's where he would put his best shots. He had to take them out, and because of their elevated position above the wall, they just might be able to do so.

He pressed his radio to his mouth. "RPGs, target the gun positions on the roofs."

Within moments, dozens of rockets streaked from all directions, and he smiled as explosion after explosion lit the night sky.

Niner dove off the roof, hitting the ground hard, Wings' warning coming in not a moment too soon. He rolled out of the way as Jagger dropped beside him, then covered his eyes as an RPG exploded against one of the pre-detonation screens, the corrugated steel rattling onto the ground nearby. Spock and Jimmy rounded the corner, the plan for this situation an immediate abandonment of the roof and rallying where they were now.

"Incoming!"

Sweets hit the ground as an RPG slammed into one of the prepared positions, making it past the screens. Niner helped him to his feet then looked about. "Where's Mickey?"

Head shakes from the others had him scrambling up the ladder leading to Mickey's position, and he cursed at what he saw. An RPG had obviously made it through the screens and slammed into Mickey's location, toppling the heavy sandbags.

"Incoming!" shouted someone and he threw himself flat on the rooftop, covering his head as another RPG slammed into one of the positions. He scrambled forward, peering into the pile, and spotted a hand.

"Just a second, brother, I'll get you out of there!" He quickly went to work, hauling sandbags out of the way and tossing them back into position in case another RPG found its way through. He yanked another bag out of the way, revealing Mickey's head. His friend's eyes were closed, and there was no sign of life. He reached in and checked for a pulse, and sighed with relief as he found it, strong and steady.

"My God, brother, you gave me a scare." He continued to remove the bags as Spock poked his head up the ladder.

"Did you find him?"

"Yeah. He's unconscious. I think he got hit by the sandbags when the RPG detonated." He furiously continued to free his friend and finally removed the last sandbag, tossing it back in place, protecting them from another direct hit. He quickly did an assessment on him then turned to Spock. "Give me a hand." He slid Mickey along the roof toward the ladder, and Spock reached out and grabbed their friend under the armpits. He hauled Mickey forward as Niner held his legs, when Mickey suddenly jerked.

"What the hell!"

Spock stared him in the face, upside down from Mickey's current perspective. "You fainted, darling."

Mickey sat up and Niner shoved him back down. "Get down, you mental midget! We're still taking fire."

Mickey rolled over onto his stomach. "Then let's get off this damn roof."

Spock climbed out of the way and Mickey swung over the edge, dropping out of sight as Niner scrambled forward and followed, another RPG detonating overhead as it impacted one of the screens. He dropped to the ground then rose, grabbing Mickey by the shoulders and giving him another once over, staring into his eyes.

"Am I okay?"

Niner frowned. "I'm not sure."

Mickey's eyes narrowed. "What do you mean?"

Niner flicked both his friend's ears. "I think these things got bigger."

Dawson sprinted around the corner and breathed a sigh of relief at the sight of all six of the rooftop team standing alive and well at the rally point. "You guys good?"

Niner jerked a thumb at Mickey. "He tried to buy it, but survived."

Dawson regarded Mickey. "You okay?"

"Yeah, just a little shaken up. It's not every day you have an RPG go off two feet from your head."

Jagger punched him on the shoulder. "Next time listen to Wings when he tells you the bad guys just ordered your position targeted."

Mickey patted himself down, finding his earpiece dangling off his vest. He pressed it back into place. "I guess it fell out."

Niner grunted. "No surprise there. Nobody ever designed them to fit Dumbo wings like those."

Mickey flipped him the bird. "Careful, squirt, your protector isn't here."

Dawson looked up as another RPG streaked past, missing the mark. "I think they're starting to run out."

Niner agreed. "Yeah, I noticed that when I was up there saving his sorry ass. Let's hope they're stupid enough to waste them all. It would mean we'll have free reign up there."

Another RPG detonated against one of the screens, sending it toppling to the ground nearby. Dawson eyed it. "Maybe we'll give them a few minutes. Get some of the spare steel and get ready to reinstall the screens." He activated his comms. "Control, Zero-One. Status report, over."

"This is Control. Your hostiles are holding their positions while they use their RPGs. Our analysis suggests they've almost run out, however more hostiles continue to arrive and may have more. Advise caution if reoccupying the rooftops."

"Copy that, Control. Any updated ETA on our French friends?"

"Ten minutes out."

"Copy that. Zero-One, out." Dawson cocked an ear, noticing the silence. "That can't be good." He jerked a thumb up. "Back up there, ladies. And Mickey?"

"Yeah?"

"Duct tape that damned thing in your ear if you have to. I don't want you off comms again."

Niner clasped his hands in front of his chest. "Please please please, can I do it?"

Ibrahim stared through the smoke, uncertain whether the barrage had been successful. In the faint moonlight he had spotted something odd mounted around the rooftops, and when the RPGs began detonating off them, he realized they were pieces of metal designed to explode the warheads before they reached their targets.

Ingenious.

He had to remember that for their own fortifications.

At least a few RPGs had made it through and hit the positions on the rooftops, but without knowing if anyone was actually there since the guns had been silent, he had to question whether it had been worth it. Had they just wasted most of their RPG arsenal on what ended up being little more than a light show?

Had *he?*

One thing he was certain of was that if anyone had been on the rooftops, they weren't there now, which meant they might have a clear shot at reaching the walls, which was key. He had noticed a curious pattern when staring at the carnage surrounding the base. Except for a few areas, all the dead were more than ten feet from the wall.

They had a massive hole in their defenses. They appeared to have no coverage outside the wall except from the rooftop, which due to the angle meant a huge blind spot.

If they could make it there.

It would be dangerous, and as he thought about it, he could think of only one man to lead the charge. He clicked on the talk button. "Lawan, are you there, brother?"

"Yes, I'm here."

"Have you noticed that they can't cover close to the wall?"

There was a pause. "Yes, I see that."

A sly smile crept up one side of his face. "I want you to lead the charge. In the name of Allah, get our men to that wall. Once we get there, we can use the grenades to kill all those infidel pigs. Can you do it?"

The challenge was out there, broadcast over the airwaves to every single commander within the organization. It would be impossible for Lawan to refuse and the bastard knew it, if the delay in his response were any indication.

"You know I can."

He had to suppress the cackle that threatened to erupt. He had forced his greatest rival into near-certain death. He might die a martyr, but he would be dead, and no longer a challenge to his leadership.

"Then do it."

Lawan issued the order to advance over the radio and men moved in from all sides, picking up speed as Lawan urged them on. Ibrahim spotted him, sprinting toward the wall, screaming "Allahu Akbar!" at the top of his lungs, fear, rage, and fervor in his eyes.

He was a man who knew he was about to die.

US AFRICOM Base Camp N'Djamena

Outside N'Djamena, Chad

Colonel Waters slammed her office door shut and grabbed the phone, jabbing Line One. "Bill, we've got a situation developing and I need your help."

Brigadier General Bill Gillespie cleared his throat into the receiver and Waters winced, moving the phone from her ear for a moment. It was a nasty habit the man had, but other than that, he was a good one.

And her ex-husband.

They hadn't given up on their marriage due to a lack of love, it was their careers that had gotten in the way. They were both too ambitious to sacrifice their own career so the other could succeed. And now they had both succeeded, and she saw stars in both their futures, not just his.

He finished his disgusting habit, something she had told him about repeatedly. "What's the situation?"

"We have a Delta team trapped on a Forward Operating Base in Nigeria. They're surrounded by hundreds of Boko Haram, and the Nigerians are refusing to let us send in help."

"From what I hear, they managed to get a Chinook with an FOB in a Can in there."

"You heard about that, did you?"

She could almost hear his eyes roll. "Of course I heard about it. What were you thinking?"

It was her turn to roll her eyes. "That I didn't want another Benghazi."

He sighed. "I'll do what I can to protect you."

"I can take care of myself."

"Don't be a fool."

She bristled. Maybe they had divorced for more than their careers. "Let's drop this. I need a favor."

"You're right. What can I do for you?"

"Do you still have that Ghostrider used in Mali a few days ago?"

"Why, what are you thinking?"

He knew her too well.

"I want you to fully arm it and send it here."

"So it can be stolen by Aussie mercenaries?"

She smiled. "You really are up to speed, aren't you?"

He laughed. "Always." He became serious. "You realize you're the second person who's called about that aircraft in the past hour?"

Her eyebrows shot up. "Really? Who else?"

"I'm thinking CIA."

"Huh, I received a similar call earlier about the Chinook. What did you say?"

"It's already inbound. They should be landing at your base in ten minutes."

She smiled broadly. "You know, Bill, it's times like these when I remember why I fell in love with you."

He laughed. "Because when you need heavy firepower, I always deliver, even in the bedroom?"

She roared. "Oh, Bill, you always could make me laugh."

FOB Ugurun, Nigeria

Lawan sprinted toward the wall ahead, his pulse pounding in his ears with fear, a pit of rage roiling in his stomach over having been outmaneuvered by Ibrahim. When their leader had been killed, he had wanted to take over the organization, but was convinced that whoever led next would only do so for a short time—he would be betrayed by a rival and killed. It was the only reason he had backed Ibrahim.

But the man had survived. And thrived. Even Lawan's own men thought Ibrahim was a great leader. When he had heard of the defeat here this morning, he had recognized it as an opportunity to perhaps sow division and take over as leader, to take his rightful place at the head of Boko Haram.

Yet he had been outplayed. The moment Ibrahim sent that radio transmission for all to hear, there was no choice. The wall had to be reached, and it had to be with him leading the charge.

He didn't want to die. He feared death as any normal person would. Yes, they were told that dying in the name of Allah granted them guaranteed access to Jannah, and should it be true, he would be content to spend eternity there enjoying the spoils of war. But what if it weren't true? What if it was all just a story told to fools by a fool so many years ago? He had a good life here. Most in the West wouldn't think so, but since he had no idea how they lived, he only had his own experiences to compare against. Because of his position, he was wealthy, he had all the women he could want, he had men that admired him and were fiercely loyal, and he was able to leave his home to rape and pillage whenever he pleased.

It was a very good life, and if the Koran was to be believed, after this good life was over, an even better one would be awaiting him in the afterlife. But why shorten one great life to enjoy an even better one that might not be real?

Yet here, now, as he sprinted toward the wall and the enemy's guns opened up on them, he could only curse Ibrahim for cutting short the bliss he now lived.

If I survive this, you're dead.

"Here they come!" shouted Niner as he peered through his scope. The orders still stood—hold your fire. They wanted as many of them in the open as possible before they unleashed another volley, though this might be the last. The .50s were almost out of ammo, and once they were, all that was left that could target outside the compound were the six of them on these rooftops.

Not enough by any stretch of the imagination.

He checked his watch. Seven minutes. Seven minutes until the French arrived. Even if it were only a single pass, just one attack helicopter could do significant damage, and perhaps put the fear of God into these assholes. The Nigerians were less than three hours away now. Some of those inside the wire might survive until then, but he doubted it would be many if any. If he were the Boko Haram commander, he'd just toss torches or Molotov cocktails over the wire to set fire to the buildings, then in the confusion, breach the barrier. Once enough of them were inside, it was over.

"BD! They're getting awfully close!" yelled Jagger.

Spock cursed. "I think they all have grenades in their hands!"

A flare screamed into the air and burst, Dawson issuing the order. "Open fire!"

Niner squeezed the trigger then moved on to the next target, not wasting any time to check if the man had gone down—he just assumed his aim was true, and the valuable second that assumption purchased allowed him to increase his kill rate.

The .50s opened up from the six Nigerian positions, the thunder deafening and reassuring. He continued to fire, as did the others, and significant damage was clearly being done. It was almost enjoyable if it weren't for the fact it was human lives he was taking. He had no guilt, of course, as these were murderous lunatics, but there was no joy in the killing, just satisfaction they couldn't hurt anyone inside anymore.

He spotted something that had him poking his head up. The blind spots between the coverage provided by the .50s had been made obvious by the lack of carnage in what resembled triangular-shaped havens extending out from the barriers between each gun position.

And it appeared as if the enemy had figured it out.

"BD! Looks like they've figured out the blind spots!"

"Copy that! Rooftop, target the blind spots!"

Niner continued to fire, as did the others, concentrating on the spots the .50s couldn't cover. So far, no RPGs had been fired, which suggested they were either out, or had given up on that tactic for the moment. With the level of accuracy these idiots had shown earlier, the leadership might have decided they would lose more of their own to friendly fire than their enemy might to successful hits.

Something rattled one of the pre-detonation screens and he recognized the sound of a metal grenade rolling down the corrugated steel. "Grenade, Number Three Center! Take cover!"

He ducked as the metal-on-metal scraping stopped, the grenade dropping to the ground below. The detonation shook the entire building, but it was over and none of his concern. He opened up again on the hostiles, wondering why the past ten seconds had felt like the seven minutes they needed.

Dawson scrambled to his feet and rushed toward the blast site. "Everyone all right?" Voices sounded off around him, no one indicating they were injured. It appeared the grenade had been blocked by the screen overhead then dumped onto the ground. Much of the blast had been absorbed by the Hesco barrier in one direction, but one of the buildings had taken some shrapnel damage. He poked his head through the biggest hole. "Is everyone all right in there?"

A woman, gripping several children against the far wall, nodded. "I-I think so."

Dawson smiled at her then shoved a thumbs-up through the hole. "Keep away from the outer walls!" he reminded those inside as another grenade warning was shouted from the other side of the compound. The explosion rocked the area, but he let it be, Red covering that zone. He would take care of it and report back if there were anything to be concerned about.

But there already was something to be concerned about. The enemy had figured out their weakness. If they had time to set things up properly, they would have had sandbagged towers at the corners and centers that extended beyond the barrier enough to cover the entire wall. There would be no blind spots for the enemy to hide in. Yet that was for a perfect world, and this wasn't it. If they could just last five more minutes, the tide could be turned.

"Here they come!" shouted Ledger from their kill box.

Dawson wanted to head over to help, but unless the call went out that it was needed, he had a job to do here.

Please, God, give us those five minutes.

Ibrahim watched as his brave warriors, led by his greatest rival, rushed the walls. Dozens more were dead, but at least two had managed to throw grenades that had made it over the wall, the rest falling short and exploding against the barrier that frustratingly held. And equally frustrating, perhaps more so, was that Lawan was still alive, racing toward the wall, eyes wide, screaming "Allahu Akbar!" the entire way, inspiring those who might falter around him.

It was a sight to behold.

Perhaps he would have made the better leader.

It didn't matter. He was the leader and intended to remain so. But after this, if Lawan survived, he would be heralded as a hero with Allah's blessings, for any other man would have died. He would become an impossible to resist rival. If Lawan survived the night, there would be no chance to kill him, for he would be surrounded by his supporters, and he would challenge the leadership before the sun set on tomorrow's sky.

Ibrahim raised his weapon then glanced at the others surrounding him. "Fire at the rooftops. We need to provide our brothers cover." Weapons rattled around him, targeting the sandbagged positions, but as Ibrahim fired, his aim was lower, and he squeezed round after round at his rival, whose head swiveled toward him, shock and terror on his face as he realized what was happening as the ground was torn up around him.

"Ibrahim!"

Lawan had picked up the burst of gunfire from his left, at least a dozen AKs opening up, but it wasn't until he noticed targeted rounds whizzing past him from the left instead of directly ahead that he realized what was happening. At least one of those guns was firing at him.

And it had to be that bastard Ibrahim.

There was no doubt now the man intended for him to die, and his archrival would succeed unless he could figure out what to do. He scanned the area ahead and spotted a motorcycle lying at an angle atop the two men that had probably been riding it. He made a beeline for it, covering his head uselessly, then cried out as he dropped behind the twisted cover.

The gunfire continued all around him, several bullets pinging off the metal frame of the motorcycle, but it appeared he was, for the moment, safe from Ibrahim. As long as he stayed here, perfectly still, he might survive long enough to get the drop on the bastard himself.

But this would be a long, cold night in the dirt if he were forced to lie here until this was over.

Ibrahim smiled at the sight of Lawan crying out then dropping. He peered across the battlefield, still lit by the American flare, but couldn't find the body. Lawan had fallen behind a pile of corpses and motorcycles, out of sight, and it had him wondering if the man were actually dead, or just faking it.

Either way, the rivalry was over. If he were dead, then he was no longer of any concern, and if he faked his death to lie cowering among the bodies of the brave warriors that had fallen before him, and remained there while others fought his battle, he would be shunned by the survivors, no longer a threat for leadership of the organization.

No matter what, he had won the battle for the leadership, and with the number of warriors now reaching the wall, it appeared he was about to win the day as well.

His radio squelched. "Imam, come in! Imam!"

"Go ahead."

"Helicopters, sir! I count six helicopters passing overhead, heading directly for you."

Ibrahim cursed. "American?"

"No. French!"

His eyes narrowed. Why the hell would the French be getting involved? Could they have been mistaken about who was behind that wall? The French actually scared him more. They didn't bother with politics or niceties. They simply went in and took care of business. "What kind of helicopters?"

"I don't know. Small. Like attack helicopters, I guess."

He frowned. Small and fast, with heavy weaponry. Far harder to shoot down than an old Huey with a side-mounted gun.

This could be about to get ugly, and they had lost enough troops already.

What the hell do I do?

Ledger squeezed the trigger on Ginger yet again, taking out another of the bastards trying to make it through the kill box. So far, the defenses were working, but grenades were getting tossed over the walls of the compound now, and one well-placed throw could put an end to them.

Clarke fired one of the American's M4s beside him. "It's been a long time since I've had some fun."

Ledger didn't bother giving him a look. "My idea of fun is a Friday night with a Sheila you won't see Saturday morning. If this is your idea of a blast, then you need to seek professional help when this is done." He fired again as someone poked their head out from under the loader's bucket.

"Lay me on a couch and I'll be sleeping long before I'm—grenade!"

Ledger spotted it sailing over the loader and directly toward them. He rose and tossed Ginger in the air, grabbing her by the muzzle then swinging her like a cricket bat. The stock smacked the grenade back toward the loader as a hand grabbed the back of his shirt, dragging him back down as it erupted not ten feet from his face. He slammed onto his back, atop Clarke, as the blast washed over them, the sandbags protecting them.

"You all right?" asked Clarke from under him.

"Nah, yeah, I'm good."

"Then get off me before I make you buy me dinner."

Ledger laughed and scrambled back to his position, giving Ginger a kiss. "Good girl."

Clarke took up beside him. "We need to get you a girlfriend when this is all over."

Ledger took out another nutbar. "If we get out of this, I'm calling your sister."

Approaching FOB Ugurun, Nigeria

Lieutenant Colonel Richelieu turned his head slightly to the left, his gunner sitting behind him having spotted their destination first.

And he cursed.

The sight before them was eerie. A dark landscape lit dimly by the moon and stars with a donut of activity ahead—a dark hole where almost nothing could be seen, then a ring around it of constant flashes. A flare launched, revealing the truth, and they both gasped at the sight. The encampment was entirely surrounded by what appeared to be hundreds of the enemy, their weapons pouring lead onto the defenders, grenades exploding, some inside the wire, some outside.

They were on the brink.

"This is Team Leader. Prepare to engage. Remember, single pass, but make it a complete three-sixty. I want to lay as much ordnance as possible on them before we leave. Don't worry about hitting the barrier with a stray shot. It's filled with sand. Let's just leave here intact, with as many Boko Haram as possible dead. We're the only hope these people have."

A string of acknowledgments from the others filled his ears and his gunner grunted. "The Americans couldn't do this?"

"Politics. Apparently, the Nigerians are forbidding them to enter their airspace, or they'll cut off all future cooperation between the two countries. It's a power play by the Nigerian president who's up for reelection. If this happened six months from now, the Americans would be welcomed in. Right now, he needs the Muslim vote, and playing favorites with the infidel doesn't look good."

"Nuts."

"No shit." He pushed forward on the stick, guiding them into the fray when suddenly the gunfire stopped and the enemy retreated. He frowned. "I guess they heard we were coming to the party."

"Fashionably late."

"This is Team Leader. Watch where they end up. We might be hitting the tree line instead." His eyes narrowed as he spotted the long line of motorcycles to the north and south. "And on our way out, choppers one through three soften up that southern road, four through six the northern. We don't want the reinforcements feeling left out."

Chuckles and acknowledgments responded as his gunner activated the weapons systems. His comms squawked in his headphones. "Tango-Whiskey-One, this is Command, come in, over."

"This can't be good." He activated his mic as he guided them in. "This is Tango-Whiskey-One, go ahead, Command, over."

"Tango-Whiskey-One, this is a priority message from Command. You are to abort immediately. I say again, abort immediately. Acknowledge, over."

296

He cursed as he slammed a fist against the console. "Command, we are within sight of the target, about to engage. They are surrounded by hundreds of hostiles. We can save these people. Request permission to proceed, over."

"Negative, Tango-Whiskey-One. You are to abort and return to base immediately. Acknowledge, over."

A flurry of curses erupted as he shook his head, damning the politicians whose orders they were required to follow. "Acknowledged, Command, aborting mission, returning to base. Tango-Whiskey-One, out." He switched channels. "This is Team Leader. We've been ordered to abort and return to base."

Protests erupted in his ears and he agreed with every one of them. But it was beyond his control. He was a soldier and he did what he was ordered. If he ignored his orders and engaged anyway, it could create an international incident that cost even more lives down the road if they lost the cooperation of the Nigerian government. There had to be a reason for the abort order, and whether he would ever know what that was, he highly doubted it.

He banked them hard, away from the now once again hopeless battle, and said a silent prayer for the brave men and women now left to their own devices to survive until relief arrived.

If that wasn't canceled as well.

Operations Center 2, CIA Headquarters

Langley, Virginia

"What the hell is going on?" cried Leroux as the six French helicopters turned around and headed back to their base in Chad. "Get me…" He stopped. There was no one to get. This was a Hail Mary done through back channels. There was no one to call to protest, to ask why.

Yet he knew.

Politicians.

Child spun in his chair. "Bunch of cheese-eating surrender monkeys."

Leroux grunted, though wasn't prepared to condemn the pilots only following orders.

"They were the last hope they had," murmured Tong as she stared at the retreat. "What are they going to do now?"

Leroux shook his head as he stared at the aerial shot provided by the Reaper. When the choppers had been on their final approach, the enemy had backed off en masse and were now hiding in the tree line. The base was safe for the moment, but once Boko Haram realized the threat was gone, they would attack, with the knowledge nothing would threaten them again.

He slammed his fist on his station, rattling everything on it and startling those around him. He raised a hand. "Sorry, people. Just frustrated."

"You're not the only one," said Therrien. There was a pause. "Umm, boss, check this out." Therrien pointed at the screen as a new image appeared. Leroux squinted at it as the doors to the operations center opened and Morrison entered.

Leroux turned to him. "Do you know why the French just aborted?"

Morrison glanced at the screen, frowning at the tactical display showing the six helicopters racing back toward Chad. "Yes, I do. The president asked the French president to recall them."

Leroux's jaw dropped as his eyes shot wide. "He did what?" He sprang from his chair, jabbing a finger as the display. "Does he realize he just condemned all those people to death?"

Morrison held up a hand. "Before you fly off the handle, let me explain. There's more going on here than you realize."

Leroux drew a deep breath and held it for a moment as he struggled to regain control of his rage. He leaned to the side, looking past his boss. "Sonya, let Bravo Team know that the French choppers will *not* be coming."

FOB Ugurun, Nigeria

"What complete and utter bullshit is that?" cried Niner from out of sight on the rooftop.

Dawson didn't have an answer for him, but couldn't believe his ears either. Control had just informed him that the French had aborted the mission with no explanation given. He had a sense the woman on the other end of the line had more to tell, but was holding back for some reason. This cowardly act, he was certain, had nothing to do with the pilots or crew. He had fought alongside the French on many occasions, and they were not the white-flag-waving military of old.

This was politics yet again.

He activated his comms. "Bravo Team, Zero-One. You just heard that. The French are not coming, but the Nigerians still are. They're about two and a half hours out. We need to hold as long as we can. Rooftop positions, keep thinning the ranks." He faced Buhari. "Nigerian teams, prepare to repel anyone who gets inside the wire. This is it, people, this is our final stand. It's been an honor serving with each and every one of you, and I still believe God is on our side, and in the end we will prevail. But if we don't, they better make an effin' movie about this cockup, because heads somewhere need to roll. Zero-One, out."

Red joined him and Buhari, as did Ledger. "Well, mates, let down once again by the powers that be."

Red grunted. "This is bullshit."

"Agreed," said Dawson. "But we all know the situation. Surrender is not an option here. We fight to our last breath. If one of us dies, it might be the next guy that lasts long enough for relief to arrive. Or the last." He turned to Buhari. "Make sure your men know we don't surrender. We fight hand-to-hand if we have to. Boko Haram will slaughter them and the civilians in horrible ways for what we've done here. We've killed hundreds of them. We've done the impossible already, and now we have to do the impossible again. I don't know about you, gentlemen, but I have no intention of dying here tonight. I have politicians and bureaucrats to punch in the throat back home."

Red slapped him on the arm. "Me too. Let's kick some more ass. I want my death scene in the movie to have men and women alike bawling."

"Here they come!" shouted Niner as a roar erupted from the tree line, Boko Haram once again emboldened now that the choppers could no longer be heard.

Dawson resumed his position and closed his eyes for a moment. He didn't believe a word he had just said. He was going to die. They all were. It was inevitable now that they had been abandoned yet again. There were simply too many, half the .50s were out of ammo, and the enemy had discovered their weakness.

It was over.

He pictured Maggie back home and his eyes burned.

I'm so sorry.

Niner opened fire, making every shot count. They were running low on ammo for the MP4s, and he didn't want to switch to the less accurate AK-47 lying beside him. Hundreds were rushing the perimeter with more still arriving by motorcycle. It was hopeless, and he was a Korean Davy Crockett. He heard his best friend Atlas down below, directing villagers as they filled in the gun nests cut into the wall by hand as the gunners ran out of ammo. And as each .50 fell silent, the horde closing in picked up their pace.

They would be over the walls in no time.

Then it would be over. It was just a matter of math.

He fired again, continuing to pick off the enemy as his brothers did around him, the cause hopeless but still worthy. This was the end for all of them, but he would go down fighting before he would let any of these barbarians lay a finger on one child.

But in the end, he would fail.

And never have the opportunity to bring his own child into this ridiculous world.

A grenade detonated at the entrance to the barrier and Ledger checked his weapon yet again. "This is it, mate."

"Today is a good day to die," replied Clarke in his best Klingon impression.

"I didn't know you liked Star Trek."

"Who doesn't?"

"Wow, what a wasted friendship we've had that to this date we never talked Trek."

"We can start now."

Ledger fired a round into someone a little too curious. "Favorite TNG episode."

Clarke fired, another down. "The one where Picard learns to play the flute."

Ledger took out another, noticing they were coming quicker now. "Not how I would have described that episode, but definitely one of my fav—"

A grenade dropped into their position and they both stared at each other for a moment before diving over the sandbags and into the open. The grenade detonated and Ledger quickly checked himself then grabbed the little guy, making certain he still had all his favorite body parts. He turned to see Clarke wincing, clutching at his lower leg. Blood oozed through his pants and Ledger reached for him when gunfire broke out. He dropped back to the ground, reaching for Ginger lying nearby, then switched it to full-auto, emptying the mag on the half-dozen that had made it inside.

"Falling back!" he shouted, warning the Nigerians around the bend that friendlies were coming through. He grabbed Clarke by the collar and hauled him to safety as he glanced at their previous position, destroyed, along with the ammo left behind.

Ginger was now useless.

"They're over the wall!" shouted Buhari from the Number Three side.

Red's voice responded as M4s rattled from his team. "We're taking care of it."

The M4s fell silent as Dawson spotted the enemy pouring over the wall at the far end. "We have multiple hostiles coming over at the one-two corner. Keep clear of the wall." He aimed his weapon and opened fire, single shots, well-aimed, ripping down the length of the encampment, eliminating the half-dozen that had made it over within seconds, but more were coming.

This was it.

"This is Zero-One. We need all guns except the rooftop outside, now!" He continued to fire down the line as more came over the wall. "Buhari! Get the civilians out here!"

"Yes, Sergeant Major!"

Dawson reloaded and continued to fire, joined by Spock and Atlas and half a dozen Nigerian regulars, but there were just too many. Someone cried out behind him and he risked a quick glance. It was one of the Nigerians, a round caught in the shoulder. Another cry and Dawson stopped paying attention, instead continuing to fire, single shot, making the rounds count, for their ammo was quickly running out.

They were about to die.

Wings lay helplessly in the bed, the two women assigned to help him trembling on either side of him, their ministrations forgotten. He could hear the cries of the brave soldiers on the other side of the thin walls as they succumbed to the overwhelming firepower of the enemy, along with the wails of the families taking refuge in the other buildings, and it was heartbreakingly frustrating.

He should be in this fight.

He should be out there with his comrades.

"We are winning, brothers! Keep pressing forward! Kill them all!"

The transmission sent a chill through him, and the women whimpered. One of them stood and pointed at his M4. "Please."

He glanced at it then looked up at her tear-filled eyes. "Do you know how to use it?"

She nodded. "They showed me."

He reached up a hand and she took it. He squeezed it. "Good luck." He handed her the gun and the spare magazines, and she left out the door, joining the fight for her family and friends.

They were all soldiers now.

Dawson hugged the barrier, firing at will along with the others, ejecting another empty mag. "Last mag!" he shouted as he opened fire again. The enemy was pressing from the far end of the FOB, near where the sandpile had once stood tall, and it was providing them with enough cover to gather in numbers.

He heard something behind him and his heart ached at the sight. Dozens of women were emerging from the buildings, hugging the walls, all gripping AK-47s. The fear in their eyes was heart-wrenching, but the pride he felt at this moment in his fellow human beings was overwhelming. He pointed at one of Buhari's men. "Coordinate them!"

"Yes, Sergeant Major!"

Dawson returned his attention to the battle ahead of him while new guns entered the fray from behind. Ledger's position had fallen silent a few minutes ago, but had opened up again from a different prepared location, suggesting the enemy was making headway behind him.

A woman screamed but he didn't have time to check, as there was nothing he could do. If she was dead, then she had been spared what was to come. He fired his last round and slung his M4 then drew his Glock.

"I'm out!" shouted Niner from overhead.

"Coming at you!" yelled Jagger, no doubt tossing over a mag.

Something shook the ground outside the wire, the massive impact almost knocking him off his feet. He glanced over at Buhari. "What the hell was that?"

Buhari shrugged.

Another impact, then another, pounding in rhythm, passing along the outside of the wall he was protecting, had everyone stopping except his team, who took advantage of the distraction to continue killing the enemy.

Then the distinctive sound of scores of rounds from a 30mm ATK GAU-23/A autocannon joined the chaos, and Dawson almost cried out in joy. He activated his comms. "Control, Zero-One! Is that what I think it is?"

"Affirmative, Zero-One. A Ghostrider has engaged, I repeat, a Ghostrider has engaged."

Cheers erupted from his men as they heard the report, the Nigerians cowering, still not aware this new gunfire was friendly. Dawson pointed at Buhari. "Get the civilians back inside! That's friendly fire!" He emptied his Glock in the direction of the enemy. "Control, Zero-One. Tell Ghostrider that we've lost the southern end of the camp. Lay down fire for twenty meters inside the wire."

"Copy that, Zero-One, relaying now."

The pounding of the 105 mm M102 howitzer continued, each high-explosive shell pulverizing the ground outside, the hundreds of rounds from the autocannon turning anything that might have survived into flesh bags. There was a slight pause then the overrun area of the FOB was hit and hit hard, explosion after explosion decimating the enemy, and within moments, there was no one left to fight.

The Ghostrider resumed targeting outside the wire and Dawson listened for any Boko Haram still fighting, but heard nothing. He pointed at Buhari. "Sergeant Major, take your men and do a sweep of the base. Make sure we don't have any uninvited guests."

"Yes, Sergeant Major." Buhari gathered his men and they swept toward the dirt pile, searching in every foxhole, under every building, any place they might hide, as Dawson climbed a nearby ladder to get a better look. He found Red already doing the same.

"It's a beautiful thing, isn't it?"

Dawson agreed as he stared out at the carnage. From somewhere in the night sky streaked round after round of heavy caliber gunfire along with rounds from an airborne howitzer. There was no defense against it if you didn't have air-to-ground capability or air cover.

The Ghostrider was the great equalizer, and today it was their savior.

He closed his eyes for a moment, saying a silent prayer of thanks, and asking God's forgiveness for anything untoward directed His way he might have said over the past few hours.

They had won the day.

Ibrahim stared in shock at what was happening. He simply couldn't conceive of the firepower on display in front of him. All the guns of every Boko Haram member in the entire region couldn't rival it. And his men were being slaughtered. Every single last one of them.

He started his motorcycle and gunned the engine, propelling himself toward the road and possible safety as the attack continued to his left, the explosions and bullets making a circuitous route around the base and closing in on him. He twisted the throttle, sending more power to his wheel and he squeezed the brakes as he reached the ditch, killing some of his speed as he leaped back onto the road, those already there scrambling to turn around.

He paused, taking one last look at the scene, then gasped.

Lawan collapsed back onto the ground with satisfaction as the wall of death approached. He had survived so far, but this was the end, yet he would die satisfied that the last shot he had ever fired had killed that piece of shit Ibrahim. Yes, they would both probably meet again in

Jannah, where perhaps he would get to kill him once more, but that was a risk he was willing to take.

He pushed to his knees and closed his eyes, staring toward the heavens and Allah, his hands out, palms upward, as he said his final prayer, the ground shaking around him as the Americans rained death from above down on his brothers.

And for a moment, just as the round that killed him exploded, he hoped Jannah wasn't real, so that Ibrahim could never enjoy the spoils promised a warrior of Allah.

Operations Center 2, CIA Headquarters

Langley, Virginia

"Ghostrider-Six-One, this is Control. Recommend you target anything on the road, north and south for five klicks, over."

"Copy that, Control. Adjusting targeting."

Morrison smiled at Leroux. "So, better late than never?"

Leroux shook his head. "Earlier and we might have saved lives. Even just letting the French do their thing."

"You're right, but that's politics for you. It's an election year. The president couldn't have the French saving the day under his watch. Our little idea, however, embarrassed him into acting, as did the threat of that recording the sergeant major made being released to the public."

Leroux's eyebrows shot up. "Did you tell him that?"

Morrison shook his head. "No, I just showed him a message Dylan sent me, promising to do just that, and the president issued the order. Luckily for us, we had some brass that took matters into their own hands and pre-positioned that Ghostrider in the area on a training mission after they received your call requesting its status." He faced the room. "You all did excellent work here today. You saved a lot of lives, and any that were lost were not your responsibility. This is on Washington." He smirked. "I'm sure you'll all hear about your contributions on the nightly news."

Chuckles and snickers washed through the room and Morrison patted Leroux on the back. "Good job, son."

Leroux sighed. "Thank you, sir. It was a team effort, and I think I can speak for all of us when I say it was personal this time. Very personal."

FOB Ugurun, Nigeria

Dawson stood on the rooftop, surveying the area as the Ghostrider continued to circle high overhead, its guns silent. Helicopters pounded in the distance as the Nigerians were finally bringing in their precious choppers, now that they felt it was safe to do so. Buhari's men had secured the FOB, and were now making the rounds outside the wire, searching for survivors and finding none.

Hundreds of Boko Haram were dead, perhaps most of the 500 Langley had estimated were there. The Ghostrider had shredded the road in both directions, leaving few alive, the occasional sound of a motorcycle engine revving in the distance the only sign of life.

But there had been a cost.

Sweets and Jagger had been wounded though only slightly, Wings was slowly dying, but with choppers inbound he would hopefully survive, Clarke had a bad leg wound but he would recover as well once evac'd, but the worst of it had been taken by the Nigerians.

Without body armor, Buhari had lost twelve men, with another eight wounded. And inside the buildings, their thin walls providing little protection, ten civilians had been killed, and another twenty-two wounded.

But none had been taken by Boko Haram, none subjugated to the horrors that had been in store for them.

Spock stared up at him from below. "You okay, BD?"

Dawson nodded. "Never better. You?"

Spock smiled as he was hugged by yet another villager. "Just remembering why it is I do this job."

Dawson chuckled. "It's easy to forget sometimes, but something like this..." His voice drifted off as he shook his head, at a loss for words. Spock laughed as two young girls ran into his arms, and Dawson couldn't help but smile as his friend, whom he knew had been having doubts about his future, carried them off.

Dawson stared out at the battlefield and wondered if those ultimately responsible were dead, or had they lived to fight another day. He sighed at the futility of it all, for even if the leaders had died here today, tomorrow there would always be another fanatic to take his place.

And he and Bravo Team would be here, standing on the wall, so those back home could sleep soundly without fear of those who would do them harm.

THE END

ACKNOWLEDGMENTS

I love Bravo Team. I've been writing these characters for over a decade, and each time I write one of their scenes, I find it so easy, as I know them so well. I could probably fill volumes with these guys just talking on a Friday night or a Sunday morning. It might be a fun exercise someday.

As I've said before, I put a lot of tidbits from my own life in my books, and this one was no different. One of them was Chris Leroux's dislike of The Big Bang Theory when he watched it the first time. I lasted ten minutes before turning it off and turning to my daughter and saying, "I can't believe this is the number one show in Canada." Now I can't get enough of it. I've binged it at least half a dozen times and another binge is probably coming soon.

Another is the recreation of the beans around the campfire scene from Blazing Saddles. I used to love that movie when I was younger, though haven't seen it in years. I do remember that when watching that scene, I would almost pass out from laughter. I'm not sure I want to see it again, because maybe now, in my much more mature age, I might no longer find it as funny. I'd hate to destroy those memories, especially these days where nostalgia is so important.

Though I must admit, a good fart joke still cracks me up.

As usual, there are people to thank. My dad for all the research, Ian Kennedy for some info on FOBs and defensive tactics, Brent Richards for some weapons info, Ian Davidson for some motorcycle info, and, as always, my wife and daughter, my late mother who will always be an angel on my shoulder as I write, as well as my friends for their continued support, and my fantastic proofreading team! As well, I'd like to thank my Facebook followers for some character name suggestions, including Michael Brown, Ralph Kurtzman, Wendy Hartling, and a whack of my Aussie Facebook followers for some of the slang used here (any mistakes are my own!) including Susan Toland, Luisa Ciaglia Mulholland, Simon Jackson, Simon Warren, and Lesley Hall. Thanks, mates!

To those who have not already done so, please visit my website at www.jrobertkennedy.com, then sign up for the Insider's Club to be notified of new book releases. Your email address will never be shared or sold.

Thank you once again for reading.

Made in the USA
Middletown, DE
11 February 2023

24633725R00194